'I owe you an apology.'

'I spoke of you and your family yesterday in a way that was like to give offence. I should not have done so.'

'You had no idea who I was.' A small smile touched the Earl's face, instantly lightening his forbidding expression. 'I suspect, though, that knowing who I was would not have changed your opinions one jot.'

'It might not have changed my opinions,' Susan replied honestly, 'but it should have made me a little more circumspect about voicing them.'

'Only *should*?'

'Should!' She gave a slight answering smile then. 'I could not honestly guarantee that it would! I fear I have a tendency,' she said, 'to speak my mind.'

Janet Grace studied English and American Literature at Kent University, taught English in schools and to foreign students, supervised a playgroup, fostered disturbed adolescents and taught craft, child development and sex education at a Technical College, before turning to writing. She is happily married and lives in a large ramshackle farmhouse in Nottinghamshire with her husband, three children and a menagerie of animals including dogs, cats, three rats and a parrot.

Previous titles

ISABELLA
FOOL'S HEAVEN
A MOST UNUSUAL LADY

SHARED DREAMS

Janet Grace

First published in Great Britain 1992
by Mills & Boon Limited

© *Janet Grace 1992*

Australian copyright 1992
Philippine copyright 1992
This edition 1992

ISBN 0 263 77640 9

Masquerade is a trademark published by
Mills & Boon Limited, Eton House,
18–24 Paradise Road, Richmond, Surrey, TW9 1SR.

Set in 10 on 10½ pt Linotron Plantin
04-9204-85074
Typeset in Great Britain by Centracet, Cambridge
Made and printed in Great Britain

For Tim, Simon, Cathy and Sam.

CHAPTER ONE

'Oн, probably, George. I dare say.'

Impatient irritation slid through the Earl's tones before he had time to modify them to his usual impeccable good manners. He forced a smile.

'I am sure you are right.'

He had not in fact been listening to the opinionated bluster of George Winston Le Grade Sharp Pembleton, having disliked him ever since their schooldays together almost twenty years previously. Obviously one of the disadvantages of returning to Chene after so many years away was going to be the renewal of just such unwanted acquaintances.

George smiled back, wrinkling his plump pink cheeks happily, but the Earl caught a look of sharp, resentful comprehension in the small blue eyes. He was relieved when the other horsemen caught up with them along the winding path that slunk along the woodland's edge, and his brother, Oliver, called George back.

'Look! From here you have a good view over the hedge to the line I would want to take for the canal construction.'

The other local gentry, all neighbours of the estate at Chene, crowded their horses into the gap in the hedge to peer across the fields. They were interested in this new talk of coal-mining and canal-building in the area: wary, suspicious, but sniffing riches in the air.

Sir William Gantrey, with his swollen red nose, made room for George Pembleton beside him, and began muttering about land boundaries, and the whereabouts of coal-bearing seams of rock. Colonel Parkins scratched his scant hair and rumbled some query.

Seeing all his guests absorbed in Oliver's enthusiastic conjuring of canals from green-pastured contour lines,

7

standing up in their stirrups to point and speculate,
dismissing cottages and copses in sweeping gestures, the
Earl allowed his horse to amble quietly on down the
path, and round a bend among the trees, until he was
out of sight. He drew a deep breath, straightened his
shoulders, and smiled. He was certain Oliver's enthusiasm would win the gentlemen's necessary co-operation
and support for his plans, and he wanted to escape their
company just for a moment.

He barely gave a glance to the small figure awkwardly
dragging a woven wattle hurdle along the path. The drab
browns of her clothes sank her into the insignificance of
peasantry among the shadows of the hawthorn trees that
overhung the track. Hearing the chink of the bridle,
however, she turned and paused, and his eye was caught
by the pale of her face in the gloom, as she rested her
slight weight against the hurdle. She pushed a strand of
brown hair out of her eyes. He was startled when she
spoke to him.

'I apologise for troubling you, sir, but I would be
grateful for assistance.'

Her voice was low but clear, educated and well-bred.
He frowned, surprised, and studied her more closely.

The face looking up at him was neat rather than
beautiful, the features regular. The eyes were grey, and
regarded him steadily from beneath tidily arched brown
eyebrows, the nose was small and straight, the mouth
clearly delineated against the pale skin and showing a
firmness that hinted a determined character. Brown hair
was endeavouring to escape from beneath a plain straw
chip bonnet, and a smear of green lichen from the fingers
that grasped the hurdle showed where she had pushed
the strand from her forehead. Such clothes as the Earl
could see behind the wattle were indeed brown, but not
drab. The muslin dress was a pale coffee colour, and was
topped by a darker, fine wool shawl.

Her expression cooled noticeably at his scrutiny, and a
hint of arrogance raised the brown eyebrows. It seemed

she mistook his frown for irritation, for she continued defensively, or disparagingly, he was uncertain which.

'Oh, it is not for myself. There is a child hurt. Young Jimmy Peters from the cottage by the mill.' She gestured briefly down the path. 'He is a little further on, beside the track. I am afraid he has broken a leg. I have fetched this hurdle to carry him on, but I cannot lift him alone.'

She was looking at him with guarded hopefulness that would slip quickly into disdain. The Earl of Chene, feeling that, having suffered Pembleton's company for a day, he did not deserve this further infliction, nevertheless knew his duty as a gentleman. He gave a small resigned sigh, then allowed his dark face to relax into a smile as he swung himself down from the saddle.

'Naturally I will help,' he said briskly, taking the hurdle from her. 'If you could just lead Bo'sun? Have you sent your maid for help? Surely you were not walking out alone?'

He was not a particularly tall man, nor particularly handsome, with his crisp black hair, heavy black brows, craggy features and reserved dark brown eyes, but he was certainly accustomed to people agreeing to his suggestions, and promptly, the girl thought, when he answered her thus. He handed the reins to her, lightly hoisted the hurdle under one arm, and strode on down the path, without waiting for her reply.

Miss Susan Finderby, at twenty-four years of age mistress of her grandfather's house, and herself accustomed to managing her own affairs, gave his retreating back a look between amusement and exasperation. She ignored his ludicrous comment about a maid, treating it with the contempt it deserved and, with a quiet word of encouragement to the enormous black horse who was blowing gently at her neck, she started after his retreating madder-brown riding coat and spotless buckskin breeches.

Susan Finderby's afternoon had been, had he but known it, far more frustrating than the Earl's. Her meeting with the vicar to discuss the building of a village school, a project dear to Susan's heart, had again foundered. It was through no fault of the vicar's, but she had been striding back home to the manor deep in angry thought when she had, almost literally, stumbled upon young Jimmy, and been obliged to turn her thoughts to his aid.

Now they leapt back to the problem of the school. Despite some success in fund-raising, the selection of a suitable site remained unresolved. The plot that had seemed ideal, that she had walked over visualising the building, was a paddock of unused, well-drained ground in the village centre, easy of access and close to the church. It now looked as if it would be unobtainable, and Susan had fumed and fretted at the problem longer than she had intended at the vicarage, and throughout her walk home. It still worried at her mind.

'Where is the boy?'

The abrupt voice from ahead interrupted her reflections. The man had not paused to look back, but continued to stride onward, assuming she would follow.

'Just around this corner,' she called, justifiably indignant.

Jimmy Peters was lying where she had left him, leaning back on a mossy mound at the bole of a tall ash. Always small for his age, he looked much younger than his eleven years. His face was rigid and pale beneath the beading of sweat standing out on his grubby brown skin. Smudged tear tracks patterned his cheeks. He opened his eyes, but showed no surprise at the arrival of a stranger with Miss Finderby.

At least, Susan thought with relief, the man she had waylaid was calm and competent. With the minimum of fuss he knelt to examine the boy, looking first at the leg, obviously misshapen by fracture, then gently feeling the other limbs for further damage.

'How did the accident happen?'

He was asking the boy, but Jimmy, gasping sharply as the man moved him slightly, seemed beyond speech.

'He told me that a group of them had been playing in

Farmer Trask's field there, over the hedge,' Susan replied quietly, watching his hands move firmly over the child's body. 'The little fools were riding the dairy cows, trying to race each other. Farmer Trask was understandably not amused. After shouting at them fruitlessly, it seems that he put Hercules, the old bull, into the field. If you were a local man you would know about Hercules. Suffice it to say the cow races ended abruptly, everyone scattering for home. Unfortunately Jimmy fell awkwardly from the cow. In his panic he managed to drag himself out through the hedge, for he was afraid Hercules would trample him. He was lying here when I found him.'

Jimmy's eyes had been flicking from one face to the other as she told this tale, and he had clutched at Susan's hand, but he had not flinched further at any of the stranger's probings.

'It seems to be only the leg that is hurt,' the gentleman said, straightening up, and looking down at her in a way that made her wonder if she had indeed smeared lichen all over her face while pushing back her hair. 'We will need to splint that leg before moving him.'

The man was not in fact paying any attention to Susan at all, she realised. His mind was on the task before him. He was casting his gaze about thoughtfully until his eyes lighted on some palings filling a gap in the hedge. With a grunt of satisfaction he strode over and pulled a couple of the wooden stakes roughly out of the ground, banging them against the hard earth of the path to shake off the mud. He handed them to Susan.

'Set these on either side of the child's leg,' he said, frowning, and began to unwind the snowy folds of cravat from about his neck. 'Unless you have any overwhelming desire to rip strips from your petticoats we will have to contrive to fix the splints with this.'

Susan quietly untied the cream silk sash from her dress and set it beside the cravat.

'I dare say we will manage better with both,' she remarked calmly.

He gave her a sharp glance, and a short laugh.

'Indubitably. Thank you.' He glanced back down the track. 'I was riding with friends who should be catching up with us at any time, so it will not be necessary for you to help in carrying the hurdle, but I would be grateful if you would assist while I splint the boy's leg.'

'Of course.' Susan's reply was tart. 'I had been intending to do it myself.' She had only required assistance, not to be dismissed as an irrelevance, she thought, crossly.

She moved over to speak reassuringly to Jimmy, explaining gently what they intended to do. The dark-haired man was frowning, studying the boy's leg, then suddenly looked up and caught her gaze. His eyes were so dark in the shadowed light beneath the trees that they seemed black, unreadable.

'Hold his hand, would you, please? And try to keep him still. I will need to straighten the leg before we can splint it ready to move him.'

There was an undertone of grim anxiety in his voice, and Susan knew that he would inevitably hurt the boy. She gripped Jimmy's hand, and rested her other hand on his shoulder, before giving a short nod of assent.

He straightened the leg in one firm, steady movement. Jimmy tensed rigid, screamed on a high, wavering note, then, blessedly, fainted. Susan flinched, and swallowed hard, feeling the blood drain from her face. She stared hard at the mossy floor beside where she crouched.

When she raised her head again it was to the sound of men's voices, the clinking of bridles, and Bo'sun snorting breathily. The awaited riders were coming towards them down the track. She studied them with a wary interest, but, although she thought one of the men was old Colonel Parkins of East Gridby, the others she did not recognise.

'Turned surgeon, have you, Marcus? This is very sudden!' One of the men, as dark as Susan's helper, was laughing. 'You'll be setting up a barber's pole next!' His amusement turned to concern as he drew closer. 'How is the lad? Looks a nasty accident. Let me give you a hand.'

The man he had called Marcus smiled briefly.

'Thank you, Oliver. We need to carry the boy to his cottage. Down near some mill, apparently.' He raised his voice slightly. 'If you gentlemen could be so good as to take yourselves back and request refreshments from Bowdler, my brother and I will join you as soon as we are able.'

The young man, Oliver, was about to dismount, when Susan, who had been ignored by them all, perhaps because they assumed her to be no more than the poor child's mother, noticed a large man with a round pink face, who urged his horse forward. He swung himself down to the ground beside her, and flung his reins over to Oliver.

'Let your brother go on back and do his business as a good host should,' he said jovially. 'I'll give you a hand with this hurdle. Where are we off to?'

'Ah. Thank you, George.'

The dark man's tone was neutral, not enthusiastic, but the rest of the riders moved on, promising to leave two horses waiting by the mill for the litter-bearers. The two who remained lifted Jimmy gently on to the hurdle and set off down the tracks, with Susan left to walk beside them, steadying the child.

'How did this accident happen?' the pink-faced man, who carried the front of the hurdle, enquired. The question was more to make conversation than from any interest, Susan thought, watching his broad back straining the seams of his riding coat. She said nothing.

The dark man, Marcus, with the craggy, thoughtful face, explained the story Susan had told. The other snorted.

'These stupid cottagers' children. They deserve whatever comes to them. Just think of the damage to the cows. The farmer is quite likely to lose any calves they're carrying.' He shifted the weight of the hurdle irritably, jolting the boy, who was still, Susan hoped, unconscious. 'They shouldn't be allowed out to make a nuisance of themselves. Ought to have a job of work to do.'

'Where they *ought* to be is in school!' Susan burst in angrily, angered as much by the way they ignored her existence as by what was said. 'And so they would be if I had my way. Not running wild to cause damage to others and themselves, but improving their minds and prospects, and the quality of their lives.'

The man George turned his head in sharp surprise, but it was the dark man who responded with unexpected interest.

'Is there no school?' he asked. 'Why can they not attend?'

Susan frowned. The way these men had ignored her seemed somehow to compound all the frustrations of her discussions with the vicar.

'There is no school because we have no funds, nor anywhere suitable to build one,' she responded shortly. Then she drew breath. 'Or, to be more truthful, we have raised some funds, though nowhere near enough, and the ideal plot of land we had chosen, and earmarked for building, we have now discovered to be unobtainable.'

'Why is that?' the dark man asked, with genuine concern.

'Because,' Susan responded grimly, 'it is owned by the Earl of Chene.'

There was a short pause, a charged silence that perplexed Susan. The dark-haired man had an expression of blank surprise. It was the other man who, after a few moments, asked, with a restrained avidity that was also puzzling, why that should be such a problem.

'It is obvious you are not a local man,' was all she would curtly reply.

'So enlighten me!' he persisted. The back of his neck was red with the exertion of carrying the litter, but she thought he grinned, privately.

Susan frowned, then sighed. Jimmy's hand was limp and cool in hers, but his face was twitching in little spasms of pain. They had left the shelter of the wood now, and were making their way down the slope of a meadow to the line of willows that marked the banks of the stream. The whitewashed walls of the mill could be seen, and the row of cottages under rotting grey thatch, one of which housed the Peters family.

'Well? Why such a problem?'

'Leave it, Pembleton!' The dark man's tone was sharp.

'No, no! Don't spoil fun. I am keen to know why the Earl of Chene is so unapproachable. Aren't you, Marcus?'

Susan could feel the dark man's anger. Exasperated at them both, she answered with quick irritation, 'It is nothing of great interest. If you were a local man you would know that the Chene family has never interested itself in the welfare of the area surrounding its estates. Indeed, has shown an arrogant disregard for all our concerns. Perhaps they lack any social conscience. Who knows? But certainly any attempt we have made in the past to deal with them has brought nothing but curt rebuffs from their agent, and I see no reason why we should expect better this time.'

She paused, then began again, more coolly, striving to be fair, 'But of course they do not use the house, and thus can have no commitment to the area. Why should they care?

'So,' she continued, with an edge of contempt for the man George, and his impertinent probings, 'you have your answer. Nothing interesting. Merely frustrating for those who wish to build schools. Look, there is Mrs Peters. I will go ahead and explain what has occurred.'

She hurried away down the meadow before either man had a chance to respond, and by the time they had carried their burden down to the cottage, and past the gaggle of wide-eyed children, slatternly mothers with babies on hips, yipping dogs, shrieking hens and hissing geese, to deposit the boy on a straw mattress on the floor of a foul smelling cottage, she had vanished down a narrow path, away from their road back to Chene. She was hastening, they were told, to fetch the doctor.

There was nothing left for the Earl of Chene to do but continue his ride home in the company of George Pembleton.

CHAPTER TWO

SUSAN was lucky to catch Dr Broadby, who had his sleek bay cob saddled up ready for a trip down to Finderby Lake for an hour or two of fishing. He gave a reluctant grimace, but called indoors for his bag, and was away towards Mill Cottages within a matter of minutes, leaving his housekeeper standing on the stone steps of his square, red brick house, shaking her head and muttering, though whether over Jimmy's misfortune, or the doctor's deprivation of his fishing trip, it was hard to tell.

Susan stayed just long enough to tell her tale again for that lady's edification before continuing on her way to Finderby Manor.

It was late afternoon now, and Hephzibah would be offended that she had been left to prepare the food alone, glowering at the pots hanging above the fire in the great open fireplace, and muttering angrily under her breath about packing her bags and seeking a position in a house where a modern, efficient, easy-to-use, easy-to-clean, won't-burn-everything-a-body-tries-to-cook kitchen range had been installed. Susan smiled to herself. She had heard it all *so* many times. One day, she promised herself, she would give Hephzibah a range. She had no doubt it would be rejected as an ill-tempered monster within a week.

There were no modern improvements at Finderby Manor, and through the windswept winter months it was bone-chillingly bleak in its sea of trampled mud, but Susan felt for her home the unquestioning love that grew from a deep-rooted sense of belonging. Her family had lived here for more generations than she could number, ever since the site had first been occupied, or so her grandfather believed, and she never caught sight of it ahead of her across the meadows without a small thrill of

16

content. She paused, as she often did, on the low stone arched bridge that crossed the stream.

The track that led on before her was level and smooth, the flower-speckled grass that covered it, like the rest of the meadow, cropped short by grazing sheep. Sometimes, in winter, the lazy, chuckling summer stream would well and swell in the heavy rains, and burst its banks, flooding in grey waves over the meadows and leaving the manor perched above the swirling waters, marooned on its rounded island. The earliest settlers had wisely made use of that natural knoll, left in the flat expanse of the river valley.

The river itself now lay a mile away across the fields, its tempestuous onslaughts tamed by farmers and millers, but in the early days it must have been a dangerous companion to her forebears. They had occupied the knoll, and strengthened it against attack, whether by men or floods, by means of two great mounded banks encircling its rim, and building their home secure in the centre, as safe as Noah's Ark.

The present house was old, although certainly not the oldest that her family had occupied there. At one end, huge trunks of darkened oak supported a heavy thatched roof, with walls timber-framed and white-painted. The other end of the house was stone-built, with thick walls against the sleet and storms, and small deep-set windows. It contained the great high baronial hall where her ancestors had feasted, and boasted, and enforced the law for many miles around. Now that hall was unused, and only the draughts touched the threadbare banners that hung like dim memories on the high walls, and only the creeping sunbeams watched the drifting dust-motes of their slow disintegration.

Susan stepped out briskly across the drowsy, sun-warmed meadow, and up the steep banks into the walled manor gardens, rubbing her fingers in the leaves of rosemary and sage, rue and lavender as she passed them by, releasing their fragrances into the lazy air. She followed the lichened brick path round to the back of the

house, where the thatch bristled above her like ponderous grey eyebrows, raised occasionally in surprise over
tiny dormer windows.

A bright rectangle of sunlight stretched over the stone-
flagged kitchen floor from the open door, and determined
rays pushed their way in at the tiny window-panes, but
none reached to the fire, and at first Susan could not see
Hephzibah in the gloom. Then she noticed her, standing
on a wooden stool to reach down plates from the oak
dresser.

'I'm sorry I'm late,' Susan said. 'What can I do to
help?'

'It's all done, Miss Susan, as well you know, coming
in at this time.' The old woman's voice was creaky with
indignation. 'What would your grandfather have had to
say if I had waited for you to get home before I cooked,
I'd like to know? So you'll have to eat what I've done,
and you'll have to make do with it.'

She climbed nimbly down from the stool and set the
plates on the long deal table. Small, thin and wiry,
nimble despite her hunching, crooked back, she
reminded Susan of an irascible mouse.

A leg of lamb was turning on a small spit at the front
of the fire, the smoke jack above clicking as it turned,
and Susan walked over automatically to spoon the basting
juices, sniffing appreciatively as they trickled over the
blistering fat. She peered furtively into the bubbling pans
that hung above the flames.

'That's a rabbit stew you're poking your nose into, my
girl,' said Hephzibah truculently, appearing at her elbow
and making her jump. 'No good your sniffing at it as if
it was the pig's dinner. You'll eat it and you'll like it.
Then there's the roast meat, some cold chicken from
yesterday, boiled cabbage, and a dish of parsnips. There
would have been peas,' she finished pointedly, 'if there
had been anybody here to shell them.'

Susan grinned at the old woman affectionately.

'Where are Becky and Anne? They could have helped.'

'Becky's out in the dairy. She should have the butter

made by now, and be bringing in the milk. And I set Anne to work on the sheets, putting sides to middle. Your lumping great brother pushed his feet through another last night. I didn't *think* I'd be needing them here.' She sighed gustily. 'I *thought* I'd have the help.'

'I could tell you why I'm late.'

Susan smiled, knowing the old woman's boundless curiosity.

'Just talking on to that Vicar Stanbridge, I dare say.' She turned away to the table, reluctant to betray any interest.

'Oh, no. I left Mr Stanbridge all of two hours ago.'

Susan took off her shawl and hung it behind the door, taking down a white cotton apron as she did so, and tying it about her waist. Then she sat down in the rocking-chair beside the spit, where she could lean forward to baste the meat as required, and twisted the metal guard around to keep the worst of the heat from her face.

She was watching Hephzibah's back view, all patterned calico and apron-strings, with amusement.

'So you dawdled and gossiped. That's not news,' the old lady grunted, provoked.

'No, indeed, I didn't dawdle. I was obliged to hurry. And I only gossiped briefly to Mrs Miles at the doctor's house, for she needed to know where he was going.'

Susan knew the old woman would not be able to resist such a bait. Hephzibah marched firmly over to the opposite chair, sat herself down, and glared.

'You tell me, right now, what you mean, Miss Susan.'

Susan told the tale of her afternoon's adventures, from her disappointments with the vicar up to the departure of Dr Broadby, with some enjoyment. Any event out of the common way was an excitement in Finderby. Hephzibah shook her head in slow disbelief, then her eyes widened at a sudden thought, and she raised her gnarled hands up to her mouth, gazing at the young mistress of the house in horror.

'Those men! It will be them! Sure as eggs! What other

gang of strangers would there be in the area? Common cut-throat ruffians without a doubt. And to think you escaped with your life! Dear Lord preserve us, for we shall all be slaughtered in our beds like pigs for the salting.'

'Heppy, dearest, what *are* you talking about? They were gentlemen out for an afternoon's riding. Nothing more. Why should they not ride here?'

'Skulking along the shady track by Kerne Wood, instead of taking the King's high road through the village? What sort of gentlemen would they be? No, no. Take my word. You met. . .' and her voice dropped in gratified awe as she realised what she was saying '. . .you met the Gradely Gang! You did, as ever was, and you came away to tell the tale. Praise the Lord!'

'The Gradely Gang?' Susan was bewildered.

'Well. . .' Here Hephzibah paused and smiled knowingly, gratified at being able to turn the tables on Susan in this game of gossip. 'Of course I *would* have told you before if you'd been back. . .'

But she could not resist hurrying on to share this juicy morsel of gossip from the village.

'I heard it from Mrs Blaythorpe at the baker's. Do you remember that burglary over at Long Needham? When the footman had his head broke open? And the coach that was stopped on Bell's Moor? And the robbery of Lady Cray's diamonds only the day she arrived home from London? All so greedy and cruel? They are saying it is all the work of one gang! Just the one gang. And there have been other crimes for sure, what with highwaymen two a penny and a body not safe to go out.

'The Gradely Gang, they call them, though nobody seems to know why, and 'tis mortal sure they'll strike again, ruthless and bloodthirsty as they are. It freezes the marrow in my bones to think of you out there and speaking to them as bold as brass. How could you, Miss Susan? How *could* you? To go speaking to strangers, and them murdering villains as anyone could tell?'

Susan could not suppress a smile.

'But those attacks all happened miles away! If they happened at all, for you know how these tales always grow in the telling. I dare say it was no more than Lady Cray losing her reticule at one of the coach-stops, or the footman helping himself to teaspoons at Long Needham.' Susan spoke mischievously, knowing how Hephzibah hated to have her stories undermined. Then she took pity on the old lady's look of hurt. 'Anyway, if the magistrates know who this gang are, why, they are probably halfway to catching them, if they don't have them clapped in gaol already. As for its being the Gradely Gang in Kerne Wood, I am sorry, Heppy, for I hate to disappoint you in such a wonderful surmise, but it would mean they were a gang of gentlefolk, not ruffians, for gentlemen they all were that I met, I give you my word.'

Hephzibah sniffed disparagingly. She was clattering round the table, making up a tray of food to be taken up to old Lord Finderby's room, where he lay in frustrated helplessness in his bed.

'And how would a green country girl like you know a gentleman from a honey-tongued villain, I'd like to know? Heh? How many gentlemen do you ever meet, Miss Susan?'

Susan laid the plates around the kitchen table. Since her grandfather's illness, which had confined him to his room, and the death of Aunt Catherine, their mother's sister, Susan and her brother Jeremy had taken to eating in the kitchen, sharing their food with their servants, as had generations of their ancestors before them.

'I know Eustace Chapley-Gore,' she remarked meekly.

The snort Hephzibah gave in reply was adequate to express her opinion of *that* gentleman, however.

Marcus, sixth Earl of Chene, and his brother Mr Oliver Carlleon would have been surprised and amused to learn that they had been condemned out of hand as brutal ruffians.

They were sitting on either side of a small fire in the library at Chene, which the Earl had ordered lit after

dinner, for despite the warm summer day the evening
was cool. The last streaks of light were fading from the
sky, framed in the panes of the long, elegant windows,
and the bats that swooped and hawked were invisible
now, but the Earl did not bother to bestir himself to call
for the great swagged velvet curtains to be pulled. There
was a deep peace in the room. The air was softly scented
with leather from the orderly shelves of books, and
beeswax, and apple logs burning. The shelves, which
covered every wall from floor to ceiling, creaked comfortably as they settled down for the night. The dowager's
harp stood blissfully silent.

Oliver stretched out his long legs towards the blaze.
His dark hair, in a 'Brutus crop', was brushed back to
curl lightly on his forehead, and softly on to his collar.
His eyes, a lighter brown than those of his brother, were
thoughtful. He critically eyed his pale pantaloons for a
moment, and his black Hussar buskins, their tassels
dangling almost to the floor, then looked up and smiled
with deep satisfaction.

'Thank God they have all gone home! But it was worth
it, Marcus. Every tedious minute of conversation, even
suffering old George Pembleton, and Colonel Parkins's
endless doubts. They are with us now, every one of
them, and every one committed to a financial investment
in the canal, in addition to agreeing to it crossing their
land. I never hoped for as much. As soon as the Act is
cleared through Parliament we can begin work.' He gave
a very boyish grin. 'I have waited so long for this day.
Studying methods and practice with Bridgewater and
Brindley and Gilbert, all the time I was dreaming of
opening up our mines here at Chene. We can link straight
into the Grand Trunk Canal, and all our transport
problems will be solved.'

'As will be the problem of the constant flooding in the
mines, if you can truly succeed in taking the canal direct
into the hillside to the coal face, and draining the flood-
water off to fill the canal.'

Marcus was lying back in his chair, his dark eyes half

closed in the shadowy light, twisting the stem of his glass slowly round and round between his fingers. At each twist, the gold of his signet-ring caught the light from the candle that stood on the small rosewood table beside him, and winked lutescent, while the glass flashed sharply silver.

Everything about Marcus seemed a little stronger than his brother, more exaggerated perhaps, more harshly drawn. Although he was some inches shorter in height, people tended to think otherwise, for he was broader-shouldered, and muscular, giving an impression of vital energy, ill-contained, which made him seem the larger of the two. His hair was darker, black with hints of blue in it, not brown, and cut shorter, for it grew thick and unmanageable if not sternly cropped. His eyebrows jutted heavier, shadowing eyes already dark and, with his hook of a nose, giving his face a natural expression of aloof arrogance that could make him daunting to approach. But his mouth was firm-lipped and generous above the determined chin, and laughter-lines were there to relieve any expected severity.

He looked half asleep, but, as Oliver knew, with Marcus such an appearance was likely to be deceptive.

'It has been done before,' he said. 'The Worsley mines use just such a system most effectively. You should come with me to see them. They have fifteen miles of underground waterways within the hill there now, with boats constantly loading to carry away the coal. It is effective and it is profitable. I know we can do the same here.'

'You visit your mines, Oliver. I'll take your word for it. It is steam engines I want to view. Once we have the canal open, so we can move the goods in bulk, I shall be building the most modern cotton mill in the north of the country.' He smiled. 'There will be nothing to rival Chene, little brother. Nowhere in England!'

They sat in a companionable silence. Both were aware that they would soon be expected to join the Dowager Countess of Chene in her drawing-room to partake of bowls of tea and polite conversation, and neither was keen to make the move.

'An unfortunate business, that child's accident,' Oliver remarked idly. 'I thought you were like to explode when George pushed forward to assist, but it was better for me to bring them all back and point out the rest of the proposed canal route. Who was the boy? Was that his mother, poor girl, or a sister?'

The Earl was silent for some time, and Oliver wondered if he had indeed fallen asleep, and thus left Oliver to entertain his mother alone over the tea-tray. He was debating whether to risk awakening his brother when Marcus spoke.

'No,' he said thoughtfully, as if he had been giving the matter long consideration. 'She was no relation to the boy. She had merely encountered him lying there. Though she obviously knew him.'

He paused, then, when Oliver was about to get up to go to the drawing-room, continued, 'She was an articulate young lady, of singularly strong convictions and forthright opinions.'

Oliver was uncertain whether his brother was expressing admiration or criticism, amusement or disapproval.

'She sounds a dragon to me,' he remarked, losing interest and standing up. 'And speaking of which, Mama will be expecting us to take tea. Come on. Do your duty.'

Marcus gave a slow smile.

'I am sorry, Oliver,' he said. 'Had you forgotten? There is still Lord Finderby we have not approached. That corner of his land is essential if the canal is to take the route we wish. I will write a letter to him now to arrange a meeting, and it can go over first thing tomorrow.' He frowned suddenly. 'Father never mentioned why they didn't speak, did he? I hope to God it is a quarrel long since forgotten, and won't raise an ugly head to hinder our plans.' He shrugged lightly, dismissing the matter. 'Go on. You go ahead and join Mother.' He laughed up at Oliver's face. 'I shan't be long,' he said.

CHAPTER THREE

'Who is it, Barnaby?'

Barnaby was standing at the kitchen door, a hand irresolutely on the latch. His bulky figure in stained cord breeches, and a heavy leather waistcoat, black and greasily impregnated from years of intimate contact with the Finderby cattle, effectively barred the entrance.

Susan did not look up. She was resting her hands on the great kitchen table, staring down at the list of linen that Hephzibah had just presented to her, chewing her bottom lip as she contemplated its unwelcome news. The items were listed in three columns in Hephzibah's shaky script. 'Good for use', 'For mending', and 'For rags and dishclouts'. The last list was much the longest, despite evidence that Hephzibah had given some sheets a reprieve, and moved them across to the centre column.

'Tis a fellow with a letter. Says he's a groom from Chene, and the letter's from the Earl. Says the Earl is back. They've opened up Chene House again!'

Barnaby's incredulity at such a claim was loud in his tones. Susan stared up in amazement at the kitchen doorway, and Hephzibah paused, open-mouthed, a pile of greasy plates in her hands.

'Well, invite him in, Barnaby,' Susan said, straightening up.

'And you,' Hephzibah put in busily, waving a dismissive hand towards John Wilkes and Jeremy, who were waiting with undisguised curiosity, shuffling their coarse knitted stockings on the flagstones, 'get back on out to your work.'

John grinned amiably, still chewing on the last of his ham and eggs, and slouched across to the door, where his boots, forbidden in Hephzibah's kitchen, awaited him.

'Who is the letter for?' Jeremy asked, as the unbelievable visitor, a groom from Chene, ducked his head and
entered the kitchen.

'For Lord Finderby, from the Earl.'

'And Chene is truly open? The Earl himself is there?
They are moved back from Bath?'

The groom was young, with a fresh pink face, and the
buttons of his uniform straining over a broadening chest.
He nodded, then coloured up as they all stared at him,
uncertain whether they were mocking him with their
amazement. He mutely held the letter out in front of
him, uncertain to whom he should deliver it.

Jeremy took it.

'Lord Finderby is my grandfather,' he explained, but
he carried the letter over to Susan.

'What should we do?' he asked quietly. 'Grandfather
will never read a letter from Chene.'

Susan held this extraordinary epistle, and turned it
over and over in her hands, staring at it, as if it might
thus be persuaded to give up its secrets.

She looked up abruptly.

'You go on out with Barnaby and John,' she said. 'I
will cope with this.'

'Are you sure?'

At seventeen, now that his grandfather was paralysed,
Jeremy was beginning to think he should assume the
mantle of man of the house, and certainly all matters
dealing with the farm were deferred to him, although
accompanied by heavy advice. But over more complex
matters the habit of relying on his sister died hard.

'Yes, Jeremy, thank you. There is nothing you can do
to help. This is a matter I must handle.'

She smiled at the boy with a small shrug, and he
nodded.

'Strange to think Chene is occupied again,' he ventured, but she had already turned away, and he went out
to pull on his heavy working boots, and join the men.

Hephzibah had immediately taken the shy young
groom into her care. He was seated at the table clutching

a tankard of ale, and looking gratefully at the plate of ham she had set before him, and the loaf, and lump of new butter. Becky was ogling him blatantly from the other end of the table, renewing his blushes.

'Sent out without his meal,' Hephzibah muttered disapprovingly to Susan. 'These great men think of nothing but their own convenience.' She drew Susan across the room and lowered her voice. 'Whatever will you do with that letter? The boy needs to take back an answer.'

Susan paused only briefly, then looked at Hephzibah straight.

'I shall open it myself, Heppy, and see what this Earl has to say.'

Hephzibah paused, staring into space, then folded her thin lips tight, and nodded.

'Yes. It's for the best,' she said, and turned briskly. 'Rebecca Marsh! Where is your modesty? Off to the dairy with you now!'

Susan left the kitchen, which was redolent with smoke, and ham and frying, and went through into the small parlour, which was very much her private room. Her desk was set by the window to get the best of the light from its tiny panes, but today she flung open the casement to the sunshine, and let in the stiff breeze to flick the scents of cowbyre and sheep, hayfields and herbs through the room, briskly dispelling the musty overnight air.

She sat down, and looked at the letter more closely. The paper was thick, crisp and expensive, the seal on the fold stamped with the Earl's own ring, showing the lion's head peering out from a wheeled chariot, a pun on the family name—Carlleon. She turned it over. The writing was elegant but decisive, spreading her grandfather's name boldly across the front.

She briefly wondered whether to take the letter upstairs. Grandfather's dislike of the Earls of Chene was not a reasoned thing. It was rooted back two hundred years, from a time when the grateful Queen had helped

herself to vast acreages of Finderby land in lieu of some
financial debt. It had been unpaid by a Baron Finderby
who had rapidly, and uncharacteristically, slipped from
royal favour. The land was handed to a new, ascendant
star, the sweet-talking, newly wealthy Carlleon, along
with an earldom, for unspecified, but probably dubious
services rendered.

The Finderbys had forgiven neither Good Queen Bess
nor the Earls of Chene, but whereas Queen Bess was
long gone, beyond earthly recriminations, the Chenes
still remained, secure in possession of the lost Finderby
acres. The gulf between the two families had remained
rigid under generations of resentful Finderby Barons,
ignored by uncaring Earls at Chene, and had also grown
more inevitable, as the decline of the Finderby family
fortunes increased the social void between them.

It was all no more than legend and story to Susan and
Jeremy, however. For almost twenty years the old Earl
had suffered from a succession of illnesses, and the
family had resided entirely in Bath for the last fifteen
years, allowing the Earl to take the waters and seek the
ministrations of the best physicians, while his agent, Mr
Blake, ran Chene with a scrupulous, meticulous, unge-
nerous hand. It was extraordinary to think Chene would
be open and occupied again, exciting perhaps, for the
neighbourhood. Her mind turned momentarily but
speculatively towards her plans for the school. But it
would doubtless refuel all Grandfather's long-subdued
disdain towards the family.

Susan thought of her grandfather's frail health, and
the paralysis that left him humiliated and frustrated,
cursing furiously and bitterly against a fate that had dealt
him such an old age. More particularly, she thought of
the disturbed night he had just suffered, along with his
dour and crabbed old valet, Alfred. With any luck he
would be sleeping now, and perhaps Alfred also. She
could not disturb him with the letter. More, she could
not risk bringing on another attack.

With sudden decision she broke the seal, and spread

the crackling paper smooth on the desk. Its message was short. His lordship requested the pleasure of a meeting with Lord Finderby at the earliest opportunity to discuss a matter of business. It was signed simply, 'Chene'.

The words strode boldly over the paper. Not words to be ignored, or trifled with, Susan thought, with a frown of irritation. But what business could they possibly have with Chene, after the families had not communicated for two hundred years?

Susan pulled open her desk drawer and selected a sheet of paper, then reached for her worn silver writing tray. She gently shook the little inkwell, eyeing the contents critically before unscrewing the top. She chose a quill and carefully trimmed the end. Then, folding her lips together every bit as decisively as the Earl might have done, she penned a neat reply, sanded the ink and tapped the paper clean, folded it firmly and stuck it down with a wafer. The Earl of Chene, she wrote starkly on the front, and went back through to the kitchen.

Susan stopped with a grunt of annoyance, and untangled the bramble that had snagged into her skirts. The road to Chene ran between big hedges here, and the centre of the track was slimy with determined mud despite the heat of the day. Keeping to the verges, Susan walked in a dusting of pollen and lush greenery. She smiled briefly at the memory of Hephzibah's horror.

'Go yourself, Miss Susan? How can you consider such a tom-fool notion? Only yesterday you barely escape with your life from this gang, and now you intend to walk five miles alone. Can't you wait until the men are not using all the horses? You could arrange to borrow the doctor's gig. Are you wanting to be murdered in your shoes? Are you? And then you think you can dance in to his lordship at Chene and expect him to talk business. What sort of fool are you, Susan Finderby?'

But, 'I told him two o'clock,' was all Susan would be goaded into replying. 'I should be leaving now. Please don't tell Jeremy when you send out the men's lunch. I will tell him what has occurred this evening.'

And she had calmly tied her tidiest bonnet over her unruly brown curls, and brushed some fluff from the skirt of her habit. Her smartest garment, its jacket and skirt were of rust-brown broadcloth, the waistcoat of white, ribbed dimity. It was, she thought, presentable, but businesslike. She did not want it ripped by an encroaching bramble.

She carefully disentangled herself, and stepped out down the road.

By the time Susan turned in at the great lodge gates of Chene she was hot, dusty and tired. She had not been to the house before, and the distance had seemed further than the five miles she had supposed.

The gatekeeper, puzzled as to how to place her, with her dust-soiled shoes and skirts but her quiet courtesy, willingly brought her a glass of small ale. When she had drunk, he pointed out a footpath that avoided the elegant curves of the ornamental drive, lined with graceful lime trees, and its gravel newly scored by the narrow wheels of speeding high-sprung carriages. The footpath travelled straight between the trees of the park. It had once regularly carried the feet of those who needed to reach their destination with energy left for a day's work. It looked freshly in use again.

Predictably, the path brought Susan out of the trees towards the side of the house, where it then continued to wind its way to the nether regions. She paused and surveyed the building before her, uncertain where to go.

It was a vast frontage, of red brick, edged and trimmed in white stonework. At either end a wing stood proud, ornately turreted at each corner, and a matching turret in the centre of the building topped the great pillared porch. Serried rows of windows stared with blank, daunting arrogance, not *at* her, Susan felt—they would judge her not worthy to claim their attention—but indifferently over her head. A low brick wall with iron palings above, and a massive central gate divided the park from the inner area about the house.

Straightening her hat, she stepped out from the shelter of the trees, and walked purposefully across the expanse of lawn that fronted the huge red brick gateposts. The drive swept up to meet her, and swerved neatly in between the open wrought-iron gates to the gravelled courtyard that extended before her to the massive front door. Setting back her shoulders, and tilting up her chin, she marched over the gravel, the crunch of her feet disconcertingly loud and intrusive.

It was with considerable satisfaction that she heard a distant clock solemnly toll the hour, and strike twice. Without hesitation she walked under the overhanging arches of the porch, vast enough for a coach and four to drive beneath to discharge its passengers safely, and tugged vigorously at the iron bell-pull. A sonorous clanging sounded within.

The Earl had been waiting for his visitor in the library. The letter brought back by his groom had been brief, informing him, in plain, decisive script, that Lord Finderby was unable, through illness, to reply himself, but the writer was prepared to represent the family interest on his behalf. It was signed simply, 'S. Finderby'. The Earl hoped that this would not prove an inconvenience. He frowned over the plans laid out on the library table. The way the land lay, that corner of the Finderby estate was important for them.

The library door stood ajar, and the Earl was listening with half an ear, waiting for Bowdler's discreet knock announcing S. Finderby's arrival. It was with surprise that he distinguished the voice of the dowager, raised to an affronted shrillness. He walked hastily over to the door and down to the main hall. Surely his mother could be persuaded to be affronted somewhere else, he thought, with a spurt of anger.

'You have no business, Bowdler, to admit this. . .this person by the main door. Have you learnt nothing after all these years? Send her around to the kitchen entrance if she has come to seek employment.'

'Excuse me, madam. . .'

The voice was female, quiet, gently bred, and oddly familiar.

'Hold your tongue, girl. Insolence will not get you a post in this household, let me tell you, nor will travel-soiled skirts. Now be off with you, round to the back of the house, where you belong.'

'Your ladyship, the young person tells me ——'

'Bowdler. . .' The Dowager Countess of Chene's warning tones shook with annoyance.

The Earl quietly entered the hall. A small, straight figure, half hidden in the shadow near the massive oak door, moved forward into the pool of light that flooded down the stairs and silhouetted the dowager as she poised, quivering with rage, halfway down the final flight.

'My name is Finderby,' the girl said, coolly, tilting her head back, eyebrows raised in what could almost have been disdain to return the irate Countess's stare. 'I have an appointment with the Earl.'

Bowdler was shrugging apologetically, though whether to the dowager, the visitor or the Earl—just noticed with much relief—was uncertain.

The Earl took a few steps forward, a slight frown on his face as he studied his visitor, and the dowager turned on him immediately.

'Is this true, Marcus? Have you an appointment with this creature?'

'Mother, I fear you are over-exciting yourself.' His voice was coldly repressive. 'Certainly I have an appoint-ment, a business appointment, with Miss Finderby. I will be speaking with her in the library. Miss Finderby.' He turned to her and bowed, noticing the shocked surprise that crossed her face as she recognised him, then how she deliberately removed all expression, and regarded him neutrally. 'If you would be so good as to accompany me? Please excuse us, Mother. Some refreshments, Bowdler, if you would.'

Her face was pale and set, but she ignored the outraged noises from the dowager, and accompanied him undaunted down the passage and into the library. She turned to face him as he closed the door.

'It appears, my lord, that I owe you an apology,' she said firmly. 'I spoke of you and your family yesterday in a way that was like to give offence. I should not have done so. I am sorry.'

She was regarding him steadily, her grey eyes wide beneath the brim of her hat.

He was surprised at her directness.

'It is not important.' He gave a frown. 'You would not have spoken at all had you not been goaded by Pembleton. You had no idea who I was.' A small smile touched his face, instantly lightening his forbidding expression. 'I suspect, though, that knowing who I was would not have changed your opinions one jot.'

'It might not have changed my opinions,' she replied honestly, 'but it should have made me a little more circumspect about voicing them.'

'Only *should*?'

'Should!' She gave a slight answering smile then. 'I could not honestly guarantee that it would! I fear I have a tendency,' she said, 'to speak my mind.'

'I too, Miss Finderby. Come and sit down. Though I must also apologise. My mother is. . .' he paused, surprised at how angry that outburst of his mother's had left him '. . .she can be over-hasty in judgement, and not quick to see her mistakes.'

Susan gave a small shrug. She did not like to admit, even to herself, the hurt of that encounter in the hall, which she had hidden in her mind beneath an angry contempt.

'It is not important,' she said.

The library, like everything else about Chene, was huge. Susan's jean half-boots tap-tapped across what felt like half an acre of honey-gold polished wood beside the heavy tread of the Earl's top boots. She could not suppress a surge of envy as she glanced at the row upon row of calf-bound volumes, begging to be explored, the wooden ladder set ready to reach the topmost shelves. The room was in one of the corner towers, she judged, from the views framed by the long, small-paned windows on two sides of the room. Their heavy green curtains were looped back by tasselled sashes.

As they reached the fireplace, and two deep chairs near a large table which was covered in piles of papers, Bowdler pushed open the door at the far end of the room, and advanced with a large silver tray.

Settled eventually in her chair, her small glass of ratafia and an even smaller biscuit on a silver dish on the table beside her, Susan folded her hands neatly in her lap and fixed the Earl with a steady gaze.

'I have come as you requested,' she said. 'But I must confess that I cannot imagine what business there is to discuss between us.'

'The building of schools, perhaps?' the Earl replied drily.

She coloured faintly.

'That,' she said, 'was not in your mind when you wrote to my grandfather.'

He had not known her relationship to the Baron. He wondered briefly about the family circumstances that should necessitate her responding to his letter. Surely there was a father, an uncle, a brother?

'No,' he replied, 'you are right. I wished to discuss plans that my brother and I have for developing the estate here at Chene, and which have bearing upon your grandfather's land at Finderby.'

He paused, and frowned again, stood up, and walked to lean against the mantelpiece, looking down at her.

There was no fire burning, but it was neatly laid ready, Susan noted, and had been newly swept after recent use. At Finderby no fires were lit, except for the kitchen and grandfather's bedroom, after the end of March. She tried to feel disdain at the Earl's extravagance, but failed. She

smiled as she imagined a vivid picture of him, all
aristocratic arrogance, frugal and huddled about his
kitchen fire, as they so often were at Finderby in the cold
evenings.

He was studying that small private smile when he
spoke abruptly, interrupting her wayward thoughts.

'Is there no man in your family to whom I could
speak? You say your grandfather is ill. When do you
have hopes for his recovery? Or is there no one else?'

He watched the small chin tilt higher. Hephzibah
would have recognised that glint in her eye, and sighed.

'Contrary to all popular male belief,' she began, enun-
ciating her words with haughty clarity, 'to be female is
not to be devoid of all intelligence, sir. My hearing is
unimpaired, I have no difficulty in distinguishing the
words you say, and am well-versed in their meaning. So
far, of course, you have said nothing to any purpose, but
I dare say you will come to the point in your own good
time. When such a time comes I will, naturally, give you
concise and logical answers. No masculine attributes are
necessary for this process.'

The Earl's brows snapped together in a dark scowl
that would have caused his brother Oliver to back away
hastily, and had even been known to daunt the dowager.
Susan gazed steadily back at him, quite unperturbed,
though two spots of colour on her cheeks betrayed the
upsurge of anger.

'Right,' said the Earl, grimly. 'As you wish, Miss
Finderby. My brother and I are to develop the existing
coal mines at Chene, and build a new manufactory for
cotton. In order to do this effectively we need transport,
and ideally water transport. We wish to build a canal
from the mines to eventually join up with the existing
Grand Trunk Canal, thus giving us access to the water
network throughout the country, and to the sea. This
development will bring considerable prosperity, and has
been greeted with enthusiasm by all the other landowners
who will be affected. They plan not only to allow
development across their land, but also to invest in the

scheme, thus doubling their possibilities of financial returns from the venture.'

He was aware that, in his irritation, he was speaking brusquely. A small voice in the back of his mind was telling him to pause and approach this indomitable small figure differently. He angrily silenced the small voice and spoke on.

'A section of the canal needs to cross a corner of the Finderby estate. The business I wish to discuss is the terms by which we will develop that corner, whether we buy the land outright, or lease it, or whether your family wish to see the donation of the land as an investment entitling them to an agreed share of the canal's profits. There may very possibly, from our research, be coal on the Finderby land also. A share of the canal would enable you to develop this profitably.' He glanced at her dusty, unfashionable habit. 'No doubt this will prove a considerable incentive.'

He paused again. Her face had paled, though whether as a result of his aggressive approach, or with regard to the content of what he had said, he was unsure.

'Have you no comment, Miss Finderby?' he asked, with scathing politeness.

She looked at him, her eyes reserved and thoughtful.

'No,' she said. 'Not immediately. I would like to see a chart of your proposed canal if you have one.'

'Of course. If you would come to the table.'

He could not understand why she was irritating him so much, driving him to speak so abruptly, so unwisely. Surely he could ignore her eccentric outspokenness and sell his plans better than this? She was only a drab brown country girl with dust on her skirts. Her straw hat barely reached his shoulder. His taste in the gentle sex was renowned to be for acquiescent, statuesque, raven-headed beauties with ice-white skin, not brown-skinned, brown-haired dabs of girls who spoke their minds quite careless of his consequence.

He pointed to the chart laid out ready, and showed her the proposed line of the canal, the existing coal workings and the hoped-for expansions, and where coal might be found at Finderby. The lace ruffle at his wrist slipped from his dark green coat sleeve to brush the paper as he stretched.

Susan studied the map in silence for some time, then calmly went back to her seat, and refolded her hands on her lap. She frowned for a moment in thought, then looked up at him squarely.

'You seem to have been open to the point of bluntness with me. I shall therefore return you that compliment.

'I do not believe there is any possibility whatsoever of Finderby land being used to help accrue your profits. My grandfather holds precious every acre of family land to leave intact for my brother. Even were that not the case, I cannot imagine that he would ever bring himself to have dealings with a representative of your family. His opinions of them have been held too long.

'Furthermore, I could not recommend your scheme. You talk only of profit, and financial returns from your coal and your factory, nothing of the land you will scar and the lives you will blight. Well, I have seen coal workers, sir, and, worse, I have seen cotton mills, and the abysmal conditions for men, women and young children within them. They are despicable places, run by despicable men.'

She stood up, preparing to leave. 'I inadvertently gave you my opinion yesterday. I have seen nothing today to change that opinion one iota. I am sorry. Your profit-making canal will have to manage without the Finderby acres. Good day to you, my lord. I can see myself out.'

So shocked was he by her response that his face was rigid, his jaw clenched, and his black eyes blazed. It was with a superhuman effort that he relaxed his gripped teeth, his bunched fists, and drew breath.

'Wait, Miss Finderby.' His voice was harsh. 'We should discuss this further. You are misjudg-ing. . .misjudging these plans. . .'

She had walked halfway down the great room. She turned and looked back at him.

'If that is so, then naturally I am sorry. Be that as it may, nothing else is altered, and I can see no reason to prolong what is patently a fruitless discussion. Goodbye, my lord.'

He slammed his fist down on to the table in fury and strode down the room after her, his footsteps thundering like a battle-drum.

'Then go, Miss Finderby, go. Throw away this opportunity. We will manage quite well without your family's paltry acres.'

He grabbed the door-handle ahead of her and stood glaring as he flung it wide.

'In that case,' she said tartly, 'there is no cause for such an unseemly display of anger.'

She preceded him down the corridor to the hall. Bowdler leapt up from his chair and hurried forward.

'Miss Finderby is leaving, Bowdler.'

'Yes, my lord.'

The man swept forward and held the door wide with a flourish.

'Goodbye, my lord,' Susan said, standing on the doorstep. The gravel outside seemed to stretch endlessly away before her. She suddenly felt absurdly small and forlorn, all her bravado drained away. She held out a stiff hand. He shook it briefly, and stood back.

'Goodbye, Miss Finderby.'

He stood scowling in the doorway, then turned and strode furiously back to the library, scattering a mound of papers from table to floor with a sweep of his arm. From the window he could see her small figure, brave in its rust-brown jacket and skirt, like a winter robin, trudging across the gravel towards the great gate. He gave a growl of impatient fury, hovered angrily staring after her, then strode back out to where Bowdler waited in the hall.

'Order a carriage,' he ordered abruptly, 'to catch up with Miss Finderby, and drive her home.'

'Yes, my lord,' returned Bowdler.

'Well, hurry up, man.'

'Yes, sir. At once.'

Then, to the butler's retreating backview, 'Bowdler. . .'

'Yes, my lord?'

'No. Leave it! Let her walk.'

Bowdler stared sombrely as the Earl swung round on his heel and stalked back to the library.

But Bowdler had a soft spot for anyone who could look the dowager's fury in the eye with unconcern. The Earl was not to know, he reflected to himself, if he was suddenly to remember an urgent errand to be discharged in Finderby village, and was to send the groom Benjamin Foot with the gig. And if he was also to suggest that Benjamin look out for a young lady in need of a lift, that was none of his lordship's concern either.

Bowdler quietly pushed open the baize door that led to the back of the house, and the stable-block.

CHAPTER FOUR

'YOU went to see him?' Violet's pale blue eyes were wide with exaggerated horror. 'Susan, how could you? How did you dare?'

Susan regarded the girl who sat staring at her across the kitchen table with considerable exasperation.

It was a source of disappointment in Susan's life that Finderby village yielded no more congenial young lady of like age and breeding to be her friend than Violet Netheredge. The daughter of a general long-since deceased, she now lived in genteel semi-poverty with her mother, who compensated for the loss of her husband by caring instead for her nerves.

It was inevitable that Susan and Violet would see much of each other, and Susan had discovered that, provided she restricted their conversational topics to village tittle-tattle, and discussion of the latest fashion plates, she could keep her temper with Violet very well. Today, however, she felt irrationally irritated by Violet's gleeful probing.

'I went because somebody had to, and there was no one else. Jeremy——' she glanced apologetically at her young brother, sitting glumly in the rocking-chair listening '—is too inexperienced to undertake such a visit. It was purely to discuss a business proposition—a proposition which I turned down. I have every hope that that will be the end of the matter.'

Violet gave a pout.

'Tell properly, Susan. Everyone wants to know. What is he like?'

'Who?' Susan enquired infuriatingly and concentrating on the sheet she was mending—one of the casualties listed by Hephzibah the previous day.

'Why, the Earl of Chene, of course. Mama says he is

one of the most sought-after bachelors in Britain! Here, on our very doorstep! Is he young? Is he good-looking? Is he amenable? Will he be entertaining?'

Susan shrugged irritably.

'There is nothing of interest to say.'

But she knew she could not avoid Violet's inquisition, and would only fuel mischievous and misguided speculation should she try to do so. With a sigh she rested her mending in her lap, and spoke with decision.

'The Earl is about thirty years of age. He is dark-haired, dark-eyed, dark-skinned, and his character is reflected in his colouring. He is arrogant, domineering, short-tempered, and hoping to make a great deal of money by exploiting a great many unfortunate people. He gave no indication at all that he intends to do any entertaining. I should turn your hopes elsewhere if I were you, Violet.'

'Well!'

Violet was well pleased at having goaded such a promising picture of villainy from her friend. If the newcomer to the neighbourhood was not to be slain by her own feminine charms—and Violet was not entirely blind to her status in the marriage market—then she preferred a villain to be gasped over in a friendly huddle of whisper and surmise.

'What was his business proposal?' she enquired eagerly.

Susan shook her head impatiently, already regretting her outburst.

'I suppose it is no secret. Half the men of the area have joined him, it seems. He hopes to build a new canal to open up the Chene coalfields and to provide transport for a new cotton mill. He wished to bring part of the canal across our land. I explained Grandfather would not consider any change to the estate. That is all.'

'I wish I had gone with you, though,' Jeremy put in, in wistful tones. 'I would dearly like to have seen the charts.'

He did not elaborate on his disappointment, however.

He had done all that on the previous evening when Susan
had arrived back, driven in a smart gig by Benjamin, the
same groom who had called in the morning with the
letter. Becky had trotted over from the dairy with a great
jug of fresh milk just as they arrived, and persuaded
Benjamin to stay for milk and scones, while Susan had
explained all that had occurred. Jeremy's heart had
burned with excitement at the thought of canals, and
mines, and mills, of machinery and steam engines. He
would give anything to be involved in such a venture.
But he knew his grandfather and his sentiments quite as
well as Susan, and he was a realistic boy.

'Why? Would you have chosen to defy your grandfather, and build canals with Lord Chene?' Violet asked
innocently.

Jeremy scowled. He disliked Violet intensely. She
reminded him of a rabbit, with her pale, inquisitive face,
and prominent front teeth, but she filled him with
unease. He had a secret fear, which he had not dared to
present for Susan's critical comment, that Violet was
watching him grow, like a gardener with a recalcitrant
seedling, only waiting for him to be old enough before
she would pluck him and swallow him up. He regarded
her warily, and treated her to all the incommunicative
gawkiness of which seventeen was capable.

'Of course not,' he grunted with a glare, and slouched
outside.

Violet gave a tittering giggle at having thus provoked
him, and turned back to discuss the progress of Jimmy
Peters' leg, which, she thought, was paining him less
than he probably deserved. Violet considered small boys
an uncouth breed, due regular physical punishment to
teach them civilised behaviour. She was not best pleased
when Susan merely commented that she had sent a
hamper of good things up to Mill Cottages that morning,
and received favourable reports.

It was late that afternoon, after Violet's welcome
departure, that Susan accepted what she already really
knew—that she would have to tell her grandfather what

she had done. Immobilised he might be, but his friends regularly visited, and Violet did not hold the monopoly on gossip in the village. Word would get back. The lesser evil was to explain to him first.

She checked with Alfred that he was awake and fit for conversation. The old valet stood shaking his grey head in the dark passage outside the bedroom door, the boards creaking beneath his feet as he shifted his weight.

'He's as good as he'll ever be, Miss Susan.'

'Be ready with his draught, Alfred. I am afraid he will be angered when I tell him, and you know how upset he can get.'

'I'll be ready, Miss Susan. Better you tell him than some meddlesome body from Finderby. Get on in with you.'

She smiled.

'Thank you, Alfred.'

Lord Finderby lay, as he always did, propped on a mound of pillows in the huge four-poster bed. The great wooden posts were coarsely carved, and black with the touch of generations of Finderbys. Above, the brocade tester hung faded and worn. The bed had been mute witness to all the violent emotions and upheavals of a hot-blooded family; it had seen them born and suffering, loving and weeping, raging and dying. If dark family rumours spoke true it had even been a passive accomplice in murder, when an early Baron had smothered an inconveniently barren wife with its pillows, and brought a wealthy child bride to shiver in fear among those same pillows not six months later.

Susan walked quietly over to the bedside.

'Hello, Grandfather.'

The sharp brown eyes, bright as her own, swivelled round to fix her with a glare. He grunted.

'So. How are you, my girl?'

His speech was slow, a little slurred, but as forceful as ever.

'I have come to tell you of something that has

occurred. I have dealt with it, I hope in a way you would approve.'

He frowned. He hated to be reminded of his uselessness.

'Tell me.'

It was not possible to sit down. If she was seated, Lord Finderby could no longer turn his head, with its shock of white hair, far enough to see her. It was necessary to stand, as she had stood by his desk, confessing her crimes, as a child.

'Chene House is open again,' she began, watching the twitching of the formidable white eyebrows. 'The Earl is back in residence—the new Earl; his father died some eighteen months ago.'

'I know that, girl. I haven't lost my memory, more's the pity. So what is this Chene puppy up to?'

'We received a message requesting an interview with him,' she continued cautiously. 'To discuss a business proposal. I travelled to Chene yesterday and spoke to him.' The look on her grandfather's face was ominous, and Susan hurried on. 'He is proposing to build a canal to open up his coalfield, among other ventures. He wished to take the course of the canal through part of our land—that corner by Soggett's old mill. It would run through Packman's Piece, the Dog-Leg Field and Square Meadow. I checked the charts carefully. It seems it is the level, low-lying ground they need. He wanted to know if we would sell or lease the land to him, or join in the venture ourselves. I told him we would not have dealings with him in any way at all, and took my leave. I hope I did right, Grandfather.'

'By God, I should think you did.' The veins on the old man's forehead stood out alarmingly. 'Damned confounded Chene impudence. Haven't they got enough of our acres? Must they claw more of my inheritance, of young Jeremy's future? Never! Never, never, never. He would have to see me dead to touch a square foot of my land.'

He paused, panting, and to Susan's relief Alfred came

stolidly in with a large bottle and spoon to administer the draught left by Dr Broadby.

'Curse you, Alfred, take that mess away.'

Ignoring the outburst, Alfred silently poured out a spoonful.

'Damn you, I will not have it. I am busy with my granddaughter. Kindly wait outside, sir. I will have words with you later.'

Alfred held the Baron's head still with one sturdy but affectionate hand, and neatly tipped the spoonful down the old man's throat at the start of the next tirade.

'You're an old fool to over-excite yourself so, my lord,' Alfred grunted, straightening the pillows as his charge coughed angrily. 'Miss Susan dealt with everything just as you would wish. No need to fret yourself at all.

'Not that he ever listens to me,' the valet concluded to Susan with a toothless grin, and retired to sit in a chair by the window.

Resentful, but calmer, the Baron looked at Susan.

'God-damned old fool.' There was resigned affection in the words. Then, 'Thank God my blood runs true in your veins, my girl,' he said. 'You knew what to tell that Chene whelp, though I doubt if you knew the words he deserved. If ever that damned upstart asks again, give him the same reply. Or better, set the dogs on him and have done.'

Tempers at Chene were no better. It was well-known among the staff of the household that his lordship had inherited his mother's sharp tongue, short temper, and liking for his own way, but he was a controlled, caring, fair employer with a leavening sense of humour, which led to his being treated with wary affection, whereas the dowager, with her spiteful outbursts and carping tongue, was universally disliked.

Since the brief visit by Miss Finderby, however, the staff had walked as if on the proverbial eggshells, and often that was not carefully enough.

'For heaven's sake, Marcus,' Oliver exclaimed, a

couple of days later, in a rare outburst of criticism of his brother, 'it is not Bowdler's fault you failed to get the Finderby agreement! No need to bawl him out of his shoes.'

Marcus swung round furiously. They were walking round the back of the house to the stables, Oliver having suggested they go out to ride, privately hoping the exercise might go some way to soothing his brother's exceedingly savage breast. Everyone had suffered the blastings of his anger, even the dowager, and that was surprising, for she had hoped to please her elder son by remarking that Miss Finderby was merely a dirty, drag-gle-tailed guttersnipe who traipsed unattended around the countryside no better than a tramp, and thus deserved all his anger and contempt, yet at the same time was quite beneath his notice. Marcus's scathing response on her habit of untimely and ill-chosen comments had been masterly, and had driven the dowager to retire, affronted, to her room for the rest of the day.

Oliver returned Marcus's baleful glare with no hint of dismay, but an ironic twitch of a raised eyebrow. The expected outburst of fury died unspoken. Marcus looked at Oliver as if he had only just taken in the sense behind the words, then blinked.

'Have I really been so bad?' he exclaimed, ruefully.

'Worse!' remarked Oliver.

His brother stared gloomily at the ground ahead, slapping his riding crop angrily against his boot as he walked.

'Oh, God, I am such a fool!' He turned to face Oliver. 'How could I have mishandled that interview so badly? So that some officious, opinionated chit of a nobody can effectively scupper all our plans? How could I have been so inept? Lord knows, it is not that I lack experience in persuading fair maidens. Most of the time they are tripping over their feet trying to dance to my tune before I have even played it.'

'An ease of conquest,' Oliver returned drily, 'which

has perhaps disadvantaged you when meeting a young lady who is apparently impervious to your charms.'

'Impervious! Oh, more than impervious to my charms. She considers me, if I remember aright, a despicable man, and lacking all social conscience.'

Marcus had attempted a casual tone, but had betrayed an understandable bitterness.

'But that is absurd,' Oliver began, startled. This was something of that interview with Miss Finderby that his brother had not previously confessed. 'You, of all men! But why?'

The Earl shrugged.

'Whoever knows why women believe anything? Forget the wretched girl. I am sick of her. Come. We can ride over towards Riggerby and Guysthorpe and gallop back on the long stretch by Beacon Hill. I want to look at what Blake has been doing with those far fields.'

It was not until they were returning from their ride, and ambling at an easy walk down the drive, that talk again returned to the problem of the canal.

'You know it is possible to re-route the canal,' Oliver began tentatively. 'If Colonel Parkins does not object to the change of route across his land, all the rest affects only the Chene estate. I have studied the plans at length over these last two days. We would have to cross the river, of course. . .'

'And there you have the objection. With the expense of another aqueduct I fear the whole scheme would become prohibitively costly. As it is it will stretch our resources to the limit.'

'Once you are moving the coal in any quantity the canal will pay for itself within a few years.'

'But I need capital for the rest of my plans. You know how much it means to me, Oliver. That will not be a paying venture for a very long time. And I need the capital now to finance it. I don't have that money if everything has gone on aqueducts and extra miles of canal.'

Oliver looked at his brother's brooding expression. He

moved with an unconscious grace to the easy stride of
the lean grey horse, but his gaze was set in the blank
distance, and his mind far away.

'Perhaps I could go and call on the Finderbys,' he
ventured. 'Try to start the negotiations afresh. I have
had my successes with the ladies as well, you know!
Perhaps my boyish charm will succeed where your manly
assertiveness failed. It is so important to us. It would be
worth the attempt.'

The Earl was silent for so long that Oliver was
wondering if he had even heard the suggestion. Then he
gently reined in his horse. They had just emerged from
the trees, where the drive swept round across the lawns
to approach the imposing inner gates or led away to the
rear of the house and the stable-block. Marcus turned
his brooding eye towards the great expanse of house
before them, then he turned to Oliver.

'Thank you, but no. I will call at Finderby myself. It
is, I believe, my problem to solve.' He paused. 'I was at
fault in my treatment of the girl. Whatever her opinion
of me, it is for me to cure.' He gave a rueful grin. 'I
promise I will endeavour to contain my vile temper.' For
a moment he sat looking down at the riding crop he was
twisting round between his fingers. 'You see, the curious
thing is, I would hazard a guess that Miss Finderby's
views and my own are actually very much the same.'

A nudge from his knee sent the horse ambling amena-
bly on towards its stable. Oliver gave a sharp, surprised
glance at his brother's retreating back, his mouth open
to exclaim, but then he closed it thoughtfully, and
followed in silence.

CHAPTER FIVE

THE day the Earl chose to renew his acquaintance with Miss Finderby was an unusual one at the Manor, for it saw a morning without Hephzibah in the kitchen.

Susan had left the house early, walking down into Finderby village with calls to pay at Mill Cottages, to Mrs and Miss Netheredge, and the vicar, as well as to the couple of small shops. No one expected her speedy return. Thus when Jeremy arrived unexpectedly back from the fields, having somehow contrived to gouge an ugly gash in his forearm, and Hephzibah had discovered, to her mortification, that the last of the salve had been used on John Wilkes's broken head several weeks previously and had never been replaced, she felt obliged to don her shawl and run instantly down to Dr Broadby's house, leaving Jeremy rocking peaceably alone by the fire, nursing his bandaged arm and supposedly watching a mutton hotpot.

It was with hopes of relieving his boredom that Jeremy jumped from the chair and strode out to the back door when he heard hoofbeats entering the yard. Raising his good hand to shade his eyes, he studied the newcomer, who was looking about him, uncertain where to go. Seeing the lines of the lean grey horse, the cut of the madder-brown riding coat, and, above all, the dark hair and dark, frowning face, Jeremy felt a twinge of excitement.

'Can I help you, sir? Let me take the horse, then you can come inside.'

The Earl looked round to see a boy beneath a small overhanging porch at a doorway of the house. Above his head the old grey thatch curved its warm folds to the house roof like a blanket of snow over a mounded rabbit warren. The boy was on the brink of manhood, but with

49

none of the overgrown awkwardness so common to that age. He was of no great height, but with a lithe, compact grace that promised strength and agility in the man to come. His hair was a shock of brown curls, his skin tanned by the weather, his expression alert, eager, intelligent. Without a doubt, he was a close relative of Miss Finderby.

'Thank you,' said the Earl, dismounting readily and allowing the grey to be led away and settled in a stall. He followed the boy into the house.

The Earl was not commonly entertained in kitchens. Even when visiting his tenants, and his long residence in London and Bath had precluded much of that, he was usually ushered into damp and formal best parlours. It was clear, however, that no thought of its unsuitability had crossed the boy's mind.

'Sit down, sir. Would you care for a glass of ale? Or the cider is very good? There would be scones if Hephzibah were here, but there is certain to be bread, and fresh butter.'

He eyed his visitor hopefully.

'Before you so generously feed me,' began the Earl curiously, 'don't you wish to discover my business, and who I am?'

The boy gave a disconcerting grin.

'Well, it is difficult, sir! You see, I believe I have a very good notion as to who you might be. And if I should be right, Grandfather's orders are to set the dogs on you immediately. But, of course, you might *not* be, in which case naturally I would offer you hospitality. We do to everybody who calls. Then if I were to discover my mistake *after* you had accepted food and drink——' his expression was engagingly confiding '—I could hardly set the dogs on one who has eaten at our table, could I?'

The Earl for once found himself quite at a loss to know how to respond, but he did have a lively sense of humour. He set aside the dent that this ingenuous pronouncement should almost certainly make in his self-esteem, and gave a slow smile.

'Bread and fresh butter sounds most tempting,' he said politely, 'and the cider, since you recommend it.'

Jeremy laughed.

'Right away, sir.'

In fact it was difficult for the boy to prepare the food with only one usable arm, and the Earl saw him wince as he brought the bread out from the pantry.

'A new wound?' he asked.

Jeremy nodded, unwilling to make anything of such a trivial hurt. 'I cut it this morning.'

He was surprised when the visitor appeared beside him at the pantry shelves. They raided them cheerfully together, and in fact it was the Earl who sliced the bread and spread the butter before sliding it on a plate across the table to Jeremy, and sitting down opposite, looking perfectly at home.

'Jeremy Finderby,' said the boy, his smile conspiratorial, and held out his hand.

'Marcus Carlleon,' said his guest, 'Earl of Chene.'

And they shook hands.

Jeremy gave a sigh of guilty pleasure.

'I was sure it must be. And I did so want to hear about your plans,' he explained, suddenly a little shy, 'for the canal, and the mill, and the mine. I would dearly love to see such things, especially all the machinery—steam engines—you know?'

Marcus nodded.

'I have an interest in steam engines myself,' he said carefully. Much as he liked what he saw of the boy, and was amused by his welcome, he could not do business with a child. Nor even consider using the boy's enthusiasm to put pressure on Miss Finderby.

'I cannot really discuss business with you, in the circumstances,' he said apologetically.

'Oh, there is no business to discuss,' Jeremy admitted, without rancour. 'I told you what Grandfather said about you and the dogs. Not, of course, that he has seen them recently. I mean, look at Ranger!' He peered under the table, to where an antiquated mastiff lay sprawled, its

stertorous breathing a constant background to their
conversation. 'He hasn't any teeth left. And Riddle, out
in the yard, she isn't much better. I think you would
survive the attack comfortably! But that isn't the point,
is it? Grandfather will never do business with a Chene.
He hates all your family. When Susan confessed she had
visited you he was so angry it almost brought on another
attack, and he told her the only way you would ever
touch an acre of Finderby land would be over his dead
body.' The boy gave a reluctant smile. 'So, you see, there
is no business to discuss. I would love to hear about your
plans, though. Just. . .well. . .just to think about what
we might have done.'

The Earl was staring down into his mug of cider,
frowning. He looked up at the boy's eager, apologetic
face.

'Well. . . I have the maps in my saddlebag,' he said. 'I
will bring them in.'

When he returned, he paused before spreading them
on the table.

'Tell me, Jeremy,' he asked, his curiosity genuine,
'why *does* your grandfather feel the way he does? Whatever has my family done?'

'Taken all our land, of course!' Jeremy was offhand
about such self-evident stuff. He was hopefully eyeing
the maps. He was startled when the Earl exclaimed,

'What *do* you mean?'

'Don't you know?'

The boy's amazement was obvious. The Earl shook
his head.

'Tell me,' he said firmly, 'from the very beginning,'
and he sat down expectantly with the maps still folded
under his hand.

'Well,' Jeremy began, a little self-conscious, 'it goes
back a long way, our claim to the land. Do you really
want the whole story?'

The Earl nodded, and the boy grinned and sighed.

'I suppose it all started with a King. An early Celtic
King whose kingdom was all this land around us, and

his palace was here, on our mound. His name was
Taliesin. He had a beautiful wife called Olwen, and three
beautiful daughters. After some years of peace the Saxons
came, and their leader was a thane called Find. They
were fighting for land, and Find wanted this kingdom.
There was a terrible bloody battle all over those
meadows, down towards the river——' he gestured with
his hand, his mind on the story '—and the Celtic King
and most of his men were slain.

'But when Find came triumphant to the palace strong-
hold Olwen came out of the gates and defied him. He
would have to slay her, she cried out, before he could
take the palace. He fell in love with her at that moment,
and swept her up in his arms, but she reached inside her
cloak for her dagger, and she stabbed him.'

The boy paused, and looked up, feeling a trifle foolish.

'That's how I was always told the story, sir. Anyway,
she nursed him till he recovered, and somehow learned
to love him, and they married, and he became thane of
all that kingdom. She bore him sons, and married them
to landless Celtic Princesses, and her grandsons also. She
long outlived her husband, and she ruled all the family
until the day she died, as did her Celtic daughters-in-law
after her. It is because of Olwen that we Finderbys are
small and brown like Celts to this day! Anyway, the
thanes of Finderby remained strong until the Norman
invasion, always living here at our Manor.

'In keeping with family tradition, the thane in 1067,
whose name was Ralph, made no argument with the
Norman invaders, but hastily secured his position by
marrying a high-born Norman lady called Adela. She
ensured her husband became a Baron, and a powerful
one. We remained a powerful force over all this land
hereabouts, all the original Celtic kingdom that is our
inheritance, until the reign of Queen Bess. The Baron
then, Andrew, made some foolish speculations. He lost a
great deal of money. Worse, he somehow managed to
direly offend the Queen, and could not pay her the sums
she demanded in compensation. She confiscated his

lands, and gave them instead to an upstart kitchen boy
made good, and gave him an earldom, setting him higher
than the Barons in their own land, to their eternal anger
and shame.'

He suddenly recollected to whom he spoke, and had
the grace to blush.

'I am sorry, sir. I did not mean to insult your family. I
was telling the story as our family tell it. So that you
understand.'

'Thank you.' The Earl paused, studying the boy's
earnest face. He was amazed. He had had no inkling of
this dark thread of bitter resentment twined about his
inheritance of Chene. 'I had no idea. No idea at all.'

'I expect,' Jeremy remarked, viewing his tale in an
unexpected light, with one of those abrupt shifts towards
maturity of which seventeen-year-olds were disconcertingly capable, 'that they tell the story rather differently
in your family.'

'If you had met my mother,' his guest announced
drily, 'you would realise that it is a story we have never
told at all. Our family origins are decently draped in a
few of the mists of time. My mother, though,' he added,
'would give her eye teeth for a pedigree that pre-dates
the Normans!'

Some thought seemed to amuse him briefly.

'Strong-minded women seem to be a characteristic of
your family,' he remarked, to no apparent purpose.
Then, seeing Jeremy's eye stray yet again to the charts,
he took pity, and spread them out.

Susan arrived home much earlier than she had
thought. Violet and her mother had borrowed the vicar's
gig and pony, and gone to pay calls in the neighbouring
village, and the vicar himself had walked over to the
family of an old shepherd whose wife was slowly dying.
Meeting Hephzibah, she had agreed to let that lady enjoy
a gossip round the shops, while Susan, who was worried
at the news of Jeremy's injury, hurried home with the
salve.

She had pulled off her wide-brimmed hat and shaken

her brown curls into cheerful disarray about her face as she walked briskly into the kitchen, but she stopped, rigid with astonishment, just inside the door. Two faces looked round at her from the table, where they had bent together over a shuffle of papers. One, a mixture of guilt, amusement and pleading eloquent beneath his brown curls, the other. . .

'Why are *you* here?' she asked coldly. She hung her hat behind the door, then took off the pretty Norfolk shawl, which she had worn around her shoulders, crossed over her breasts and tied behind her back. She came over and set her basket on the table, her hands still gripping the handle. 'Why?'

The Earl had stood up, watching her. The clever reasons and arguments for his visit, and to advance his purpose, that had run so convincingly through his mind as he rode over, now floundered and found no voice.

'I needed to make you an apology,' he heard himself say, simply.

She had nerved herself for another outburst of anger, demands for the land, threats. The simplicity of his statement shook her. She stared at him, confused, and was shamed to feel a hot blush of colour run over her face.

'It is all right,' Jeremy put in, anxious that his sister's dislike of their visitor should not upset the tentative friendship he had made. 'I have explained that there is no question of doing any business over the canal, told him what Grandfather said. We are just studying the plans for general interest, aren't we, sir?'

Abruptly, Susan sat down at the end of the table, and the Earl cautiously resumed his seat.

'I am sorry,' he said, 'if my visit has distressed you.'

She looked up at him from studying her fingers, which were plaited before her on the table-top.

'You should not have come here,' she said, her voice low and angry. 'My Grandfather would be distraught with fury were he to discover you were under his roof.'

'That is my fault,' Jeremy put in defensively. 'I invited him in before I had asked his name.'

'And you saw fit to entertain an Earl in the kitchen?' Susan asked, turning on her brother with perverse irritation.

'I didn't *know* he was an Earl,' Jeremy replied reasonably, 'not until after we had got the food out. And he didn't mind at all. He had to cut the bread and spread the butter himself, actually. I couldn't manage it with this arm. Don't worry, Sue. Grandfather need never know. It is absurd to keep up the sort of hatred he has, over something that happened so long ago. Do you know, it seems extraordinary, but the Chenes don't even remember the story? I had to explain it to him.'

'I asked him to,' the Earl put in apologetically. 'I wanted to know why your grandfather regarded my family with such animosity.'

'You didn't know?' she asked. She was astonished. 'Your family has no such antipathy to ours?'

He shook his head.

Susan suddenly felt very tired. She walked over to the fire and moved the kettle into the heat of the flames, reached down the teapot, and the caddy.

'It all seems rather petty to me,' Jeremy remarked loftily, his attention almost entirely absorbed by the diagram of a steam-pump that he had discovered among the maps. 'A thing of the past. Nothing to do with us here and now.'

Susan rounded on him, caddy in hand.

'But Grandfather *is* of the past, Jeremy. And he relies on us to uphold all he cares for. He is doing it for *you*. Surely you understand that? You can't betray him.'

'Lord, Susan, don't take on so. I only said it was foolish to act like Montagues and Capulets. I've already repeated endlessly that we can't join in building the canal. I'm not betraying anyone.' He turned from her, back to the Earl. 'I'm sorry, sir. Ignore the family dispute. Can you just explain this?' He pointed at a detail of the diagram.

'There is something else I wished to discuss with your sister first,' the Earl replied.

He waited while Susan made the pot of tea, watching her back view, stiff with disapproval and hurt, move about the things of the kitchen, all closely familiar to her, as they were to the boy. He reflected that he had not ventured into the kitchens at Chene since he was a small child begging titbits from the cook. He diplomatically accepted the reluctant offer of a dish of tea, and moved his chair a little nearer her end of the table.

'What did you want?' she asked warily.

'Relax; it is nothing to do with the canal,' he began hopefully, but her eyes remained hostile, and he sighed. 'It is the boy we rescued—young Jimmy Peters.'

He saw her register surprise that he had bothered to remember the child's name, and gave a small grimace of anger, instantly subdued.

'I went to call on the family on my way here. I saw the boy, and he is as comfortable as he can be, lying in the only downstairs room on a pile of straw and covered by sacking. But he is frequently knocked by the other children, tripped over by his father—especially after an evening at the Boar—even perched on by the hens. He becomes weary and fractious. There is a small room upstairs where he could be carried to rest quietly, but the thatch above it has quite gone, and it leaks at the smallest shower.'

She was frowning at him in resentful perplexity.

'However do you know?'

'I asked. Then I went up with Mrs Peters and had a look,' he said, watching her face.

Susan found this almost impossible to believe, but she could not truly think he would so blatantly lie, and her troubled grey eyes clearly mirrored her confusion.

'Why are you telling me this?'

'I would like to offer to re-thatch the cottages. It would be sensible to do the row, rather than just the one. We have a thatcher permanently employed at Chene, but I know he has nothing to do at present. I want to see my

workforce busy, partly, of course, to let them appreciate
I am back. But, more importantly, I don't like to see the
boy suffer, and the work could begin at once. But. . .'
he paused and looked down at his hands, clasped about
his bowl of tea '. . .I do not know whom to approach,
whom the cottages belong to.'

Here the Earl was not being entirely truthful. He had
talked at length to Mrs Peters, to that lady's surprise and
gratification, and knew full well that the cottages were
part of the Finderby estate, that the Finderby family was
much respected and liked, and Miss Finderby, like her
grandfather, would do all she could to help out in times
of misfortune, with gifts of food, clothes or bedding. But
it was also well-known that the family hadn't two pence
to rub together, and the cottagers might as well cry for
the moon as for a new roof. However, Marcus was not
sure he could paraphrase all that entirely tactfully.

'The cottages are ours.'

The flush of colour had again run over her face, and
she was looking at him with accusation in her wide eyes.
He realised she suspected that he must have been told.
'They are Finderby cottages and it is our obligation to
care for our tenants, not yours.' Her voice was quivering,
angry and suspicious. 'Why should you want to be
spending money on Finderby cottages?'

'For the sake of the child?' His answer was deliberately
mild.

'What do the likes of you care for a child like Jimmy
Peters? You wouldn't care if he died of exhaustion in
your coal-mine like all the other children you will send
under the ground. More likely you are hoping to improve
the properties for some scheme you have to acquire *them*
for Chene also. Or to bribe us to give you those *paltry*
fields.'

He glared at her.

'You will be good enough to understand, Miss
Finderby, that my dealings are never underhand. I have
never employed children, and I never offer bribes.'

He was icily angry. She glared furiously back at him.
Jeremy looked at them both in perplexity.

'Lord, Susan, do talk sense,' he said. 'You have been
fretting for years that you haven't the money to repair
Mill Cottages, and suffering agonies of guilt over those
miserable families. Now you get a perfectly civil offer to
do everything you have always wanted, and you treat the
offer as if it were a spoon from the devil! Ridiculous.'

He turned to the Earl.

'It is very good of you, sir. I know you appreciate that
we would have done the work ourselves if we could, but
our situation is such that it has been impossible. In the
circumstances, and for the sake of the families, and
Jimmy in particular——' he emphasised this, as his
sister opened her mouth to contradict him '——for their
sakes we will gratefully accept your offer. I am sorry we
can't do the same about the canal.'

Marcus nodded curtly. He turned back to Susan.

'Miss Finderby?'

She took a deep, angry breath, and swallowed.

'For the sake of the boy,' she said, glowering at her
oblivious brother, whose head was once again buried in
a diagram of the entrance of a canal into a drift-mine, 'it
seems we must accept. It would, I can see, be wrong of
me to deprive them.' She was still resentful. 'Though
Lord knows what Grandfather will say when he finds
out.'

'He need never know,' said Jeremy carelessly.

'I do promise you that I am doing this entirely for the
sake of the boy,' added the Earl. 'Surely, Miss Finderby,
you have been in those cottages? You have seen and
smelt the squalor. You must have felt the same. From
what Jeremy says, you *do* feel the same. How easy would
it be for *you* to turn your back on their condition if you
had the wherewithal to change it? Impossible, I suspect.
And so it is for me.'

He stood up.

'I must trouble you for my papers, Jeremy. I should
be on my way. Don't despair. The coal will not vanish

from your land. It will always be waiting for you, a gold-mine in time of need. Then, it will finance whatever you wish.'

And he took his leave, bowing courteously over Susan's hand, before vanishing with Jeremy to fetch his horse. She stood feeling uncomfortably torn, aware that she felt mean and small-minded, ashamed of herself, and yet unfairly so, for she had only defended her family's land and her own deeply held beliefs. She stared at Jeremy as if he had wilfully grown to an independent adult before her eyes when he returned, whistling, into the kitchen.

'I have an invitation to go over and ride at Chene whenever I wish,' he said with great satisfaction. 'Is that the salve for my arm in your basket? And I believe the hotpot may need attention.'

When Violet called at the Manor the following day, she settled herself, with her customary glow of superiority that the daughter of the Baron offered only such inferior hospitality, at the kitchen table. She was wearing a new straw bonnet, trimmed with ribbons to match her name, and her pale, pointed face was sharp with news. Susan poured tea, and sighed resignedly. She would have to hear it all.

'We went over to visit Mrs Bourne at Kesthorpe,' Violet began, reserving the best of the news, and helping herself to a spiced biscuit, 'to ask after her mother, who has been laid low for weeks after a fever. She was up to greet us, though deathly pale and thin, and they gave us most excellent hospitality, and a new type of cake, so tasty that I was persuaded to ask for the recipe.' She rattled on for a while describing the cake, and Mrs Bourne's new spinet, on which she could play some charming melodies, but all the time patently savouring some morsel as yet undisclosed. Susan made it a point not to ask, and bent her head over the bowl of peas she was shelling.

It was after a detailed description of the lifestyle of the

new parson of Kesthorpe, as interpreted by Mrs Bourne, that Susan finished her bowl of peas to shell, and eyed the resulting pile critically.

'I shall need to pick some more peas, Violet,' she said. 'Come out and keep me company.'

So it was out in the Manor garden, with a light breeze bringing the bleating of sheep over the old wall, and Susan squatted by the twining pea plants, picking busily into a basket, that Violet was reluctantly driven to divulge her excitement of news.

'They were all in uproar in Kesthorpe, uproar! Everyone so concerned. They wondered we had dared to make our journey. We saw the magistrate himself going up to the Hall.' She paused, and Susan eventually obliged.

'Why was that?'

'Because the Gradely Gang broke in to Kesthorpe Hall two nights ago, and took all the silver plate, and the cutlery, and the candlesticks. When the butler heard them and went down in his nightshirt with a poker, why, they caught him, and they burned his hands in embers of the kitchen fire until he told them where Lady Cowley keeps her rubies. They knew! Knew she had rubies, though she hadn't worn them since the Yule-tide ball at the Hall two years ago. They held Sir and Lady Cowley at pistol-point in their beds while they took the jewels, calm as you please, and then shot at a young footman who tried to prevent their escape.'

Violet was well rewarded. She had all Susan's attention. She had stopped plucking pea-pods and was staring at her friend.

'But that is horrible!' she exclaimed. 'The footman, was he killed?'

'No,' said Violet, a hint regretfully. 'They missed him, but made good their escape while he lay shivering in a flower-bed.'

'And the poor butler?'

'They say his hands are badly burned. It is not known if he will ever have the use of them again.'

'The unfortunate man. That is a terrible story, Violet. And so near to home.'

Indeed, Kesthorpe was no more than thirty minutes' drive in a gig. Much closer for ruffians on horseback. She shivered, and stood up. 'Let's go back indoors.'

Just before she left, Violet thought to enquire after the Earl, and whether any more had been heard of his business proposal. Susan replied with reluctance, but knowing word would soon have travelled around the village, and would reach Violet anyway. 'He called here.'

Violet's mouth fell open in astonishment.

'He showed his plans to Jeremy, but Jeremy echoed my decision, and my grandfather's, that we will not take part in the scheme. He asked permission to re-thatch Mill Cottages. For the sake of poor Jimmy. Jeremy agreed.'

'Chene? To re-thatch your cottages? Ridiculous! Whyever should he do that? He would not care for some cottage brat.' Violet was both unbelieving and indignant. 'It is some sort of bribe. A cunning way of making you agree to his plans. It must be. Why, you said he seemed a dark and wicked man. There has to be some reason to his own advantage.'

'I did consider that,' Susan said stiffly, 'and told him so. But he denied it.'

'Well, he would, wouldn't he? He would hardly admit to it! A hardened villain as he must be, with his scheming to trick other men out of their land. Mama was most distressed, most anxious for the fate of all our other local landowners, when I told her your tale of that man.'

'That was wrong, Violet, to make him out so evil. I never said half as much. You make far too much of too little.' Susan was irrationally annoyed by Violet's silliness.

'Nonsense, Susan. You are tolerant to a fault, yet I could tell how you really felt about him. And why should the Earl persist in his pestering of you, if it is not for some personal gain? Unless——' here she giggled at her own wit '—unless he is so smitten by your beauty, he cannot keep away!'

She gave a little shriek of spiteful laughter as she took her leave.

CHAPTER SIX

SUSAN went once again to visit the vicar, Mr Stanbridge, the following morning. Another thing that had annoyed her about the sudden incursion of the Earl of Chene into her existence, besides his absurd schemes and suggestions, was that all her plans and work for the school in the village, plans so cherished for so long, had been forcibly dismissed into the background by the demands of his affairs. She resented that. She was determined to seek an alternative site for the school, and give no further thought to Marcus Carlleon, Earl of Chene.

The morning was cloudy, colder than it had been of late, and the persistent wind struck chill through her red wool cloak. She took the main street which curved round the base of the hill that formed Kerne Wood, avoiding the short cut where she had found Jimmy.

The village had long ago changed its focus. Once both church and cottages had clustered near the Manor, but persistent flooding had eventually undermined the church foundations, and it had collapsed. It had been rebuilt almost a mile away, on higher ground beyond the wood, and the houses had inevitably straggled after it. Now there was a group of houses near the church, including the vicarage, and the other residences, especially the newer houses of any size, spread along the road between there and the track that led over the meadows to the Manor. The doctor's house was one of these, as was the neat red brick box with the small pillared porch and glistening sash-windows that housed Violet and her mother.

Susan passed them all briskly, calling cheery greetings to friends and tenants as she passed, and eventually reached the vicarage, a low building of stone, like that used at the Manor, but now covered by glossy dark ivy right up to the roof tiles.

She was surprised to see Mr Stanbridge, a black cloak flapping about him, hurrying out of his garden gate, his flat black hat crammed anyhow on top of his long bob wig.

'Miss Susan,' he cried joyfully, the moment he caught sight of her. 'The very person I was on my way to see. Come in, come in.' He turned to sweep her along with him back to the house, brushing past unkempt rose bushes that clawed at his cloak. 'I would have been with you yesterday if old Mistress Prudence hadn't had another turn after eating sharp gooseberries for her lunch, and convinced that fool sister of hers that she was on death's door! Had me running up there for the last rites, when by evening she was up demanding plates of pressed beef! And the callers this morning. . .well, they always tell me there's no peace for the wicked!'

He bustled Susan inside, taking his cloak and her own only to fling them carelessly over the banisters, bellowed with stentorian gusto into the gloomy depths of the vicarage for his housekeeper to bring refreshment, and threw open the door of his study.

'I have such good news for you,' he announced, a gleeful grin cracking his face as he snatched off his wig, tossed it down on to a tottering pile of erudite volumes, and vigorously scratched his bristly scalp. He waved Susan to a chair already burdened by three volumes of sermons, several dusty documents, a black cravat and a ginger tom cat, while he evicted an irate tabby from the chair behind the desk, and flung himself down before it could resume possession. It jumped indignantly on to his lap.

The Reverend Mr Stanbridge was a good friend of Susan's. She thoroughly enjoyed his brusque, irreverent manner, surging with unceasing energy and practical advice through the startled lives of his parishioners. He was somewhere in his fifties, she supposed, though it was difficult to tell, of squat build, with a square face so knobbled with warts and bristles it was impossible not to look at him and visualise a toad. His clothes hung about him in careless disarray, and his wig was invariably askew.

He was leaning back in his chair now, hands clasped across his generous paunch, regarding her with huge enjoyment, while the cat kneaded his chest.

'Such news,' he repeated, 'you will not believe! I had an extraordinary visit yesterday mid-morning, and to be truthful my mind has been reeling from the shock ever since.'

Susan couldn't help but laugh; his exuberant good humour was irresistible.

'Who was it?' she asked.

The vicar pulled himself straighter in his chair, to the annoyance of the tabby.

'His Lordship the Earl of Chene, no less!'

So pleased was he with his news that he failed to notice Susan's quick intake of breath, and the forced smile with which she followed his continued tale.

'He called in here, and sat in that self-same chair where you sit now, and asked me the whereabouts of the plot we wanted for building the school. So, not being a man to let a God-given opportunity slip, I told him. And more, I took him out, and I showed him.'

He was gesturing expansively. The cat sulked, and retired to sit on the window-sill as the vicar continued eagerly.

'Then, *mirabile dictu*, he gave me his assurance that I might consider the land on permanent lease for use as a village school as of that moment, and promised the legal papers would be drawn up and sent to me as soon as possible! What do you think of that? But then! Then— as if that were not enough to send an old sinner singing to his luncheon—he insisted on pressing this piece of paper into my hand before taking his leave, full of regrets that he was unable to stay and share my luncheon with me. I tell you, Susan, I was never more dumbfounded in all my life.'

He had thrust the paper over his littered desk-top, and was waving it at her. Susan got up, curiously reluctant, and took it. She recognised the writing immediately, and stared at it for a few moments before the sense of the words she saw before her penetrated her mind. It was a banker's draft against the London account of Marcus Carlleon, Earl of Chene, for one thousand pounds, to be used specifically for the setting up of a school for the village of Finderby.

She stared down, astounded, and memories of the things she had accused him of floated into her mind. Why had he done this? Her mind spun. It could only be because of what she had said. No one else would have mentioned plans for a school at Finderby to him. It was a scheme dear only to herself and the vicar. And now, it seemed, incredibly, to the Earl also. She did not know what to think. She fingered the paper, and wondered why she felt unable to look up and meet the vicar's eye.

To Susan's relief, his housekeeper blundered in through the door at that moment, bearing a wooden tray which held a coarse china teapot, two dishes, and some small dry cakes. A terrible old harridan of a cook graced the vicarage kitchen, and produced the most indigestible food in the village, but the vicar never seemed to notice what he ate, and he broke so much crockery by inadvertently tipping plates off the end of his desk while he ate and read at the same time that his cook and his housekeeper had now conspired to give him only the cheapest chinaware. He did not seem to have noticed this either. The village, noting the disregard he felt for his attire, so frequently muddled or torn, wondered with some amusement what privations he would be subjected to next, and when, if ever, he *would* notice.

Mrs Bunce thumped the tray on to the desk, splashed out a dish of tea, dumped a cake on a thick blue and white plate with a grimy crack across it, and held both aggressively towards Susan. After handing the banker's draft back to the vicar, she managed to take them with a friendly smile, having long ago decided that, whatever the appearances, these were not deliberate attempts to poison her.

It was only when they were both served, and Mrs Bunce had banged the door to behind her, that Mr Stanbridge spoke.

'So, my dear, what do you think of that for a welcome surprise?'

'It seems,' Susan said carefully, trying to keep the stiffness from her voice, 'that we have been misjudging the Earl.'

'Indeed, yes. Do you remember our despair at the thought of him?' The vicar gave a throaty chuckle, which turned into a bout of coughing as he lost an encounter with a lump of cake. 'Of course, it has been Blake, the agent, making decisions for so long. He, it seems, was the cheese-parer, or the old Earl, perhaps. Ah, if this is a sign of how things are to change now the new Earl is back—well, long may he stay!' He took a noisy slurp at his tea. 'What I do not understand is how he knew we were mooting a school at all, and on his land at that.'

'That was me,' Susan said. 'I told him.'

Mr Stanbridge looked at her sharply. 'Did you, now? And when did you meet his lordship?'

Susan reluctantly told the tale of her meeting with the Earl, and of all his plans, and also of his offer to thatch Mill Cottages.

'Aha!' The vicar offered his cake to the tabby cat, which turned up its nose in disdain. 'It seems Finderby has acquired a new benefactor. Welcome news, eh? Oh, don't pucker up, girl, I know you do your best. But we both know how things are at the Manor, especially with your grandfather as he is. Which reminds me, I must call on him soon. But a new benefactor. . .' She could see his mind hopefully turning over new projects, then he turned happily and pointed a stubby finger at her. 'And it must be your influence, Miss Finderby.' He grinned naughtily. 'Don't you think?' He swept up from his chair, scattering cats, crumbs, cakes and plates. 'Let's go out and study our new school plot. We have plans to make!'

And he had grabbed up his wig, hurled out of the door, flung a cloak around each of them and set off down the path before Susan could respond.

All Susan's delight at being able to plan the school was overlaid with a misery of guilt. Despite the fact that he planned a mine, where she knew men, women and even children slaved and died in filth beneath the ground, and a cotton mill; despite his rudeness and ill-temper, she had obviously somehow grossly misjudged the Earl. She, who had always secretly despised Violet and others like her for their narrow-minded prejudices, felt bitterly ashamed.

When she had arrived home from Mr Stanbridge's, having paced out the size of the school building and talked over new ideas and possibilities for its development with all the wondrous freedom that the possession of one thousand pounds capital could give, she told Jeremy what had occurred. His comments, and those, surprisingly, of Hephzibah, on the Earl's obvious philanthropy and goodwill to the village, and the Finderby family in particular, had fuelled all the niggles of guilt that had been attacking her ever since she had held that banker's draft in her hand.

She had insulted the man, doubted him, maligned him. Grandfather's sentiments had so coloured her vision with prejudice that she had been incapable of giving him a fair hearing. She had needed Jeremy to show her that it was possible to turn down a business deal without despising the man who had offered it. During the Earl's visit to the Manor, far from harassing her over the canal, he had done nothing but offer help. She was ashamed, suddenly, of Grandfather's virulent bigotry over the Chenes. As Jeremy said, it seemed absurd.

When Jeremy announced, a few days later, that he was taking himself off from farm work for a well-deserved break, and intended to go over to Chene and take up the

offer of a ride, Susan felt obliged to ask him if she could
go too. She steeled herself. She must thank the Earl, she
said, for the gift of the school. Jeremy cheerfully agreed,
and they set off together, having borrowed the doctor's
gig.

She might have had some qualms, however, if she
could have heard the conversation between Marcus and
his brother that had taken place after the Earl's return
from Finderby village.

'It doesn't seem that you even tried to change her mind,
Marcus. Did you offer more generous terms? Did you
get to speak to the grandfather? He, surely, is the key to
the situation. If the family are as squeezed financially as
would appear, why, they should be leaping at the chance
for such a sale. Yet you say you barely approached the
matter.' Oliver's voice was outraged. 'Tell me! What *did*
you do?'

They were sitting out on the terrace at Chene, the
evening sunshine making long shadows behind them,
and behind two gracefully poised statues on the corners
of the low wall that edged the terrace. There were deer
in the park beyond the gardens, and a small group was
moving slowly between copses of trees in the distance.
Marcus sat watching them. Oliver, however, kept leaping
up and pacing back and forth, full of restless frustration.
He frowned impatiently when his brother began to
speak.

'I looked at the plans with Miss Finderby's young
brother, but for interest only. He resolutely backed his
sister's decision, and I have no intention of putting
pressure on a boy to get what I want. But. . .' the Earl
paused, and gave a small smile as he glanced at his
brother's irate features '. . . I did persuade Miss
Finderby to allow me to re-roof some of her cottages.'

Oliver stared at his brother.

'Well, that must have been extraordinarily difficult,'
he said with irritable sarcasm.

'It was.' Marcus gave a curiously mirthless laugh. 'I

can assure you it was. I thought I would not achieve even that. She wanted to take nothing from me whatever. It was her brother who actually made the decision in the end.'

'So!' Oliver stood, legs apart, his lean body silhouetted tense against the turquoise and pink of the evening sky. 'If I understand this aright, Marcus, your visit to Finderby only confirmed that we cannot build the canal across the Finderby land. We know that if we try to re-route it we will run out of capital, and then all your cherished plans go for nothing. Having learnt which unpalatable facts, you promptly offer to re-roof half of Finderby village at your own expense?' His voice was shaking with incredulity. 'And you expect me to believe this? Yes?'

'You exaggerate somewhat, but that is broadly the picture. Except that I forgot to mention to you that I also called on the local vicar—an eccentric named Stanbridge—and donated a plot of land and one thousand pounds towards a village school.'

'Marcus! Marcus! Dear God, have you quite taken leave of your senses? Why? Why did you do that? Or——' his face brightened '—is it a subtle bribe to encourage Miss Finderby to our way of thinking?'

Marcus frowned.

'It seems that you and she think uncommonly alike! That was her immediate reaction to my offer to re-roof the cottages. I dread to hear what she might say when she learns about the school. But no. It was not intended as a bribe. Should she even suspect such a thing, we would lose any chance of her goodwill. The village needs a school, and I happen to own the land on which it can be provided. As you also may have noticed, I happen to care about such matters. I won't be pressing Miss Finderby about the canal at present, and her grandfather is both bed-ridden and quite set against us. We shall just have to wait a little longer, then maybe reconsider.' He stood up. 'But I can assure you of one thing. She will never even contemplate doing business with a man whom she considers to be every kind of heartless villain. The only possible way to secure Miss Finderby's co-operation will be through a mutual interest in philanthropy.'

Oliver stared, then suddenly gave a guffaw of relieved laughter.

'You had me panicking, Marcus. Despairing of ever building my canal. But I might have known. You're a cunning devil. You're playing a deep game, with your schools and cottages, and in the end you'll win the way you always do. You have set out to snare opinionated little Miss Finderby through doing good works!' He laughed again. 'Wonderful, just wonderful.'

'Well, you must think what you like, Oliver,' the Earl replied, and went indoors.

Susan made her stiff little speech of apology and thanks in a pleasant drawing-room at Chene that looked out across the terrace where the conversation between the Earl and his brother had taken place. Jeremy and Oliver were also there, listening awkwardly to her brave declaration before setting off to ride together.

She had not intended to be invited in. She had told Jeremy that, after she had briefly spoken to the Earl, she would walk in the woods of the park until he had returned from his ride. Certainly she had expected the Earl to ride. She had not expected an introduction to the unfriendly-eyed Mr Oliver Carlleon, the Earl's younger brother and a keen canal engineer. Oliver would, the Earl announced firmly, be more than happy to ride out with Jeremy. They could, he said, discuss the finer points of engineering the while.

She had looked the Earl squarely in the face, although her small gloved hands were clenched tight together, while she tautly begged his pardon for all the insults and aspersions she had heaped upon his good name, and thanked him for the generous donation to the school. But she tilted her head higher and glared, all indignant fury, at the brother, Oliver, when she happened to glance round and noticed him behind her, grinning trium-

phantly at the Earl. She could accept when she should
apologise, but she would not stay to be humiliated and
insulted.

She began to panic when Jeremy and Oliver vanished
in mutual accord to the stables, keen to leave the
proximity of such an emotionally charged young lady,
and left her staring, dumbstruck, across the room at the
Earl of Chene.

'Please,' he said neutrally, 'sit down.'

He crossed the room and tugged the dark velvet bell-
pull, requesting refreshments when Bowdler glided
silently into the room.

There was a difficult pause while they waited. The
Earl walked to the window and stared out as if he could
find nothing to say, while Susan, utterly unaccustomed
to a role of self-abased humility, could only sit dumbly,
wondering how soon she could escape. An obsequious
young footman appeared with a tray, and backed out on
a blank-faced bow when he had placed it on a table and
the Earl had nodded and waved him away.

The Earl poured them each a small glass of excellent
sherry, then sat down.

'I would be most interested,' he said, 'to hear of your
plans for the school. But first, how did you come to be
interested in such a venture?'

Instinctively she shot him a suspicious look, but he
appeared all genuine enquiry, and she mentally rebuked
herself. She took a long sip of sherry—very encouraging
to the faint-hearted—and then, determined to do her
duty and make amends for past injustices, she began to
talk.

She described, tentatively, her own search for an
education. She mentioned briefly her lonely struggles
with an alphabet book and primer, omitting any reference to the bright butterfly mother who had amusedly
dropped them into the lap of her odd, studious child,
but never thought to sit with her to open them. Then
how, later, Aunt Catherine had come and taught her,
and brought a small income that enabled them to pay for

Jeremy to be taught by the vicar. The difficulties she had encountered in gaining access to books, and the vast pleasure they had brought her, had made her acutely aware of the lack of any provision for children in the village.

'And many of them so quick, so lively-minded,' she said, leaning forward earnestly, forgetting all suspicion and reserve. 'It is quite untrue when people state that the lower ranks have neither the need nor the ability to learn to read. Any life can be enhanced by knowledge, and the tiny baby of the cottager is no different from that of the greatest lord. It is only their upbringing and surroundings that shape them to such different moulds. That I firmly believe. And those moulds can be broken.'

She paused, embarrassed but defiant at her outburst, unaware of how her passionate expression of her beliefs gave to her face an animation that was in many ways more striking, and endearing, than conventional beauty.

'You are a supporter, then, of the Jacobins?'

Shadows of concern darkened the grey of her eyes as she considered his question.

'No one could condone so much death and violence,' she said quietly, 'but much of what they believe, and hope to achieve, why, yes.' She looked at him, again defiantly, with a touch of the old aggression that he was learning to recognise. 'I believe they deserve all our respect and support. I shared in their dream of an ideal world, with justice for all citizens, and, although so much of that dream is tarnished, still. . .' She paused, then continued slowly, 'Perhaps the new century, so close now, will bring new dreamers to bring it to fruition. It *could* be possible. Reaching the year 1800 seemed an impossibility when I was a child!'

She was waiting, he knew, for his arguments, his outrage or his contempt. And, he thought with an inward smile, she would fight them every inch of the way.

'I agree with you,' he said truthfully, looking out of the window so that he would not have to see, and react to, her surprise. 'Such dreams could be possible.' Then, after a pause, 'But tell me, what happened to your parents?'

Unbeknown to Susan, he had read, with an accuracy that would have much disconcerted her, some of the omissions in her story.

'They were killed when I was seven,' she said, staring rather bleakly into the empty fireplace. 'They were driving back from a ball. It was extremely stormy. A tree fell on the carriage. They were both killed instantly.'

She did not mention that it had been a huge elm, and she had seen its scarred remains later, dismembered in a farmer's yard, ready for firewood. She said nothing of the nightmares about that huge falling tree that still, on occasion, woke her, shivering.

Nor did she mention the furious rages that had swept the house as her parents prepared for that ball, her father adamant that the storm was too dangerous, that it would be folly to venture out; her mother insisting on going, with the inane, unmoving obstinacy of a mindless wax doll. So they went. And they died. It was only later that an overheard conversation told Susan what everybody else already knew: that her mother had been disgracing herself and her family over a handsome young army captain, and it was to reach his arms that she had insisted they go that night.

'But it was not all bad,' Susan continued, burying the memories back deep in her mind, and wondering briefly why she so little resented the question. This was a subject on which she was usually sensitive. 'My mother's sister, Aunt Catherine, came to live with us, and was as much to us as any mother could be.'

Far more, in fact. It had been Aunt Catherine who had been Susan's teacher, friend, and source of all affection. And her pension that had brought a few comforts and luxuries into life at the Manor, including paying for Jeremy's schooling.

'Unfortunately she died two years ago.' She stared down at her hands in her lap. 'I miss her a great deal.'

And, thought Susan bleakly, we all miss her pension.

Even though it is possible to disguise from Grandfather how much. But Jeremy has to work the farm like a yeoman's son, instead of studying for university as we hoped.

The Earl was frowning at her when she looked up, his heavy brows drawn together in a dark line, his black eyes shadowed and thoughtful. I have offended him with my maundering, she thought.

'I am sorry,' said the Earl. 'I did not mean to distress you.'

The bleakness of expression that he had glimpsed in her face had unaccountably distressed him.

'Tell me in more detail about the school you plan. What sort of building did you have in mind?'

Here Susan was on safe ground. Her face lit up with lively pleasure. She had given endless thought to the building, and launched immediately into an animated description of rooms required, class sizes, whether to divide the children by age or by sex—for she was adamant that girls would be welcomed at her school—accommodation to be provided for a teacher, the number of teachers necessary, how to heat the building during the winter months, and a score of other details that had exercised her mind since she first dreamed of the idea.

She found in the Earl a sympathetic and intelligent listener, whose comments were both perceptive and practical. She had spoken to no one, other than Mr Stanbridge, who had so completely shared her enthusiasm, and against all expectation her heart warmed to the Earl of Chene. She gave him an impulsive smile, which lit her face with all the impassioned eagerness and delight that Jeremy had revealed when he looked at plans of steam engines. It made them, he thought, watching her, seem extraordinarily alike.

'You genuinely care!' she said, the pleasure in her voice robbing the surprise that was there of its sting. 'Why?'

He was about to answer, and he knew there were many things he might have confided to her then, but the door swung abruptly open, and Olivia, Dowager Countess of Chene, sailed into the room, full-rigged and ready to engage battle.

'Good gracious, Marcus!' she ejaculated loudly. 'Another business interview with this. . .person? And why in the drawing-room? The estate office is surely the place for such matters, not our family rooms.'

She surveyed them haughtily through an elaborate gold-handled lorgnette, sweeping her view with equal distaste across Susan, and the silver tray with the sherry and glasses. Susan, indignant and equally haughty, stared back.

The dowager was a big woman. Never a beauty, the features which had given strong, striking masculinity to her sons were in her both large and plain. Her hair, of mid-brown, was brushed back off her face and piled high on to her head, leaving nothing to soften the strong chin, wide slabs of fleshy cheek, thick brows, long nose and protuberant eyes. Of considerable bulk all over, still her bosom was massive. It travelled before her, a buttress to intimidate all comers.

Beside her, it suddenly struck Marcus, Susan was like an undaunted sparrow, refusing to be deprived of its farmyard grain by the aggression of a great gobbling turkey. He had a fondness for the impudence of sparrows, and he had never liked turkeys. He stood up, and turned to his mother.

'Mother, Miss Finderby is here, at my invitation, on a purely social visit. Her brother has gone out riding with Oliver. Do, please, come in and greet Miss Finderby. Come and join us.'

The dowager hesitated, then advanced, and condescendingly held out one limp white hand.

'How do you do, Miss Finderby?' Her tones were repressive in the extreme. She sat down on a large velvet-covered chair that creaked its protest. 'I do not believe we have already met in Town. I cannot recollect an occasion. Perhaps we frequent different—er—circles?

But, of course, I may be mistaken?' She raised her
lorgnette at Susan enquiringly.

'No, ma'am,' Susan replied, 'you are not mistaken.
We have never met. I have never travelled to London.'

'Never been to London? Good heavens, girl, whatever
sort of circles *do* you move in?'

The lorgnette moved in a leisurely survey of Susan's
unfashionable clothes, and lingered on a darn at the hem
of her skirts.

'Perhaps you spend more time in Bath?'

'No, ma'am. I have never visited Bath either. The
furthest I have travelled is to Nottingham, to stay with a
cousin.'

Susan's colour was high. She was well aware of the
pleasure the older woman was taking in baiting her, and
she determined to frustrate her by speaking the truth
with a calm courtesy, which she hoped, but doubted,
would put the dowager to shame.

'Nottingham? How strange. I believe I have upon
occasion purchased lace that was woven there. Usually,
of course, I take only the Brussels lace. But I know of no
one who *visits* Nottingham. Nottingham is not, surely, a
place one goes to. Perhaps your cousin is a lace weaver?'

She spoke as if she could not conceive there might be
any other occupant of such a place.

'In fact,' Susan gently replied, 'my cousin is married
to a clergyman.' She returned the dowager's glare coolly,
and hazarded a small smile. She was pleased to note the
woman's colour rising as she realised Susan was in no
way discomposed.

'I think,' the Earl put in, regretting having given any
encouragement to his mother at all, 'that I will take Miss
Finderby for a walk in the gardens. I dare say the others
will be back from their ride shortly.'

'As you wish, Marcus.'

The dowager was affronted, denied the upper hand,
and her farewell to Miss Finderby was curt.

As it happened, they found the ride already abandoned, for the handsome roan Oliver had been riding

had cast a shoe, and the two had trotted gently home again, and had retired to mull over plans together, with vast enthusiasm, in the library.

So Susan asked that the gig be ordered round immediately, overruling Jeremy's protests. Then, to the not unwelcome accompaniment of Jeremy's endless, eager talk of canals and coal-mines—for Susan's own thoughts were confused and she was happier to remain silent—they made their way home.

CHAPTER SEVEN

NEWS of the outrageous doings of the Gradely Gang continued to strike shivers through the gossip of Finderby. Predictably, it was Violet who had the up-to-date news of their exploits. She was standing at the gate of her house, talking to a man on horseback, when Susan and Jeremy walked past, a few days after their drive to Chene.

'Your faithful suitor is back from Bath, I see,' Jeremy remarked, scrutinising the gentleman on horseback with a marked lack of enthusiasm. 'With any luck he is busy playing you false with Violet.'

Susan followed where he was looking. She had been involved in deep inward debate about the population of village children, and the number of desks and chairs that should be ordered.

'Who? Oh, Eustace. I had not realised he was due back already. I somehow thought he was away for another week or two.'

'Which just goes to show how eagerly you count the days. Honestly, Sue, why don't you make more plain to the man just how unwelcome his attentions are? Kinder to put him out of his misery immediately.'

Susan sighed. Although she had known Eustace Chapley-Gore all her life, it was only over the last few months that he had begun to make plain that his interest in her was something more than neighbourly friendship. At first his approaches had been so obscure and tentative that Susan had been convinced she was only imagining his change of attitude, and had felt unable to repress advances which might only be the generous considerations of long friendship, more to be expected now that Baron Finderby was totally bed-ridden.

It therefore happened that Mr Chapley-Gore seemed

to feel he had established some understanding with Miss
Finderby, while Susan was still unsure both of the
reasons for his more frequent visits, and how she could,
in fairness, respond to them.

It was not that he was an impossible candidate as a
suitor. His family had been respectable minor gentry in
the area for many years. His income was sufficient for
comfortable living. He was about thirty-five years of age,
and lived with his mother at Radhill Grange, a mile or so
outside Finderby village. In many ways it would be an
ideal match for Susan.

Unfortunately he was dull, unrelievedly dull, and
Susan sometimes thought she could find no greater
reason than that upon which to reject an offer of marriage. His looks were dull—a plain, heavy face, portly
figure, and rapidly enlarging bald patch. This last had
encouraged him to begin wearing a small wig, which
made him look much older, and duller. His ideas were
as tedious as his appearance, moving ponderously along
predictable, conservative tracks. He lacked any spark of
humour, and he treated all women with the patronising
protectiveness deserved by his mother. Susan knew that
marriage to him would be a disaster for her. Probably for
them both. Luckily, he had not asked her yet, and she
hoped to discourage him from making the attempt.

'Miss Finderby! Young Master Jeremy! How do you
do? I was on my way to pay my respects at the Manor.
And now I find you out and about in the sunshine. Well,
well, well. And how have you been keeping while I have
been taking the waters in Bath? No chills resulting from
this cool wind?'

Susan felt Jeremy's instant irritation at the childish
form of address. She answered hastily, for them both.

'We have kept very well, thank you, Mr Chapley-
Gore. You are plainly healthy. What of your mother—
did she benefit from the waters?'

Mr Chapley-Gore, who liked to cosset himself, was
peeved to be judged in good health, as Susan had known
he would be. He made the best of it, however.

'We all did, Miss Finderby. I was just telling Miss Netheredge of the extensive benefits of which we became aware. Do you know——?'

He was obviously set to launch once again into a wealth of medical details, but Violet, who had listened to them once, had no intention of suffering them again.

'Mr Chapley-Gore,' she put in quickly, 'was most shocked to hear of the changes happening here since his departure. Like the return of the Earl, and the awful attacks by the Gradely Gang.'

'Yes, indeed.' Eustace was readily switched to this new track. 'Dire deeds, dire deeds. None of us safe in our beds. I must check the safety locks on Radhill Grange, and I shall go to bed with the poker.'

Susan heard Jeremy smother a snort of laughter.

'Has there been a fresh attack?' she enquired.

'Haven't you heard about the business over at Guysthorpe?' Violet was keen to tell the news. 'Just the other side of Chene—you know? Not only did they rob a house and take all the silver plate, they also brutally tortured the housekeeper to make her tell where the jewels were kept. Then, when she had been forced in agony to betray the whereabouts of the gems, and the brigands had them all, and had escaped with all their spoils, still they were not content, for it was not so very late at night. They held up a coach on the road across Guysthorpe Common and took two gentlemen's purses and their watches!'

It was hard, listening to Violet's tones, to know whether she was expressing shock or admiration. Eustace, though, had no doubts.

'Shocking business! Unbelievable impudence! And to torture a woman to gain their wicked ends. Nothing could be more despicable. A devilish man must lead them. Devilish. Why, they could be laying hands on a *lady* next! I am *most* perturbed, on behalf of my family, and——' he bowed stiffly from where he sat to both Susan and Violet '—on behalf of the charming young ladies of Finderby.'

'I think,' Jeremy remarked, with ill-concealed revul-

sion, 'that the young gentlemen of Finderby are capable
of looking after their own.'

Eustace gave a plump smile at Susan.

'Hot young heads on boyish shoulders, eh, Miss
Finderby?'

Sensing volcanic eruption beside her, Susan spoke
quickly.

'I do wish you would go on up to the Manor and visit
my grandfather,' she said. 'It would be such a kindness
to give him all your news of Bath. You must have met
many of his old friends and acquaintances. I know he is
awake now, and would appreciate a visit before he tires.'

'Of course, of course, Miss Finderby—anything to
oblige you and your family. I will go at once.'

With effusive farewells he urged the portly chestnut,
who dozed beneath him, on through the village.

Violet looked at Susan with a speculative smile.

'A little bird told me that you two borrowed the
doctor's gig to drive over to Chene the other day.' She
saw confirmation of this in their faces. 'Well, well, aren't
we moving in exalted circles, then! Visits at Chene!'

Susan's disclaimer, that it was only really to do with
the canal proposals, and the offer of the school, made no
impression on Violet's opinions.

'I was only just telling Mr Chapley-Gore how *much*
you are having to do with the new Earl—what with
canals, and roofs and schools. So *many* excuses, it seems,
that you have to see each other now! Mr Chapley-Gore,
strangely, was *not* impressed.'

Susan frowned.

'Your tongue has been over-busy, Violet. My meetings
with the Earl have been incidental, and purely in the
context of his proposals for the village.'

Violet gave a smirk, pleased, as always, when she
managed to dent Susan's reserve.

'Mr Chapley-Gore was even less impressed when he
heard more of what this Earl is like. The wicked temper,
and the grasping for money.'

She paused briefly, giving Susan a sideways, self-satisfied look.

'Have you heard how everyone thinks the Gradely Gang must be organised by someone of social standing? After all, when you think, there must be someone of intelligence behind such daring raids, and someone who would know where best to strike. Someone who has the social contacts. And, of course, someone obviously in need of money. Everyone is trying to guess who it might be. Isn't it intriguing?'

She twirled her fingers around in the ribbon of her bonnet, her glance sly.

'It is very noticeable how many more attacks there have been in this area recently. Really, just since the Earl came back. . .'

She was watching Susan now with a small smile, her pale eyes wide, making show of believing they were just enjoying sharing village chatter. She noted Susan's heightened colour, but it was Jeremy who rounded on her.

'Of all the mischievous gossips, Violet, you are the worst,' he said angrily, with far more regard to honesty than courtesy. 'The Earl is a thoughtful, intelligent, far-sighted man with plans and dreams beyond anyone I have ever met. It is a monstrous absurdity to pretend to people that you believe him to be mixed up in this gang of thieves.'

'Well,' said Violet archly, not at all perturbed by his outburst, 'the Earl certainly has a champion in you, young Jeremy! Just you be careful you don't go making friendships you regret.'

'Come on, Susan. We don't need to stand here all day.'

Susan was fully in accord with her brother's mood.

'Truly, Violet, you must not spread rumours about people in this way. And you know how Eustace can be once he gets an idea in his head. If you have fed this nonsense to him, he will soon have convinced himself it is so, and be telling it all about the neighbourhood as a gospel truth. It is most irresponsible of you.'

Violet just smiled again.

'You are overlooking two facts, dearest Susan. One, that I have *said* nothing at all. Can I help what people think? And the other, of course, is that I, and they, may all be perfectly right!'

Upon which words she swept back up the neat brick path and into her house. Susan saw the curtains drop back at one of the front windows. Mrs Netheredge had been watching, and had obviously hurried away to discover all that had been said.

'Anyway,' Jeremy pronounced crossly as they walked on, 'I had all that tale from Oliver. It is not such news.'

'You never mentioned that to me.'

'It is not very interesting. I was telling you about that steam-pump for driving mill equipment. But they didn't really *torture* the housekeeper.' He gave a chuckle. 'Well, apparently they did sit her on the kitchen fire——'

Susan gasped and looked furiously round at him.

'No, no, hold your horses! She wasn't burned. Oliver said he heard that she screeched like a captured chicken the minute they laid hands on her, and told all she knew of the jewels in a spate of absolute fury the moment she realised they had burned a great hole in the seat of her bombazine! They might have intended to scorch her, but she had so many layers of flannel petticoat that they had never a chance. And did she tear a few strips off them, by all accounts, and not over the jewels! Not a bit. It was all on account of her best bombazine. They had to gag her in the end with a dishcloth!'

It was obvious that when told this tale by Oliver Jeremy had found it very funny. Knowing his sister's odd reaction to jokes of this sort against the female sex, however, he struggled to keep a straight face. She gave a reluctant half-grin.

'It wasn't funny,' she said, attempting severity. 'The poor woman must have been terrified. Anyway, how did Mr Carlleon know?'

'Oh, I dare say the news was all over Chene. It is nearer Guysthorpe than we are,' Jeremy replied vaguely.

Susan was doubly angry with Violet when she went upstairs that afternoon to spend some time, as she tried to do each day, with her grandfather. She discovered that Eustace had spoken of the Earl, making reference to him as being obviously a most undesirable new arrival in the area, and fuelling all the old man's resentments.

She had been planning to tell the old man about the kindness of the Earl with regard to the thatching and the school, hoping, if she caught him on a day when he felt well, to go some way towards modifying his embittered prejudice. Now she felt driven to defend the Earl in face of Eustace's ponderous comments, but knew that the Baron was far from ready to listen.

'I wish you would not pay attention to Eustace's foolish talk, Grandfather. You know he has been in Bath all these last weeks, he knows nothing of Chene but what he has heard from Violet, and she has never even met the Earl. It is nothing but her spiteful talk.'

'I never expected to lie here and listen to my own flesh and blood defending a Chene, and I don't expect it now. If all the village knows the man for a villain, who are you to think you know better? Eh?'

'Grandfather——' she stood straighter, and spoke with determination '—I did not tell you before, but he has offered to re-roof Mill Cottages at his own expense. You didn't know, for I don't like to worry you, but I have despaired of doing anything about them, and they are now barely habitable. It is young Jimmy, from there, if you remember, who has the broken leg. It is largely for his sake that the Earl has got the work under way, so he can lie in comfort in the dry.'

'*He* repairing *our* cottages? Why? What devilry is he up to? What is the man's game? And why can we not repair our own cottages, may I ask?'

The tell-tale signs of his anger showed in the bulging veins of his face, and Susan called out for Alfred.

'We cannot repair them ourselves, Grandfather,' she said quietly, as Alfred stolidly delivered medicine, 'because we have no money to do so. I am grateful for the Earl's assistance, and so, I believe, must you be, little as you may like it. And, you should also know, he has donated both the plot of land, and one thousand pounds, for the setting up of a school in Finderby. No one could think that the action of a wicked man. No one. Only speak to Mr Stanbridge. See what he will tell you.'

Despite the doctor's draught the old man was gasping with fury.

'So the whelp has bought you, has he, with his bribes and promises? Quickly found the way to buy you, didn't he? Full of typical Chene cunning, taking advantage of having a mere girl to deal with. I suppose you have him busily building canals across my land where I can't see him, can't stop him? Have you? Have you? He obviously has you where he wants you! And the boy Jeremy, I dare say.'

Susan was the more stung by this because it was so close to her own initial reaction to the Earl and his proposals.

'That is absurd, Grandfather. You said I was your own flesh and blood. So I am. And you brought me up to be outspoken in the face of injustice, and support what I believed to be right. I cannot now throw away what you made me just because of your prejudice. You are doing the man an injustice. And if you would only *consider* the notion of the canal and developing our own coal supplies, why, maybe then we would have the income to repair our own cottages, and not *have* to rely on the goodness of others.'

The medicine seemed unable to quell him. The old man was furious, both at her, and at his own inability to get up and take charge of the entire situation. Susan knew she should apologise, and help to calm him down, but at that moment she could not. With a little shrug of helplessness at Alfred, she made her way out, and left the valet to soothe her grandfather's wrath.

It was with mixed feelings that she greeted young Benjamin Foot when he arrived at the kitchen door the

next morning, bearing a letter from Chene to herself and
Jeremy, and obviously very hopeful for a glimpse of
Becky.

'Come in, come in!' Hephzibah exclaimed, as he
hovered in the doorway, shooting anxious glances
towards the door of the dairy. 'Sit and have a bite. She'll
be over shortly with the milk.'

Benjamin blushed in waves of fiery pink over his
scrubbed, boyish face, disconcerted at his own transpar-
ency, and Hephzibah gave a wicked chuckle. She liked
Benjamin.

'Here.' She thumped a great pewter tankard of cider
on to the table, and bread, butter and cheese. 'I've no
doubt they sent you out without a meal again, eh? I
know how it is. And you can't be talking of milking and
butter-making with your innards all of a rumble! You
have a sup of this, and maybe I'll take a walk over to the
dairy and see how things are going.'

He gave a big, sheepish grin, beginning to get the
measure of this sharp little mouse of a creature who ruled
over the Finderby kitchen. He sat down to please her by
doing justice to her offerings, and forbore to mention the
generous amounts he had downed in the Chene kitchens
not two hours earlier.

Susan had taken the letter, and retired to her private
parlour. Penned in the Earl's distinctive hand, now
become oddly familiar to her, it invited herself and
Jeremy to spend the day at Chene in two days' time. 'My
mother,' the Earl wrote, tactfully, 'is unfortunately away
on that day, but my brother and I will be pleased to
welcome you.'

Susan knew immediately, in her heart, that they would
go. She knew Jeremy would not for the world pass over
another chance to talk with Oliver of coal-mines and
such like. Already he was planning how he would
develop the Finderby mine once he was free to take up
his inheritance, and how he could use the income it
generated to revitalise the farm, buying new stock, and
new seed, how he could travel to gain new ideas from

other farmers, and take care of his tenants as they should be taken care of. Hearing such enthusiam, Susan had no heart to stop his dreaming. No. He would go.

And she? Were she to refuse, it would seem that she too believed the rumours that wormed their way about the houses of Finderby, that she too condemned the man. She would not do that. Still, in part, she felt guilty that her own rash outburst had started Violet on this ridiculous track. Despite her grandfather's prejudice, she would not be seen to join the petty minds of Finderby. She was almost, she realised with a shock of surprise, beginning to think of the Earl as a friend. Anyway, there was much about the school they would need to discuss.

She wrote a neat note of acceptance, and took it back out for Benjamin to take on his return. Which, after establishing amid much giggling outside the kitchen door that Becky might, on occasion, be free to walk out of an evening with him, he did.

'Though only if I've nothing better to do,' Becky called after him cheekily.

Benjamin looked back and grinned.

'You'll find nothing better than what I've got in mind for you,' he said.

Susan, listening, laughed.

'You'll have to keep an eye on Becky,' she remarked to Hephzibah.

'Huh. That lad'll do nothing to upset *me*,' she said, with sharp assurance. 'But what about you? Eh, miss? Is it you I should be keeping my eye on, Susan Finderby? With that Eustace calling this morning, and then notes from Chene this afternoon. What am I to think? Well, come on. Out with it, girl. You'll not hide it from me! What did Chene say? You tell Hephzibah all about it!'

CHAPTER EIGHT

MARCUS and his brother were sitting outside when their visitors arrived. The weather had carelessly abandoned its former clouds and cold breezes, and had spread a dome of clear madonna-blue above the English countryside. The sun was already hot, but a hint of movement in the air brought a soothing susurration from the restless whisper of lime leaves. Marcus had caused tables and chairs to be set out on the lawns in the dappled shade of the great single lime that dominated that aspect of the gardens, and sat peaceably waiting beneath it, legs stretched before him, eyes closed, as if he had not a care in the world.

His brother eyed him from where he perched on the wall of the terrace. Long years of conditioning in regarding all his elder brother's decisions as unquestionably correct were difficult to throw aside, but over this business of the Finderbys and the canal Oliver still harboured doubts.

Marcus's reactions to opinionated Miss Finderby seemed inexplicably irrational: alternately furious, conciliatory, wary, defensive, or dismissive to the point of discourtesy. Now, although Marcus was commonly quite cavalier in his attitude to his clothes, Oliver had noticed—though not seen fit to comment—that his brother had chosen the pale, slim-fitting breeches, the excellently cut coat in bottle-green superfine, and the pale green silk striped waistcoat, with a care and attention to detail that was unusual. He wondered why.

He was beginning to wish he had not so actively discouraged Marcus's suggestion of inviting a house party of guests, including the particular beauty who had been absorbing his brother's erratic interest in the affairs of the heart during their stay in London. Oliver had thought it would hinder any work progressing on the canal. But it might also have discouraged invitations to Miss Finderby.

Oliver sighed as he heard the wheels of the doctor's gig crunching over the gravel at the front of the house. Not that he minded a visit from Jeremy. He was not averse to a little youthful adulation.

Susan too had had her preparations for this visit silently noted and pondered over by her younger brother. Invitations to spend a day at a house like Chene were sufficiently rare in Susan's life to make her feel quite justified in sorting carefully through her wardrobe, and the brilliant sunshine had meant that her pretty muslin dress, printed with tiny sprigs in primrose and green and ornamented with a pleated hem, would be ideal. She had added a new wide sash of primrose silk, which gave the impression of the dress having a more fashionable, higher waistline, and decorated her best bonnet with new primrose ribbons and a tiny spray of flowers. She had also spent some time cleaning her green silk pumps, and stitching a little bow of primrose ribbon to each, in order to hide a persistent stain of splashed bacon fat.

The end result, Jeremy considered, eyeing her judicially as she jumped lightly down from the gig and laughed back up at him, was unusually becoming. He wondered, briefly, to what end. Such brotherly thoughts, however, were swept aside by the appearance of Oliver around the side of the house, waving and calling in welcome.

'Hello! Isn't it a perfect day? Miss Finderby, Jeremy, it is good to see you. Yes, thank you, Benjamin, if you would take the gig now.' The groom, who had appeared on cue from the back of the house, shot a shy smile at Susan. The butler emerged solemnly from the front door. 'It is all right, Bowdler, I will take them round the outside. If you could be good enough to have the drinks sent out?'

Burying his misgivings for the furtherance of whatever plan his brother might have in mind, Oliver welcomed the visitors profusely. He led them across the gravel, and around the corner of the red brick tower at the end of the building. The house was quite narrow, relative to its length, with another smaller tower marking each rear corner. Between these spread the terrace; beyond, the gardens and lawns stretching to the park. They followed Oliver down the terrace steps, between some attractive formal rose-beds redolent of all the idleness of summer days with their heavy perfume, and towards the great lime.

Susan had seen the Earl immediately they rounded the corner of the house, as if she had some uncanny extra awareness of his whereabouts, as he stood half hidden in the patchy shadows beneath the tree. He was a little way from a pleasant grouping of chairs and tables, quite still, watching their approach. The compact vitality of his body, the evident strength in the broad shoulders and muscular thighs, the dark head tilted slightly to one side, all seemed oddly familiar to Susan, startling her with that jolt of pleasure and anticipation that the unexpected sight of a much-loved friend might bring. Then, even before she had time to analyse the impression, memories of all their discordant dealings overlaid it, and she walked, determinedly hopeful, but warily, across the grass.

He walked out into the sunshine to greet them.

'Miss Finderby.' He took her hand, and held it for an instant, looking down at her. 'I am so pleased you felt able to come.' And he smiled with a frank pleasure that brightened his dark features with an almost impish charm, as if wishing to share a delight, and promising more delight to come. Surprised and confused, Susan flushed and retrieved her hand.

'It seemed,' she said repressively, 'an ideal opportunity to discuss further our plans for the village school.'

'Of course.'

He nodded with every appearance of solemn agreement, but she was discomposed to recognise the laughter still lurking at the back of his eyes. She sat down in one of the chairs placed ready.

'What a charming spot for a summer's day,' she remarked politely.

He sat opposite her. Jeremy and Oliver had paused some distance back, deep in talk.

'So I thought,' he said, 'when I chose it.'

Susan had pulled off her white cotton gloves, and she twisted them round in her hands, quite at a loss for what to say. Then with relief she recollected that she and Jeremy had called by at Mill Cottages the preceding day.

'The thatching work has begun,' she said. 'Mrs Peters is very happy with it. We are all hoping the good weather will hold while the old roof is off. Jimmy is progressing as well as can be expected. Mostly, I believe, he is just bored.'

'Yes, I knew the work had begun. I am glad it is going to your satisfaction. Do, please, keep an eye on the progress, and let me know immediately if you have any complaints.'

'Yes,' said Susan. 'Thank you.'

She wondered what topic to try next. She felt too ignorant of architecture to initiate a discussion about his house.

It was with relief that she saw Bowdler approaching, gliding serenely over the lawns bearing a large silver tray, a footman behind him, similarly burdened. Bowdler's tray bore a vast tureen of chilled fruit punch, ideal for the day, and he began solemnly serving it out into glasses with a heavy silver ladle. The Earl brought a glass to Susan as the men retired.

'Thank you,' she said, again.

'Isn't it odd,' the Earl remarked, leaning forward in his chair, elbows on his knees, and looking down with a small smile into the glass he casually held in his long fingers, 'how extraordinarily difficult it is to begin to be distant and polite to people to whom one has become accustomed to being comfortably rude and insulting?'

And he cocked one quizzical eyebrow at her.

Susan gave a reluctant smile, and he grinned.

'That,' she replied, 'is most unfair. I have come here determined to be on my best behaviour, after having previously maligned you. You should not undermine my good intentions.'

'I should be far more maligned if I had to live through the tedium of a day of "best behaviour",' he responded, with a grimace. 'So dull. I am sure a regular dose of daily insult is far better for my soul.'

She laughed.

'Well, if you are adamant, I shall do my best to oblige, of course. But it is difficult at the moment to know quite what to insult you over. Never mind; just allow me time. . .' She pondered, half smiling, her head on one side. 'I dare say I shall manage to think of something.'

'I,' he said, 'am quite *certain* of that, Miss Finderby.'

'Quite certain of what?'

Oliver and Jeremy had belatedly noticed the arrival of the punch, and come over to help themselves. Without waiting for a reply to his question, Oliver sat down.

'Jeremy and I were talking coal-mines. He says, Marcus, that he has been down to examine the hill on the Finderby land that I suspect will bring them a generous output. He is certain he has discovered a seam in the hillside, and it could very probably be developed by taking a branch of the canal straight into the hill as we are going to do here. I shall probably call over there one day soon and take a look.'

While Marcus expressed his interest, Susan watched her brother's face, alight with enthusiasm and pride at being credited with an adult contribution to make in an adult world. This is beginning to mean so much to him, she thought, suddenly apprehensive. If only Grandfather would discuss it with him sensibly. The Earl turned and caught sight of her face.

'Oliver—why don't you and Jeremy ride over to the site of our mine?' he suggested smoothly. 'Jeremy might be less eager if he sees the mess mining can make of the surrounding land.'

Giving a slight frown at this unpromising attitude, nevertheless Oliver was more than happy to escort the boy. He was certain, quite rightly, that Jeremy's enthusiasm was impossible to dampen. Draining their glasses of punch, they were up and striding away towards the stables, hands in pockets, heads bent together in earnest talk. Susan watched them wistfully.

'I could almost wish,' she said, 'that Grandfather did not feel the way he does. That the canal could run through our land.'

'Miss Finderby! Don't say such things. You will have me seriously concerned for your health!'

She smiled, but said thoughtfully, 'No, it is true. I have never seen Jeremy so passionately involved by anything before. He works the farm willingly, and well, because he knows he must, but a business such as this, which absorbs all his dreams, would go far towards reconciling him for what he lost when he was unable to continue his education and improve his prospects. But——' she shrugged '—it is not to be thought of at present. Let us leave the subject. I have been busy considering how best to insult you, but my mind is a desert. I can only think to accuse you of a lack of courtesy in forcing me to do all the talking. Tell me instead about yourself. You asked me before why I have an interest in the school. Let me ask you, my lord, why do you? And how *can* such a philanthropic concern be found in one who wishes to own mines and mills?'

Marcus leaned back in his chair, amused.

'I never thought, whatever my multitude of other faults, to be accused of discourtesy to a lady by allowing her excessive time to speak! It is fortunate for you there are no other ladies present. I believe they would consider your reluctance to chatter would brand you a most traitorous member of your sex, not readily to be forgiven!'

'Oh,' Susan said, thinking of the conversations of Violet and other ladies of her acquaintance, 'I think I am already regarded as that. I do not seem to be able to

survive on the diet of the tittle-tattle and gossip that fills
the lives of the other women I know. It is all so
meaningless. So tedious.' Her face puckered in a small
frown. 'I enjoy discussions of purpose, arguments even,
a real exchange of ideas, a diet with a flavour of pepper
and spice. But this is most assuredly *not* seen as an
acceptable feminine characteristic in Finderby.'

A vision of Eustace's disapproving face floated into her
mind, and a flicker of despair touched her expression.

'But,' she continued, interested, pushing intrusive
thoughts aside, 'you accuse me of being an unnatural
female. Do you truly approve the time for idle prattle
commonly demanded by my sex? Do you consider it to
be necessary for femininity?'

His expression was one of exaggerated horror.

'Not in the least,' he said hastily. He laughed. 'One
thing guaranteed to send me fleeing the room on any
conceivable pretext is a gaggle of gossips. No. I believe,
rather, that I was commending you on your lack of this
characteristic.'

And he smiled at her.

For some reason Susan felt suddenly rawly self-conscious, sharply aware that she and the Earl were alone in
the spreading gardens, with not even a distant gardener
in view, and the plants all slumbering languidly in the
heat around them. She took a deep, steadying breath,
and concentrated on sipping her punch, struggling to
ignore her almost stifling awareness of his proximity.

She was glad when the Earl suggested they walk down
to the park fence, if she did not object to the heat. She
did not object at all, having grown up with no opportunity of acquiring a town young lady's horror of sunshine. The Earl offered his arm and, hoping she was
hiding her self-consciousness, Susan lightly rested her
hand upon it and allowed him to lead her across the
lawns towards the park.

'I notice, sir,' she remarked, when she felt sufficiently
composed to glance up at him accusingly from beneath
her bonnet, 'that you managed to cunningly evade my

question on the possibilities of combining philanthropy and. . .' she paused, then shrugged and continued defiantly '. . .and industrial exploitation of the poor. You assured me your interest was not in bribing my family. What, then, is it? How can you justify your attitudes?'

'My, my!' he commented quietly, his eyebrows raised. 'Industrial exploitation of the poor? You *have* been reading some stirring pamphlets!'

He felt her anger immediately, as the hand in the little white glove that had rested so uncertainly on his arm now tightened its grip as she turned to glare up at him.

'Don't patronise me, sir!'

Her grey eyes, with their thick dark lashes, were very fine, he thought, when she was angry. But he was left with no peace for admiration.

'Yes, I endeavour to read as widely as I can, *and* to form my own judgements from what I read. But I have also seen coal-mines, seen cotton mills, and been *sickened*. I consider my choice of terminology to have been restrained.'

They had stopped walking when she had rounded on him. Now that she had finished her outburst she was glaring up at him, colour high, chest heaving, lips quivering, her hand tight on his arm. For a moment they stood, eyes locked, before she flung round and began to walk on. He was startled to find his own breath quickened, and he took a moment to settle himself before he replied.

'I am sorry,' he said. 'That was patronising. I apologise.'

They walked a few more steps in heavy silence before he felt the hand relax, and she managed to look up at him and almost smile.

'I accept your apology, my lord,' she said, and she paused, clearly now waiting for him to answer her question.

Marcus was actually finding it extraordinarily difficult to offer up something that had been a growing dream of

his for many years to Miss Finderby's acerbic scrutiny.
He countered with a question of his own.

'Where did you see the mines and mills that so
distressed you?'

Susan frowned.

'A few years ago I was invited to accompany my cousin
and her husband—the ones who live in Nottingham—
on a tour of the Lakes. It was on the journey. The Lakes
themselves had a wild and rugged beauty that was
breathtaking, beyond anything that I had ever seen. But
travelling up through the Pennine hills we passed some
bleak and dismal areas.

'The mills were sited on the mountain streams to gain
the necessary power to drive the machinery, but no one
would voluntarily live in such God-forsaken places. They
were like filthy brick prisons in a landscape of treeless
desolation.' He felt her shudder. 'To form the workforce
the managers were obliged to send to the orphanages in
the cities, and coachloads of half-starved boys were
delivered, some from a hundred miles away or more, all
bemused and frightened. They had been promised
apprenticeships, and thus bound themselves by the
papers they had signed to years of starvation, misery,
cold, injuries and ill-treatment. These children were
locked up in sheds at night and guarded by day, yet still
some managed to escape and run away, often only to die
famished and cold on those desolate moors.'

She gave an angry little shrug before continuing. He
found he was acutely aware of her hand on his arm; when
she spoke so passionately of things that moved her, her
fingers clasped, or clenched. He felt her every shift of
mood.

'We stayed some days in the inn of a village near two
such mills,' she continued. 'My cousin's husband was so
appalled by what he discovered that he has since founded
a society for the protection and relief of such children.
Conditions in the mines we saw were little better.'

She looked up into his face.

'I have never forgotten the children I saw then. We

see poverty in the villages here, among the idle, the feckless, the injured or the plain unfortunate, but within the village there is always someone who will offer relief to the needy or desperate, and every cottager can make something of his garden. Families protect their own, as does the village. The poor can retain at least some tatter of their dignity.' She drew breath. 'So. Now you know what I have seen, and why I care. But what of you?'

They had reached the railing fence that divided the gardens of the house from the great park beyond. A group of fallow deer were grazing near a small copse of copper beeches some way ahead, glancing up every now and then to watch the advance of these intruders on their peace. Susan let go the Earl's arm and leaned on the railings, watching them. He stood beside her and rested his arms likewise, the elbow in the dark green wool coat almost touching that in the tight sleeve of patterned muslin. Like her, her stared ahead at the deer.

'I, too, have seen such things,' he said quietly. 'And they moved me as they did you. Such mills are unforgivable places. And, in part, I agree with what you say about the village. But it is not fair to judge those who cannot support themselves and their families as only unwilling, or incapable of work. There are keen, able-bodied men for whom there simply are no chances of regular work, and they must live in desperate poverty, trying to rely on casual farm labour, or travel many miles in search of employment, leaving wives and families unprotected. It is far from idyllic in our villages, Susan. Just a glance inside young Jimmy's cottage can tell you that.'

The use of her name had slipped out quite unintentionally. He had been thinking, in some back corner of his mind, as he spoke, how much he liked the name, and how its warm, strong sound suited her. He had not meant to say it, although it felt oddly right to do so. She made no response, however, to his unwarranted familiarity, and he thought perhaps she had not noticed.

'How does that connect,' she asked, 'with your concern over the mills?'

She stared fixedly at the deer, especially at a young buck who was staring curiously back. She had no intention of letting him see how much that casual use of her name had perturbed her. Why had he done it? What did he mean by it? She pushed her whirling thoughts aside and concentrated on his reply.

'I have long had a dream,' he was beginning slowly, and with a hesitancy that she was startled to realise was almost a shyness, 'a dream of building. . .well. . .a village, I suppose. A place of new houses, small but well constructed. . .with a school and a church, of course. . .perhaps a hospital. . .and, principally, employment. The coal-mine, the canal boats, and the cotton manufactory—honest, fair work for the men, to enable them to support their families with more than just a tatter of dignity.'

He paused for a moment.

'Mines and mills can employ many people profitably, and that fact is invariably abused by greedy men. But the hours those people work, the conditions of that work, and the wages—they are all decided by the owner. I want to be that owner, so that I can make those conditions as close as I can to the ideal, fair to everyone who works there. I want to prove that industrialists, if not obsessed by greed, can be just, thoughtful, and compassionate employers. I know I am probably absurdly naïve, but I have to try. I want my village to be a model for others to follow.'

He turned to face her.

'The initial outlay will be tremendous, but I do believe it can be done. And, although it should pay its way, it will take time. That is why the coal must be extracted cheaply, and sold to support my other building plans. And to extract it cheaply I need to transport it by canal. So there it is. That is why I am trying to develop my land.'

He seemed almost shamefaced, she thought in amaze-

ment, as he stared down at the ground between them
and waited for her comments, and she struggled to know
what to say. It occurred to her, as she risked a glance up
at his dark, brooding expression, that he had undoubt-
edly bared this dream to others once upon a time, and
had it disparaged and ridiculed. Especially by women
who liked to see his fortune at their disposal, undented
by dreams, she thought with a sharp flash of insight. Or
one particular woman. He has been hurt by someone
over this, she thought. He has learned to keep it a hidden
dream, not to be confided lightly.

She gently touched her hand to his arm in a gesture
almost of comfort, and spoke the first words that came
into her head.

'I would dearly love to help you,' she said.

He gave a sudden laugh, and, taking her hand, he
raised it briefly to his lips.

'You truly would, wouldn't you?'

She nodded, smiling, and he thought, with a surge of
amused affection, that it was probable she was already
busy in part of her mind, considering designs of the
houses, or hours of work for apprentices, or how many
pews they would need for the church!

'Miss Finderby,' he said, 'I think it highly probable
that you will be helping me. I don't imagine for one
moment you would allow me to proceed without the
benefit of your astute advice!'

He was still clasping her hand, she found, and she
pulled it back.

'You make me sound an interfering harpy!'

He chuckled, letting her go.

'Never,' he said. 'How could I? I wouldn't dare!'

His eyes were laughing, challenging her with his
teasing. Susan was glad when the inquisitive buck came
closer, venturing up to the fence, and when it bent to
sniff delicately at her skirts she could allow herself to be
distracted, and lean over to stroke the soft velvet of its
antlers.

They walked back to the shade of the tree a little later,

and drank more of the punch, newly chilled with fresh crushed ice brought from the house. Talk was easy and relaxed now, Susan full of queries and ideas about his dream village, entranced by the excitement of such a wide-ranging and ambitious plan, the Earl discovering the delight of exploring his dream with someone who brought uninhibited enthusiasm to all her suggestions, and laughed with pleasure when she found most of them already anticipated, her ideas shared.

They were walking among the rose-beds, Marcus selecting blooms for her and cutting them neatly with the blade of his penknife, and discussion had somehow moved on to places they had visited, and the disreputable escapades that had accompanied the Earl on his Grand Tour when he was little older than Jeremy, when Oliver and Jeremy arrived back. There was an air of intimacy about the couple wandering carelessly among the roses that brought Oliver to a startled and speculative halt before he hid his thoughts and walked over to join them.

Lunch was al fresco, a meal of luscious delicacies proudly produced by Bowdler, who was followed by a train of immaculately uniformed footmen and white-aproned maids, each bearing a tray. White cloths were spread on the ground, with four large cushions arranged around, and plate after plate laid down—of meats roasted, baked, pressed, jellied or smoked, salads of vegetables that Susan had never even heard of, let alone tasted before, tiny glazed potatoes, and carrots and peas, then breads, and butters and cheeses. . .

A little vision of meals in the sunshine at Finderby swam into Susan's mind, of when she would dollop her helping of whatever she had helped Hephzibah to cook on to a large plate, then wander out to perch on a favourite old stone that lay among the rosemary and lavender bushes because not one of her multitude of forebears had yet found the necessity of moving it. She chuckled.

The Earl turned to look at her, and raised a querying eyebrow.

'All this!' She smiled and waved a hand at the banquet before them. 'For four of us! It is just like a Roman orgy!'

'And precisely what do you know of Roman orgies, Miss Finderby?' His eyes were full of laughter. 'But no—don't answer that question. I am certain to be told that the slaves who waited at the orgies were subjected to despicable exploitation. . .'

Miss Finderby laughed.

'You are a fine one to talk,' she said.

She became aware of Oliver watching her curiously, but it was Jeremy who spoke.

'I don't know about Romans, but I could demolish half of this orgy single-handed. It looks magnificent. May we start?'

'Please,' said Marcus, 'help yourself. You will have to go and give your comments to my cook afterwards. I can see you are a boy after his own heart. Miss Finderby, sit down. May I make you a plateful, or would you prefer to help yourself?'

'No, no,' she said. 'One cannot possibly enjoy an orgy vicariously. I shall help myself!'

It was quiet while they ate, reclining languorously on the cushions, the spasmodic talk inevitably much concerned with what Oliver and Jeremy had looked at that morning, then drifting on to horseflesh, and horse-racing, then back to travel, and anecdotes from wild, exotic places. They spoke of the exploits of the Gradely Gang, idly speculating about who they might be, where they had come from, which houses they chose and why.

'You need to be careful here,' Jeremy remarked, waving a hand towards the house. 'It must be an obvious target, so plainly wealthy and full of fine things. I am surprised you have not suffered already.'

'I do have a large, efficient and vigilant staff, and new locks fitted to all doors and windows since our return to live here. I dare say that has quite a deterrent effect,' the Earl said, sipping his wine and not sounding in the least perturbed.

'It would be good sport if they did turn up,' said Oliver, his eye kindling at the thought. 'They wouldn't find us such easy pickings as these poor old ladies they choose to rob, eh, Marcus?'

A footman had appeared with more wine, and moved quietly round, refilling glasses, then removing used dishes.

'We shouldn't be in much danger either,' Jeremy remarked wistfully.

'Why is that?' asked Oliver, who had not, Susan reflected, seen the Manor, or he would not have asked!

'Nothing to take!' said Jeremy with a wry grin. 'Not a gem or jewel left to the family name, except for the Finderby Star, of course, and that's been locked away in Grandfather's bedroom since my mother died. Everyone must have forgotten it's there.'

'What is the Finderby Star?' Oliver's interest was no more than polite.

'Oh, some star of diamonds that is traditionally always given to the new wife of the Baron on her wedding day. They're supposed to be very good diamonds,' he grinned. 'Not that I know anything much about them. I wonder where the Gang will choose next? Maybe another highway robbery?' He suddenly sat up, a forkful of salad poised in one hand, and spoke eagerly. 'Do you think we could send out a coach with the three of us in it disguised as wealthy ladies, then when we were held up we could take them by surprise and shoot them all?'

He sounded quite taken with this flight of fancy, but abandoned it without prejudice when the Earl bluntly replied, 'No!' He and Oliver tossed the idea around for some while, though, extracting much amusement from its possibilities.

For much of the time Susan was content to listen. Every so often the Earl would catch her eye and smile, or offer her some particular delicacy.

His name is Marcus, she thought, listening to Oliver say the name with a secret twinge of pleasure. She looked at his face, the dark hair short, the heavy eyebrows mobile with humour as he spoke, the way his mouth curled up at the very corners just before his face lit up in a smile. It suits him, she thought, speaking the name in her mind. As if he had heard her, he suddenly turned to look keenly at her. Guiltily, she flushed and turned away, breathing fast.

They drank more wine, chilled in silver basins full of ice, and later the train of servants reappeared to remove dirty plates, and produce exquisite iced fruit desserts. When no one, not even Jeremy, could eat more, and everything had been cleared with silent efficiency by Bowdler's army, they lay on the cushions and chatted idly. Resting up on her elbow, looking at the three men, all stretched flat and gazing up into the softly moving lime leaves, Susan felt as decadent and abandoned as if she were at any Roman orgy. She wondered what Hephzibah would say if she could see them reclining there, waited on hand and foot. She sat a little straighter, and tried not to enjoy being decadent quite so much, but nothing took away the pleasure she found in listening to the Earl's voice as he talked quietly to Jeremy of, inevitably, steam-pumps!

Later, Oliver and Jeremy went to look at all the horses in the Chene stables, and the Earl took Susan indoors and showed her some tentative plans for his village, and they leaned over the table, heads together, and argued companionably over the appropriate size of garden for each worker, getting happily side-tracked into necessary space for potatoes, and cabbages, and a pig. It was a surprise to Susan where the afternoon had gone, when a tray of tea was served, and after that it was time to order round the gig.

It was not until they were halfway home, and Jeremy talking with an enthusiasm that demanded no response from his sister, that she realised that all the plans she and the Earl had for the village—and she realised she was thinking of it as *their* village now—*all* these plans depended upon the availability of the canal.

And the canal would have to run through Finderby land.

CHAPTER NINE

THE Earl of Chene was remarkably cheerful. Everyone noticed it. He had a smile and a friendly word for any of the staff who came his way.

Mr Blake, the estate's agent, found him whistling over the papers they had to discuss in the estate's office, and although, Mr Blake realised ruefully afterwards, the Earl had in fact decided everything to his own satisfaction and ignored all the advice from his agent that did not suit him, just as usual, he had done it in such a cheery way that it had been quite painless.

Bowdler had taken to beaming at his master's retreating back view with a slightly knowing smile. He had a very good idea about the reasons for this lordly contentment, and upon reflection Bowdler felt he thoroughly approved.

Oliver was perplexed and suspicious, and found the sight of his brother humming happily over his plans for his village, when they both knew nothing could be developed without the Finderby land, impossibly irritating.

The dowager too, returning from a welcomed few days with friends on the other side of the county, noticed the change in her usually brusque son.

Only Marcus merely smiled, and appeared to notice nothing unusual.

'Precisely *what* has happened while I was away?' demanded the dowager of Oliver one day when Marcus had just left the luncheon table, with an infuriatingly abstracted smile on his face. 'Before I left this house he was so rude and ill-tempered he was insufferable, and I was more than once sorry he is beyond the age when I could order a good thrashing by his tutor.' She glared at Oliver, reliving in her mind all the outrageously insulting

things her foul-tempered son had said to her, and her
plain face was heavy with anger. 'I come back and he is
wandering around as carefree as a poppy-field in
summer. You can't flannel me with the notion that
nothing has come about, young man. And I want to
know what!'

It did occur to Oliver that none of his brother's moods
seemed able to please their mother—well, few things
ever *did* please their mother. He felt a fleeting sympathy
for Marcus, but he was, for reasons he could not clearly
define, angry with the Earl himself.

He shrugged impatiently, unwilling to discuss it with
their mother.

'Nothing happened. We certainly have not received
the permission we need to begin work on the canal. It is
so frustrating! Lord knows why he is so cheerful. He has
been like it ever since those Finderbys came over for the
day.'

The dowager glared at him.

'Miss Finderby? *Here*?'

Her tones were icy, but then, they often were.

Oliver nodded warily. 'And her brother. A nice
enough lad, keen on canals. They came for luncheon.'

He realised too late that there might be a reason why
Marcus had not made any attempt to mention the visit to
his mama.

'Good God, what is Marcus thinking of? Has he
forgotten *all* that is due to his station? He cannot be
entertaining any rustic riff-raff that wanders through his
gates. He will be throwing banquets for the beggars and
gypsies next. Absurd! Impossible! How *dare* he?'

She strode out of the dining-room, leaving Oliver
astounded. The reaction was extreme, even for the
dowager.

From the furious sulk that later kept their mother
retired to her room in a silence that reverberated around
the whole of Chene, Oliver surmised that the dowager
had attempted to take Marcus to task. Marcus, however,
was imperturbably cheerful, merely remarking over

supper that he was sorry his mother was indisposed, and that he intended to visit Finderby on the following day to consult with Miss Finderby over her school.

Hephzibah too had noticed changes. Susan, she realised, was singing a great deal around the house, and soft catches of song would float from among the peas, or gooseberries, when Susan was out in the sunshine picking. Simple tasks like shelling the peas seemed to take her a very long time, however, and Hephzibah would look out impatiently from the heat of the kitchen to where the girl sat in the sun, and see her gazing into space, a smile playing on her lips.

Hephzibah was no fool. She pondered long and hard, regarding Susan's daydreaming figure and the flush and laugh with which she was startled from her thoughts with dubious, pursed lips. But she held her tongue, and thought fierce thoughts about the things she might do to anyone who broke her Susan's heart.

As usual, it was Benjamin who brought the note. Susan and Becky were sitting side by side at the kitchen table when he arrived, shaping pats of butter together, ready for Becky to sell in Findham market, five miles off, the following day.

Hephzibah heaved a deep sigh when she saw the way their faces shone as he bashfully tapped the open door and came in. You're envious, you old fool, she nagged herself crossly, and she made a deal of noise clattering out the cider jug, and the largest pewter tankard, and the scones she had made that afternoon.

At the table each of the girls was clutching something. Susan, as she expected, was holding a letter from the Earl, unconsciously pressing it against her bosom as she gazed entranced at what rested in Becky's hand.

'Look!' Becky held it up for Hephzibah's scrutiny. Her face was flushed pink, her pretty blonde curls bouncing from under her cap, her eyes blue as speedwells. 'Benjamin made it for me!'

It was a mouse, life-sized, and carved of wood so

skilfully that it was almost possible to believe that in a moment it would uncurl, flick its tail, and scurry off the table. Becky was smiling, stroking it with her fingertip, Benjamin watching every move of her face. Then he looked up at Hephzibah.

'I made one for you too,' he said diffidently, with an engaging shy smile. 'To thank you for all the food.'

It was another mouse, but tiny, and mounted on a pin so that it could be worn to pin a shawl. He watched her hopefully.

Startled at being remembered, Hephzibah took the tiny thing, and pinned it to her apron, frowning as her fingers fumbled.

'Well,' she said gruffly, with a small sniff, 'you are a charmer and that's for sure. Mice indeed. You have another of my scones now, and I'll fetch the raspberry jam and some cream.'

She vanished hastily into the larder. The three at the table exchanged smiles, sharing a small secret. It was impossible not to notice that the tiny carved mouse looked extremely like its new owner.

The Earl—as Hephzibah discovered when she later found his letter under the pillow as she was making Susan's bed, and *almost* accidentally happened to see the contents—had invited Miss Finderby to meet him at ten o'clock the following morning at the site of the new school, in order to finalise plans.

Susan had already left by this time, fresh and pretty in a cream cotton gown with coffee-coloured ribbons. Hephzibah could see her from the bedroom window, walking over the meadows towards the village. She shook her head and sighed, watching till the girl was out of sight. It was going to be hard if she had to trust the girl's happiness to the likes of an earl, and a Chene at that. And no one but herself seemed to be wondering what the old Baron would say.

Marcus, immaculately dressed once again, in cream-coloured breeches, deep wine-red coat and top boots, with a black hat and cane, had driven over from Chene in his curricle. This sporting vehicle was at present standing in the vicarage yard under the tender care of 'cook's lad', who took such care as was ever taken of the vicar's pony and trap. This adenoidal boy was gazing at the curricle, open-mouthed, but Mr Stanbridge confidently assured the Earl that neither horse nor carriage would take any harm.

They were standing together, surveying the plot of land. The vicar had already organised a straggle of parishioners to clear the undergrowth, and two elderly men were there as they watched, sidling mistrustfully around a large bramble, fingering their billhooks, neither wanting to be the one to tackle it.

Mr Stanbridge produced a drawing of the proposed building, but the Earl found he had difficulty in concentrating his attention. His gaze kept wandering down the road towards the Manor. He was expecting to see her arrive in the gig, unaware that this belonged to the doctor, the only working vehicles left at Finderby Manor being farm carts, and he had conjured a picture in his mind of the decisive way she would drive, sitting very straight, very much in command.

It took him a moment or two to realise that it was Miss Finderby who was walking down the street, pausing here and there to exchange greetings, pat the head of a large dog that wandered into her path, shoo aside a cluster of chickens scratching busily in the dust of the road, and skip neatly around the deeper ruts and other noxious hazards any country road had to offer.

He might have known, he thought, with that familiar mixture of admiration and exasperation which so often seemed to accompany his contemplation of Miss Finderby. He excused himself to the vicar, and hurried down towards her.

'Miss Finderby! You should not have walked all this way. Why—had I known, I would have stopped by to collect you.'

She smiled up at him. She had watched him striding

down towards her. She had known him at once. There was not another man in the village he could have been, but—I would have known him anywhere, she thought.

'Good heavens, my lord,' she said. 'I always walk everywhere, as anyone in the village will tell you. And gain much pleasure by the exercise. Those who rely always on carriages,' she said, and laughed up at him, 'become shockingly idle and over-weight.'

He offered his arm, and she rested her hand upon it.

'In that case I fear I am doomed to an obese old age in my armchair. I will drive on the slightest pretext, simply because I enjoy it.' He smiled down at her. 'Do you consider that such decadence has already left its mark? What a mortifying thought!'

'You would be a great deal more mortified, and much surprised, my lord,' she replied severely, 'were I to solemnly assure you that it had. Perhaps——' she broke off and considered, head on one side, grey eyes amused '—perhaps I should endeavour earnestly to convince you that the ill-effects are already sorely marked, and possibly—yes indeed, for it could well be true—possibly irreversible!' She chuckled. 'After all, you requested an insult every day!'

'No, no. That insult would be too cruel! I should be utterly devastated!'

'Well. . .then perhaps I shall spare you that. The day is too fine for utter devastation. But then you leave me with the necessity of searching for another insult—it is really too bad!'

They broke off this conversation to belatedly include the vicar, who had walked over the plot to join them. He had not heard more than the last few words, but the teasing intimacy with which they spoke was unmistakable. Mr Stanbridge found he was giving the Earl of Chene a very hard look indeed. Mr Stanbridge had a great fondness for Susan Finderby, and would not take kindly to watching her hurt by this striking stranger from London, no matter how philanthropic his gestures.

He watched the two of them as they discussed the

school. Susan was very decided in her ideas, her small, neat figure animated and busy as she pointed, gestured and paced out distances, quite unselfconscious, and all the more entrancing, the vicar considered, for being without a single feminine wile. The Earl walked beside her, agreeing, or questioning points she had overlooked, always watching her, Mr Stanbridge realised, surprised and partially comforted, with a lurking amusement which was mingled with, unless he was much mistaken, both affection and pride.

Susan was in full spate over the facilities needed for the older girls.

'Girls?' The Earl interrupted and spoke quite straight-faced. 'I had no intention of including girls. Surely *they* do not need any education?'

She rounded on him with a fury that had him flinging up his hands in mock surrender, unable to hide his laughter.

'You were teasing me?' she asked accusingly, needing to be certain.

'I couldn't resist it! You were so very earnest. And your eyes sparkle so magnificently when you are angry! I am sorry!'

'So you should be. I consider the education of girls to be no matter for humour.'

Susan was trying hard to keep upon her dignity, but the smile that hovered behind his dark eyes, and quirked up the corners of his mouth, was irresistible.

A small boy had run up to Mr Stanbridge, puffing and important with news. The vicar came over to them.

'I am sorry, I must leave you. Not,' he said drily, 'that I believe you need my assistance. Young Gabriel here tells me his mother's new baby is sickly and not expected to last the day. I must go down to Bogbean Cottages. But I meant to tell you—I have been in touch with Master Norris of Findham. He is willing to undertake the work here as soon as is convenient. If you are agreed on the plans we can send word. Let me know. Good day to you, Miss Finderby, my lord.'

With a swirl of black cape, one hand clutching hat and wig precariously askew on his head, he was gone.

The Earl and Miss Finderby had just finished pacing the plot, and mentally constructing busy classrooms, and had everything agreed to their mutual satisfaction, when Susan looked up, and her heart sank. Violet and Eustace Chapley-Gore were walking up to join them.

'Susan!' Violet's shrill voice called an arch greeting. 'No, don't tell me! You are busy planning your little dame school for the villagers' children. Has she told you, Mr Chapley-Gore, about all her mad schemes? I can't *imagine* why anyone thinks such people should need educated children, can you? So odd! But then, Susan is always full of odd ideas, aren't you, my dearest friend?'

Violet giggled, casting simpering and speculative glances towards her friend's dark companion, who was regarding her with a steady look she could not interpret from under his heavy dark brows.

Mr Chapley-Gore frowned, giving her comment due consideration.

'Concern for the less fortunate is doubtless our duty, Miss Netheredge,' he pronounced heavily. 'None the less, I do not feel it is necessarily appropriate for a lady to become involved in such plans as these. Such details are more properly the business of a man.'

He looked here to the unknown gentleman who accompanied Miss Finderby, but he was disappointed. Although that gentleman afforded him a brief but courteous nod of greeting, his sentiments did not meet with approval.

'I do not think you would ever convince Miss Finderby of your point of view,' the man said, 'nor would I wish you could. She, and others like her, have far too valuable a contribution to make in our society.'

Seeing Eustace more than ready to take up the point of what, in his view, were the appropriate concerns of a lady, Susan hastened to interrupt by performing the introductions.

'Miss Netheredge, Mr Chapley-Gore,' she said. 'I

would like you to meet the Earl of Chene, who has had so great a part to play in bringing my plans for the school to fruition.'

Hands were shaken politely. Violet was plainly thrilled to view at close quarters the man upon whom she had speculated so much, and engaged him in wide-eyed conversation, her rabbity teeth prominent with every smile, as she watched eagerly for tell-tale signs of his villainy.

Mr Chapley-Gore looked suspicious and disgruntled. The understanding he had of his relationship with Miss Finderby clearly precluded her wandering unescorted about the village with a Town-bred sophisticate, and in particular with one who lacked, if rumour spoke true, any gentlemanly principles at all. Indeed, the man could well be sunk in every kind of wickedness and depravity. He glowered as he walked beside Susan, unwilling to leave her in such a man's company, but unhappy at allowing Miss Netheredge to then expose herself to such an influence.

'I have seen less of you recently than I would wish,' he remarked to Susan discontentedly. 'Twice I have called and you have been out. You seem,' he sounded accusing, 'to lead a very busy life.'

'Indeed I do, Mr Chapley-Gore,' Susan assured him briskly, discovering in herself a terrible desire to giggle at the sight of his small, cross, pouting mouth, and the petulant frown that creased his smooth pink forehead. 'I am much involved in planning the school, and it keeps me as busy as even I could wish. But I am pleased to see Violet has been entertaining you. I am sure you find much pleasure in each other's company.'

'Yes. Yes, indeed. Miss Netheredge——' and his voice was heavy with comparisons '—Miss Netheredge is invariably at home, and her embroidery is charming.'

Susan might have been able to preserve her dignity had not the Earl glanced across at just that moment and caught her eye. She was forced to smother a burst of giggles behind her gloved hand, and fish desperately in her reticule for a handkerchief to pretend a bout of sneezes.

Violet, having discovered the Earl to be a reserved companion—she could even have dismissed his lack of small talk as dull had she not been so sure of his wickedness—had resorted to admitting him to her confidences. She was regaling him with a tale of the misdoings of some schoolmistress of whom she had once been told, whose behaviour was so dire, it was said, that she drowned herself in the village pond, or it might have been a river, but then it was all one, and that was the sort of awful consequence one must expect, was it not, bringing schooling into a village?

Listening to this nonsense with half an ear, for she had been told warning versions of the tale on several previous occasions, Susan was not surprised when the Earl firmly stopped at the vicarage gate and excused himself.

'It has been fascinating to make your acquaintance, Miss Netheredge. Your servant, sir.'

They could see his curricle in the yard. It was quite the sportiest vehicle Susan had ever seen in the village. Violet raised her eyebrows, and made a simpering farewell, eager to be rid of him, so that she could watch Susan's face as they all discussed him. It was a shock when he spoke again.

'Miss Finderby?'

He held out his arm to her in the most matter-of-fact way, as if he quite took it for granted that she would accompany him. Susan hovered only for a moment. She knew that her choice now, however small it might appear, was saying something decisive. She glanced at the faces of Violet and Eustace, and at the horrid mix of petty emotions she could read there.

'Thank you, my lord,' she said firmly, and took his arm.

She could hear the beginnings of Violet's outraged exclamations as they moved away. The Earl frowned.

'Have I made things difficult for you? I did not mean to. I only wished to save you the walk home.'

'It is not important. It would be impossible to escape the strictures of Violet's tongue, and if she lacked the truth to comment upon she could invent a figment of her imagination. But she will find an eager ear for her nonsense in Eustace. He is aggrieved with me. He fancies himself to be my suitor.'

'Your suitor?' The words burst out with greater ferocity than the Earl had intended, and he glared down at her, eyes dark and angry, mouth a hard line. He paused a moment. 'Surely not,' he continued more calmly. 'I fear you can have nothing whatever in common.'

'That is quite true,' Susan admitted ruefully. 'Insurmountably true in my eyes. But I am very afraid that he believes that his good influence will eventually so improve me that I will fit his ideal of the helpless little lady. Believe me, I have tried to point out to him his error!'

'So I should hope. It is a ridiculous idea.'

The Earl's brows were knit in a heavy scowl, and he sounded once again every bit the ferociously opinionated man she had first met. But this time she had no quibble with his opinion. 'And this Miss Netheredge?' he continued.

'She is. . .well, I suppose she is my friend.'

'Miss Finderby,' the Earl remarked, and continued with a casual rudeness of which she found she thoroughly approved, 'if that woman is your friend, then for pity's sake spare me introductions to your enemies. Surely you have more congenial companions than that empty-headed tattle-monger?'

Susan gave a small shrug.

'Apart from Mr Stanbridge, my lord, you are the first person I have met in Finderby who has truly shared in my ideas. If you have found many friends in your life who think as you do, then believe me, sir, you are fortunate.'

He was handing her up into the curricle as she spoke. It was much higher from the ground than the gig to which she was accustomed, with vast curved springs,

and it dipped and swayed as he jumped up beside her.
The Earl tossed a coin down to 'cook's lad', and waved
him away from the horses' heads. They fidgeted
restlessly.

'You are right, of course,' he said reflectively, pausing,
and holding the animals back. 'I have many friends, but
I probably share with them no more of my ideas than
you with Miss Netheredge, and their talk would doubtless sound quite as foolish to you. Even Oliver does not
share my dreams.' He urged the horses forward, and
swung them out of the vicarage gate, and off down the
main street of Finderby village. 'To Oliver the canal is a
longed-for challenge, but only as an exercise of his
engineering skill. The rest he sees just as my eccentricity.
He is prepared merely to tolerate it.'

The Earl's attention was now quite taken up with his
driving, all those same hazards which had enlivened
Susan's walk the horses choosing to regard as dangerous
novelties, never before encountered. However, their
wilfulness was no match for the Earl, and they were
forced to pick their way at a decorous and well-mannered
trot. Susan, however, had ample time to notice that most
of Finderby village seemed somehow to have materialised
on its doorstep to watch her progress, as she swayed high
above them in elegant luxury behind a pair of fine-
matched greys, being driven, quite unchaperoned, she
was forced by their looks to realise, by the Earl of Chene.

The Earl ignored the turning to the Manor, and drove
the short stretch further that took them to Mill Cottages.
He paused there to speak to the Chene thatcher, and
approve his work, ensuring that Susan was happy with
all that was being done, and to enquire of Mrs Peters as
to Jimmy's welfare. To Susan's surprise he produced a
basket from beneath the seat, containing fruit from the
Chene hothouses, which he gave to her for the boy. It
was only after that that he turned the greys back towards
the Manor.

He gave them their heads along the smooth grass track
across the meadows, and they sprang forward, making

nothing of their load. The curricle winged smooth and swooping through the summer air, whipping up a wind that snatched at Susan's bonnet ribbons, and slicked her dress tight against her body. She was clutching on her bonnet, flushed and laughing, when they flew in great bounds up the double embankment that surrounded the Manor, and landed with a flourish in the yard. John Wilkes came stolidly out of a barn, and took charge of the horses.

'Will you come in for some refreshment?'

Susan had impulsively asked, and the Earl had accepted, before she had given thought to where she should take him. She could not feel it right to take him into the kitchen, despite a certainty that he would not, in fact, object, and the only other room likely to be ready to receive visitors was her little parlour. For some reason she shied away from inviting him into the intimacy of that room. It was the heart of her privacy. She hesitated, unsure, embarrassed.

'There is a stone seat down by the wall beyond the herb garden,' she ventured. 'Would you care to sit there and enjoy the sun?'

Before he could answer, Hephzibah appeared beside them.

'You *both* go and sit down,' she said, shooting a fiercely warning look at the Earl, however, which strongly reminded him of the looks his nanny had given him in nursery days, warning him to be on his very best behaviour. He smiled. 'I'll bring you something on a tray,' she told them.

'Thank you, ma'am,' he said, then, 'Don't worry,' he added.

She gave him a brief, considering nod. 'I'll not be long.'

'Is Grandfather any better than he was earlier?' Susan asked, before the old woman scuttled away.

'No, dear. He has had a bad morning, but I believe he is sleeping now. Don't fret about him.'

She went in.

'Why should she worry?' Susan asked.

The Earl smiled.

'She shouldn't,' was all he would say.

They walked down through the herb garden, the brushing of their progress past the bushes filling the air with riches. Susan plucked a spray of lavender. When they reached the wall at the end of the garden, instead of sitting down on the bench she leaned on the wall and gazed out, twisting the sprig of lavender in her fingers, breathing in its pungent aroma.

'This is my favourite view,' she said.

He leaned beside her, staring out. They were looking out across the meadows towards the distant river. Immediately below the wall the double banks helter-skeltered down, dotted with sheep. The flat fields beyond were threaded by streams and dykes, their lines defined by fringes of reeds and willows. A blur of darker greens in the haze were the distant trees that marked the sweeping curves of the river, beyond those, in the far, thin mist, were rounded hills. Cows moved slowly, tails swishing, beside the streams, and in a further field men were cutting hay.

Hephzibah appeared, trotting through the bushes, carrying a tray of polished pewter, with a large tankard of cider for the Earl, and a glass of her special primrose wine for Susan. She set it carefully down on the flat stone top of the wall, and trotted away again. Susan was surprised. She had somehow thought that Hephzibah would make a point of staying. Watching her small, departing figure, Susan was suddenly shy of the man who stood beside her. She had dropped her sprig of lavender over the wall, and her hands felt awkward. She turned and picked up his cider, carefully handing it to him, and took her own glass of wine.

'Thank you,' he said.

She sipped the wine. It was a secret recipe of Hephzibah's, much cherished. It was an honour to be offered a glass of the flowery and sweet liquid.

'I asked about my grandfather,' she began uncertainly, looking down at her glass rather than up at him, 'because

I had wondered whether to take you to meet him.' She looked up then, her eyes asking for understanding. 'I don't know what to do, you see. I know that your canal needs to cross our land if you are to build your village. Jeremy has told me that if you alter the route there will be not enough capital left for your village to be built. I know Jeremy dearly wants to be a part of your plans.' She paused. 'Mr Stanbridge has spoken of you to my grandfather, as have I and Jeremy.' None of which conversations had been easy, she reflected, but perhaps her grandfather was not quite so adamant now in his condemnation of the man he had never met. 'We have tried to make him appreciate what you have done and what you hope to do. I thought. . .' Her voice tailed off. It was difficult to speak, when he watched her so intently, standing so close. She took another sip of wine. 'I thought that, were he to meet you, he might be convinced. But he has not been well recently, and today it would not be wise. Would you perhaps come to visit him when he has rallied a little?'

Her gaze was anxious.

The Earl placed his tankard down on the wall. He gently took Susan's glass from her hand and placed it beside the tankard. He rested his hands lightly on her shoulders.

'My dear,' he said. 'My dearest Susan. You must tell me whenever you think it is best, and I will come at once. For I know I must certainly meet your grandfather soon.'

He had pulled her gently closer to him, sliding his hands down her shoulders to her arms. She had tilted her head back to look up at him, and her grey eyes were wide and dark, her lips slightly parted. He felt her quiver between his hands, and her breath quicken so that her breasts rose and fell fast against the cotton of her dress. There was a hint of bewilderment in her eyes and her tongue flicked anxiously over her lip.

'Oh, my dear,' he said again, very softly, and he lowered his head to kiss her. It was a soft and gentle kiss, barely more than a touch against her lips before he set her apart again, and she was amazed that it could shake her so, so that she must lean back against the wall, weak and foolish, lips quivering and tears starting in her eyes, when he raised his lips from hers and let her go. She turned away to stare blinking across the fields, ashamed at the force of her response.

'I am sorry,' he said quietly. 'I had no intention of distressing you.'

He laid a hand lightly on her shoulder. She shook her head, unable to trust her voice to speak, and felt his hand lifted away.

'Susan,' he began, 'I would like. . .'

He paused, looking with an odd, twisted expression at the small, set shoulders, the tiny waist, the brown curls that escaped beneath her bonnet. There was nothing about her that fitted what he had always believed to be his feminine ideal, but no other girl in all his long and varied experience had filled him with the inescapable mix of emotions with which Miss Finderby had mysteriously entangled his heart. It had happened even before he had been aware that it possibly could happen, and now, caught in a dispute over a piece of land, and generations of family hatred embodied in her grandfather, he did not know quite what to do about it. Nothing in his easy and agreeable previous flirtations had prepared him for such a situation.

'Miss Finderby,' he said, his voice low with emotion. 'Susan. You must understand. How can I speak now? I will have to see your grandfather as soon as possible.'

He took her hands where they lay clenched on the top of the wall, and, turning her towards him, raised them to his lips. Then, torn between an urgent desire to kiss her again and make his feelings abundantly plain to her, and the ambivalent position in which he was placed towards her family, which made discretion the only honourable course, he abruptly took his leave.

Susan stayed at the wall, staring blindly across the fields, her emotions a whirling turmoil of confusions, dreams and hopes.

CHAPTER TEN

LORD FINDERBY slept lightly. The long, immobile days did not tire him, only wearied his mind with their tedium. At night dreams and reality blurred into a mix of angry, anxious, frustrated thoughts, and time dragged or sped in a curious dislocation. He knew every inch of the tester above him, and judged the hour by the colour and shadow that crept over it. The door was always open to the adjoining room where Alfred slept, and his grunting snores often punctuated the Baron's long hours.

It was still deep darkness, with no hint of the greys of dawn, when the Baron heard movement in Alfred's room. The sharp cracking and creaking was puzzling, until the old man realised it must be the window opening. Had Alfred heard some disturbance outside? He grunted in frustration at his own helplessness. It was so quiet for a while that the Baron almost dozed asleep again, the sounds he had heard blending back into dream, when a thud, a scuffling and a suddenly stifled cry startled him awake. Eyes wide, he strained frantically to move himself.

There were footsteps, and pushing and struggling. The door between the two rooms abruptly swung wide as two strange men hustled through it, Alfred, struggling and startle-eyed, gripped between them. The men were dressed in black—coats, breeches, boots and hats. Black scarves were tied about their faces, and their coats buttoned high to the neck, covering all trace of shirt or cravat. One of them had a hand tight across Alfred's mouth, and was twisting the old valet's arm behind his back, propelling him forward. His night-cap had gone, his white hair was rubbed on end. In his patched white nightshirt the valet looked as thin and helpless as a fledgeling bird.

There was a sound of hasty but controlled searching in Alfred's room, then a third man came through the door. Dressed identically to the others, nevertheless he was easy to distinguish. He was taller, slimmer, obviously in command. He carried an old-fashioned but doubtless serviceable blunderbuss in one hand.

'This old fool is just a servant,' he said. He glanced rapidly around the Baron's room, taking in the great bed. 'This, I presume, will be the Baron.'

Lord Finderby stared coldly at the intruder.

'Good evening, my lord.' The tall man spoke with a casual politeness edged with insolent impatience. 'You must forgive the unorthodox hour of our visit. We have come for the Finderby Star. If you will just indicate its whereabouts I believe we shall have no further need to trouble you.'

He had taken out a knife, short-handled, with a very bright steel blade, and was casually cleaning his fingernails with the point, watching the Baron from over the black silk scarf. His eyes were shadowed by the brim of his hat; the Baron could not distinguish their colour. When no answer was immediately forthcoming the man walked over to the fireplace and idly stirred the coals with his foot, but the fire had been allowed to die out through the warmth of a summer's night, and only a dusting of white ash drifted up.

'Pity,' the man said. 'Well, it will have to be the knife.'

Alfred jerked convulsively and wrenched his head free.

'Don't you tell them anything, my lord——'

A heavy hand clouted round his head, making him reel and stagger, his bare feet softly thudding on the oak boards.

'Who are you?' the Baron growled angrily.

'That, my lord, is not a question we intend to answer. If you would just tell us the whereabouts of the Finderby Star?'

'God damn your impudence. I'll tell you nothing.'

Lord Finderby glared at his questioner. Beneath the

blankets he was slowly moving his stronger hand towards the small table that stood beside the bed.

'You'll take nothing of mine, I tell you.'

His hand snaked from beneath the sheet and clutched the cloth of Nottingham lace, brought back as a gift once by his granddaughter, that lay across the table. Tugging it with all his meagre strength, he pulled it clear, and sent glass, spoon, bowl, and bottle of medicine from the table cascading in a clatter to the floor.

Below, in the bowels of the house, Ranger the mastiff began a slow, questioning bark.

'That,' said the tall man coldly, 'could have been a bad mistake. Especially for the old man.'

In a sudden lunge he grabbed at Alfred's head, jerking it forward by the hair, and with a wicked swipe of the knife he sliced the hair through, holding a pathetic handful of it aloft. He had watched the old Baron blink and flinch. Ranger barked again.

'What next?' the tall man spat. 'His ear? His nose? His fingers? Looks after you, does he? Difficult with no fingers, wouldn't you think?'

He shook the strands of white hair from his hand, and took Alfred's bony white fingers, held out forcibly by one of his tormentors.

'Will you speak, Lord Finderby?'

He swept the point of the knife along the back of Alfred's fingers, slicing each to the bone.

'I can cut a little harder next time,' he said.

Alfred's face was white, and the pattering of dripping blood filled the silence of the room. The mastiff barked again, unsure.

'It's by the fireplace,' the Baron said, abruptly ceasing to fight. 'There's a cupboard behind the section of panelling nearest to the door. Pull the corner moulding.'

His gaze was not on the intruders, but on Alfred's white face and angry, frightened eyes. He sounded suddenly very tired.

'Very wise, Lord Finderby,' the tall man drawled, moving swiftly over to the fireplace. It took him a very few moments to discover the secret of the hidden cupboard, and lift out the velvet bag that was all it contained.

He was just pulling it open to check the contents when there was a sound in the corridor outside.

'Did Ranger wake you too? I have looked around downstairs; I can't see anything amiss.'

It was a male voice, but young, not much more than a boy's. A girl's voice replied.

'I thought I heard a crash. Before the barking.'

In the Baron's bedroom the three intruders had frozen, listening. With a jerk of his head the leader indicated the others to retreat back to the window of Alfred's room.

'Perhaps it is rats in the wainscoting; they can make a devil of a racket,' they heard the boy suggest.

'Hush, you'll wake Grandfather.'

The tall intruder had shaken the Finderby Star out on to his hand. It was all of four inches across, intricate gold work set with a pattern of diamonds to mark out the star, a cluster of rubies at the centre. It hung from a chain of filigree gold studded with tiny diamonds. The tall man held it up.

'Very nice, Lord Finderby,' he murmured softly, one eye on the door. 'A credit to the family. Exactly what was wanted. But I won't extend the vote of thanks, and take more of your time. Goodnight, my lord.'

He leaned forward and, whipping up the lace cloth from the floor where it had fallen, he tied it, with harsh, deft fingers, into a tight gag around Lord Finderby's mouth. The Baron glared, furious and humiliated, vainly shaking his head.

It is probable the gang would have left then, without further harm. Certainly they showed no inclination to search the rest of the house, as if they knew it would be fruitless. But Alfred, as he was dragged backwards, slipped in the trail of blood still dripping from his hand, and, although his weight was slight, his captors, their attention on the open window, dropped him. He fell

with a clatter against a wooden chair, tipping it noisily
sideways, and hoarsely shouted, 'Help!'

With a muttered oath the tall man flung his knife at
the fallen man, whether in fury, or to stop his noise, was
unclear. His two accomplices were already at the
window, struggling to climb out. Noise could be heard
in the corridor.

'There *was* something; it's in Grandfather's room.
Come on.'

Stuffing the velvet bag inside his jacket, the tall man
backed into Alfred's room, stepping over where the old
man lay without a glance. He held the blunderbuss
poised ready. He shut the door between the two rooms
just as the door from the corridor opened, and he shoved
the body of the old valet up against the door, holding it
shut.

The second man was already on the ladder outside,
fumbling for his foothold, when the tall man signed him
to hurry and leaped nimbly out above him, forcing him
to slip and fall heavily to the ground. He stumbled up,
however, and all three were hurrying into the darkness
when Jeremy flung the window wide and shouted
furiously after them into the night. Seeing the ladder, he
at once made to climb out.

A flash and a roar broke the darkness. Particles sang
and spattered all about, smashing the panes in the
window and pock-holing the wall. With a cry Jeremy fell
back to the floor.

Susan, who had stared with shocked realisation at the
open fireplace cupboard, then ran at once to untie the
cruel gag that cut across her grandfather's face, had not
seen Alfred, where he lay pushed back behind the door.
At the shattering report she ran through, and stopped
aghast in the doorway.

Jeremy was staggering up, staring in disbelief at the
cascade of blood that sharply blotched his nightshirt. His
hand was at his cheek, blood oozing steadily between his
fingers. But Susan had seen Alfred, huddled in a
crumpled heap behind the door, and she had seen the

knife-handle protruding grotesquely from his shoulder. She ran to him, horridly aware that the soft whimperings of distress must come from her own throat, though they seemed the cries of someone far away. She fumbled with the awkwardness of panic to feel for a heartbeat.

'Can you wake the others?' she asked Jeremy, then blinked, and looked at him again. He was sitting as if stunned, on the edge of Alfred's bed, but he nodded and made to get up.

'No! You stay there. Alfred is alive. We must get the doctor.'

She pulled a blanket from the bed and laid it gently over the old valet, then abruptly put another up around Jeremy's shoulders.

'Must be the Gradely Gang,' Jeremy said. 'Need to catch them. Can't have got far. Get Barnaby and John Wilkes. . .'

But Susan had already gone, fleeing like a white ghost through the dark Manor corridors, and up the creaking stairs to waken Hephzibah, Becky and Anne. Then down to wrestle with the bolt on the back door, and out, barefoot across the yard, to waken the men from their beds above the stables. Barnaby she sent for the doctor, bareback on the hastily bridled farm horse, for the horses would do anything for Barnaby, and John Wilkes to take the dogs, and a flaming torch, and search the grounds. Then back she ran, her green Norfolk shawl still clutched tight about her nightdress, to her grandfather's room.

Hephzibah, instantly awake and alert from the light sleep of the elderly, and startling in her voluminous red flannel nightgown and laced cotton cap, had already taken charge. The girls, blinking and bleary with sleep, ran to and fro up the stairs, bringing bowls of water, and cloths, and old sheets for bandaging, and ointments. They had left Alfred where he lay, with a pillow tucked under his head, anxious not to move the knife until the doctor arrived. Alfred had not regained consciousness.

Jeremy, however, was suffering the full indignities of Hephzibah's attentions. Heedless of his masculine pride, she had stripped him of his nightshirt, and was busily examining his wounds, with the eager help of the girls, while he sat shamefaced, with no more than a strip of Alfred's bedsheet tucked about him. The scattering of shot from the blunderbuss had caught his cheek, a glancing line through his hair, three places on his chest and shoulder, and in the calf of the leg he had just swung up over the sill in order to climb down the ladder. They would all be extremely sore, but none, Susan thought with huge relief as she stared at his white face under the shock of brown curls, appeared to be life-threatening.

Hephzibah was picking shot from the wounds with a pair of tweezers, staunching the flow of blood with a handful of torn sheet, and muttering cajoling abuse at her precious Jeremy each time he flinched. Becky sat beside her now, shocked and silent, holding a bowl of water, and another dish to take the shot and used swabs. Anne squatted down by Alfred, one hand tucked under the blanket and resting on his heart, her broad country face wrinkled with worry.

'Tis beating steady at the moment,' she said hoarsely to Susan, as much to reassure herself as comfort her mistress. Susan nodded, cold with worry, and went back to her grandfather. When she had untied his gag he had gasped and choked to get his breath, then furiously ordered her through to care for Alfred and Jeremy. She sat on the edge of his bed to tell him what she had done.

'Grandfather.'

There was no response. For one absurd moment she thought he had simply fallen asleep amid all the chaos. She laid a gentle hand on his forehead. It felt frighteningly cold to her touch, with a film of sweat upon it.

'Grandfather!' she said, more urgently.

She pulled back the blankets from his chest, and, as if in a recurring nightmare, once again felt for a heartbeat. At first she thought there was nothing, but then her straining fingers picked up a flicker of pulse, and she could feel the fragile, shallow rise and fall of his chest. Frantically she turned to reach for his medicine, and

stared for a shocked, uncomprehending moment at the
bare table-top before her eyes shifted to the broken
pieces that lay about her feet. She bent down. By chance,
the base of the bottle lay upright upon its flat bottom of
heavy, greenish glass. Susan could see the air bubbles
trapped forever within it. But also trapped was perhaps
a teaspoon of the old Baron's draught. Carefully Susan
lifted it up, reached for the spoon, and dribbled it in.
She pulled open her grandfather's mouth, and tipped the
medicine inside. She stared anxiously, but there was no
response. Frantically she scoured the floor, but nothing
more had survived the breakage. Tucking the blanket
back around him, Susan took the old man's hand, and
with a sense of utter hopelessness began to chafe and rub
it, willing him to survive.

This was the scene which greeted Dr Broadby when
he breezed in some fifteen minutes later.

'I thought the shock would do his lordship no good,'
he murmured dourly, eyeing Susan as sharply as he did
his patient. 'Here.'

He reached into his black bag and brought out another
bottle of medicine.

'A spoonful every twenty minutes,' he said, and swept
on into Alfred's room.

Susan did not see them remove the knife from Alfred's
shoulder, or lift him gently on to the bed. She saw
Jeremy stagger through later on, bandaged like an Egyp-
tian mummy. He was pale and unsteady with shock and
pain, but managed still to scrape up a wavering smile for
her, while he clutched the sheet about his middle. Becky
led him away to his bed, promising with a wink to find
him another nightshirt. Susan sat on, watching her
grandfather.

Eventually Dr Broadby came out of the little room.
He came and stood beside Susan, looking down at the
Baron's still shape mounding the covers. He bent to
examine him, then spoke as he straightened up.

'It will be touch and go, my dear. For your grandfather, for he has certainly suffered another attack, and

for poor Alfred. Jeremy should come to no harm if he is
sensible. Thank heavens they brought a blunderbuss.
They meant to deter, not to kill, probably hoping to hit
several pursuers at once.

'I have set Hephzibah to stay with Alfred tonight.
Anne can bring down blankets for her and for yourself.
Becky can stay within call of Jeremy, in case he should
need assistance in the night. I assume you will stay here?'

'Of course.'

'I intend to stay until morning, unless another call
takes me away. I left Barnaby down with John Wilkes. I
want to know what, if anything, they have found. I will
call round on each of my patients in turn, through the
night. If you are dozing, you don't need to waken.'

He gave her a heartening smile, and set off down the
creaking stairs, keen to hear news of the intruders, these
men who must be the much-talked-of Gradely Gang. It
had never occurred to him that they would choose the
Manor as a likely target. He would not have thought that
the Finderbys had a groat spare to steal. Perhaps the
foolproof intelligence that reputedly informed the gang
had got it wrong for once.

It could not be hoped that an event of such magnitude
would remain unknown in Finderby. Before the plates
of ham and eggs had been set upon the breakfast tables,
or a cup of coffee sipped, everyone seemed to know that
the Gradely Gang had ransacked the Manor, torturing,
killing, maiming, looting, and even—voices dropped to
an eager, shocked whisper—even raping. The doctor
had been kept busy all night, that much was known, but,
despite the tributes given to his valiant efforts, it was
widely supposed that most of the Manor's inhabitants
were now dead.

The only thing that sincerely perplexed the village was
the consideration of what, after all the looting and
pillaging, the gang might have discovered to carry away
with them. Some hopefuls speculated on the possibility
of a hoard long hidden by the old Baron, but wiser

heads, who had visited the Manor, dismissed this. At the
end of much rumination it was generally decided that the
gang had indulged in its bout of mass torture and
slaughter in revenge when they discovered that they had
been led astray, and all the cupboards were indeed bare.

It was all very dreadful, and everyone lingered long
over breakfast, pleasurably discussing at length how very
dreadful it really was.

It was not to be expected that Violet would for a
moment wish to be seen to shirk her obligations of
friendship. She knew she was quite the closest friend
poor Susan had. As a friend she donned her bonnet and
pelisse immediately after breakfast, and set off for the
Manor, hastily forming phrases of comfort and condol-
ence should there be anyone left alive to receive them.

She was herself unclear whether to be pleased or
disappointed to see Susan and Jeremy sitting together at
the kitchen table over a late breakfast, sipping at bowls
of tea, and nibbling at slices of toasted bread and ham.
Had it not been for Jeremy's bandages, Violet would
have wondered if anything had happened at all.

'He will not stay in his bed,' Susan replied matter-of-
factly to Violet's fascinated query. 'Obstinate fool that he
is. Feels he should not leave me up to cope alone. As if
the gang are likely to return! They have taken the only
thing of value the family possessed.'

'What was that?' Violet asked, breathless and
intrigued, helping herself to a bowl of tea, as no one had
seen the need to offer her one.

Susan gave an impatient shrug. Violet was the last
person she wished to see. When she had heard footsteps
she had for a moment thought that *he* had come, that she
could lay all the burden of the night's anxiety upon him.
Her heart had leaped fluttering and hoping, then
dropped in heavy disappointment. Violet's curiosity
could not interest her. What had been taken seemed
irrelevant compared to the people who had been left
behind.

'The Finderby Star,' she said dully. 'Diamonds and

rubies. It hardly matters. It was always kept locked away since my mother died. We will scarcely notice it has gone.'

'I never even knew it existed,' Violet said reproachfully.

'There is no reason why you should.' Susan was still numbed with shock and exhaustion. 'We never spoke of it. Why should you know it was there?'

It took Violet a long time to probe the truth from Susan, and then there was precious little to know. The Baron and his valet still lay in bed, fighting for their lives, but Alfred had once regained consciousness, and given some description of the three men in black, and their demands for the Finderby Star. The men searching the grounds had found scuffed footsteps, and the place where four horses had been held. They guessed that one man waited, holding the animals, ready for a quick escape. There were no reports that anyone had heard the men come, or go. Violet was wonderfully shocked to hear of the cuts on poor Alfred's fingers, the flung knife, and the callous firing of a blunderbuss at one no more than a boy, but, despite much delicate probing, she could find no suspicion that anyone had been raped. The men had come for the Star, been prepared to go to any lengths to get it, and then left. It was as simple as that.

'It was certainly the Gradely Gang,' she said confidently. 'It shows the same knowledge and brutality as all the other attacks.'

Jeremy, who had been doing some hard thinking about the attack, nodded, reluctant though he was to agree with Violet about anything.

'Well,' she said, and her voice took on a hint of arch 'I told you so' as she slid a sideways glance at Susan, 'I can only say it goes to confirm everything I thought about the gang and who is behind it.'

'What do you mean?' Jeremy had not paid a great deal of attention to Violet's gossip recently.

'Why, that it is all organised by the Earl of Chene, of course.'

She eyed him triumphantly, eager to cheat him of his new friends.

'What nonsense! Whyever should you think that?' Jeremy was astounded. Susan stared silently and fiercely into her bowl of tea, willing Violet to go home, hating to hear his name on her lips. 'Just give me one good reason why you say that, Violet.'

Jeremy flung his challenge down confidently, despite wincing as his speech became too heartfelt and he strained his injured cheek.

Violet leaned towards him, jabbing at the table-top to emphasise her points.

'I can give you more than one good reason, Mr Jeremy Finderby,' she said. 'Just you think. Think who must be organising this gang. Someone clever, to think out and plan the raids. Someone who has access to all the best houses, and knows who owns what in them. Someone who needs money. Someone recently come to this area.'

There were spots of bright, gloating colour on her cheeks as she continued.

'No one could deny the Earl is clever, with all his plausible schemes and plans. However wicked he may be, he is full of cunning ideas that have tricked half the neighbourhood into their support. Well, you know that, don't you, Susan? It didn't take long for him to convince you to believe in him, no matter how much you saw through him at first. A victim of your own vanity, you were, so eager to drop your friends here and hurry off to Chene. Then, naturally, he has called at all the best houses since he has been back, everyone hurried to gain his acquaintance, the acquaintance of an Earl. But since his visits, so many of those houses have been attacked. Just a little odd, don't you think?'

'That is just speculation and talk,' Jeremy retorted angrily. 'You can't offer any proof.'

'Then think!' Her voice was edged with anger now at his obstinacy. 'Who needs the money?'

'Certainly not a man who has inherited Chene,' Jeremy countered triumphantly.

'Really? But what about a man who could have long led a dissolute life in the London gaming hells, doubtless running up ruinous debts? On coming in to his inheritance, he instantly plans to rip up his parkland and estates to grab out the coal in some money-making frenzy. Is he not desperate for money? Desperate enough for anything?'

Violet stared at him with a small smile.

'And have you considered why the raids never happened in this area until the Earl came back to live? Because, of course, he did not know what was here until then. His gang was no doubt busy somewhere else.'

'It is still no more than talk,' Jeremy's voice was defiant. Listening, though, Susan could tell he was shaken and unhappy at Violet's words.

Violet gave an elaborate shrug.

'Well, don't say I didn't warn you. They do say there are none so blind as those who will not see. I have been trying to tell you both for your own good for weeks, but no. You are far too dazzled by your new aristocratic friends to take heed of the wisdom of the old and true. Everyone in the village can see it but you two. They all knew, watching you——' she gave a glance that was almost a sneer at Susan's bent head '——watching you parading through the village in that vulgar curricle. They all knew where it would end. Who wanted your grandfather dead? Have you thought of that? Who wanted him scared to death by a brutal raid? Who knew he could twist you two round to get any of your land that he wanted for his precious canals once the Baron had gone? Well? Who?'

She paused, breathless, her eyes bright points of envy and malice. But her tirade had had the desired effect. Jeremy was staring at her, his face whiter than ever, the dark rings beneath his eyes sharply defined.

'You cannot believe that.'

'*Everyone* believes it.' Her voice oozed scorn. 'Everyone can see it but you. Why? Tell me now. Can you possibly suggest anyone else it might be?'

Susan knew that Jeremy was wavering. It all seemed too plausible suddenly. In the pain, doubts and confusions his wonderful faith in his new friends was draining away, leaving him troubled, open to all Violet's poison.

She raised her head at last and looked at them both.

'You have to be wrong, Violet,' she said quietly. 'You see, the gang who came must have been local to the area since before my mother died. Otherwise, they could never have known about the Finderby Star. It has never been worn since her death. Our family and that of Chene have never before communicated. Ever. It has to be someone else. There is no way the Earl could possibly have known that the Finderby Star was there.'

She held Violet in a steady look, certain she had confounded the gossip, and reassured her brother. The anguished gasp beside her took her by surprise.

'No, Susan. No. Don't you remember? It was me! I told them. At the picnic at Chene. You *must* remember. It is the only time we have spoken of it in years. *I* told the Earl about the Finderby Star. I *described* it. I even told them where it was hidden. Oh, God! It is all my fault, all this horrible attack. Violet *must* be right. It *must* be the Earl. And, fool that I am, I gave him the very information he needed.'

Violet smiled triumphantly.

CHAPTER ELEVEN

SUSAN could not believe it. Would not believe it. She sat, dull-eyed, beside her grandfather's bed, hands neatly folded in her lap, staring blindly at the opposite wall, and thought painful, heart-tearing thoughts.

Everything in her heart cried that all the Earl had told her was true. The dreams he had hesitantly bared to her, dreams she so readily shared, she could not feel he had been inventing, just lying to steal her trust. Yet, examining all that Violet had said, reason argued this must be so.

The way he had looked at her, and talked and laughed, his touch, his kiss. . . Her hands had balled up into fists, and she pressed them hard against her mouth to stifle the groan that rose in her throat. Had it all been lies? Surely not. And yet. . .

Violet's words had been so persuasive. It all made such a horrible kind of sense. A sense everyone had seen but her.

Susan knew she was opinionated. Knew she liked to make her own judgements, and not follow the prejudice of the herd. But she was not stupid. She knew that sometimes she would make the wrong decision. Sometimes the herd would be right. But not, she ached silently, not this time. Surely, surely, not this time.

Her thoughts ran in circles of misery, Violet's petty, spiteful words echoing around and around in her mind. They did sound so plausible. She understood why Jeremy had at last felt forced to believe them. It only entailed believing that the Earl of Chene was a ruthless thief, prepared to lie, torture and kill, to sacrifice anyone, in pursuit of riches. *Could* she have been so utterly blinded that she had been deceived by a man like that?

Her grandfather stirred, and moaned, and instantly

she pushed her misery away and leaned anxiously forward. But he lay still again. Anne was sitting next door with Alfred. She looked round the door.

'I heard him stir. Is there no change, Miss Susan?'

Susan shook her head, but she managed to force a small reassuring smile.

'And Alfred?' she asked.

Anne shook her head gloomily in reply. She went back to her seat out of sight, and to her pile of sheets for mending.

Susan's thoughts surged back to torment her. Especially that most damning thought of all. Only the Earl and his brother knew the Star was there. That was the inescapable truth. Could it be Oliver? Could he be the villain, the Earl merely a dreaming innocent? But a moment's reflection convinced Susan that one brother could not be involved without the other. They were too much together. Surely it must be neither, or both.

Susan plaited her fingers in tortuous knots, and racked her mind for anyone else who possibly could have organised the gang. Anyone who could have known the whereabouts of the Star. But the logical answer her mind produced, every time, made the tears run in a silent stream down her cheeks, and her heart ache in anguish.

Dr Broadby called later. He shook his head over Alfred, but said the knife wound looked no worse. There was hope. Of the Baron, he said only time would tell what the extent of the damage might be. They could do no more than wait. Jeremy he cursed as every kind of fool for not keeping to his bed, lectured him on wilfully aggravating his wounds when there was already more nursing to be done than could be coped with, and, having bullied him into his bed, came cheerfully downstairs with the boy's clothes bundled up under his arm. He dumped them on the kitchen table in front of Becky.

'And don't give them back until I say.'

Becky giggled.

Susan he ordered up to her bed to rest. Her face had a pinched, bleak look that perturbed him.

Hephzibah, resolutely putting her own exhaustion aside, honoured the doctor with a glass of her primrose wine, then grimly stirred pots of gruel over the kitchen fire while he drank it. She had heard echoes of Miss Violet's talk, and she didn't know what to make of it, but she didn't like it, not one bit.

The Earl was out on the estate with Mr Blake throughout the day after the robbery at Finderby, and he was told nothing about it. As Oliver had gone out to sup with a new-found canal enthusiast by the time the Earl returned, and no one gossiped to the dowager about Finderby, or anything else if they could avoid it, he was not enlightened until he was riding out with Oliver the next morning.

Grim-faced and angry that he had not been there when Susan needed him, he set off immediately after a hasty luncheon to ride to Finderby Manor.

When he arrived there was no one to be seen in the yard, so he put his horse in an empty stall, and made his own way to the kitchen. He took off his hat and held it in his hand as he stood peering into the kitchen doorway, which seemed gloomy after the bright sun outside. Hephzibah craned her head out of the larder, then, seeing who had come, she abandoned the cold goose she had been carrying, and came out to greet him, wiping her hands on her apron.

She had not stayed to study him when she had caught her first sight of him in the garden, though her impression had been of a well set up young man, not conventionally handsome, perhaps, but with a striking, commanding presence. A difficult man to ignore. She had liked the crisp dark hair, and the sharp dark eyes with the hint of laughter and the quick understanding. She had not resented him as she thought she would.

What she saw now did nothing to alter that favourable impression. His expression was all anxious concern. When he gazed down at her, his dark eyes filled with worry, she knew, with a small flutter of her secretly sentimental heart, just how Susan's antagonism towards this Chene intruder into her life had, all unsuspected, turned towards love.

'I am so sorry,' he was saying. 'I came as soon as I heard. Please tell me, how are all the family? How is Miss Finderby? May I see her?'

Hephzibah gave him a brief outline of the events of the robbery, and the fates of the various victims. She was uncertain how to answer his last question, however. She debated in her mind as she talked. It was clear that he was fretting to leave her and see Susan. He kept glancing hopefully up at the door through to the main house. Suddenly Hephzibah's heart went out to him. Whatever nonsense Violet had planted in Susan's mind, it was only fair to let the man have his say.

'She is very tired,' she said abruptly.

The Earl nodded. He respected the opinions of this wizened little old woman. 'I am sure she is. The strain of so much nursing must be considerable.'

'She has not been overly keen to see visitors, but. . .' Hephzibah shrugged. 'She is in her parlour; I'll take you through.'

She led him to the door of Susan's little private parlour, knocked and opened the door.

'The Earl of Chene, miss.'

Susan had been sitting at her desk, staring idly at her inkwell, a blank sheet of paper before her. She had left Anne upstairs alone, her chair in the doorway between the two rooms to watch both old men. Becky was working in the dairy. Susan had intended to write to her cousin in Nottingham. She knew that family would want to know what had occurred. But she had no energy to accomplish the task she had set herself, and gazed bleakly ahead without even picking up a pen.

She started in surprise when Hephzibah announced the visitor. When her faith in this man had been forced to crack, her faith that he would come to her had vanished also. Surely even such a hardened villain as

Violet believed him to be would not come back to gloat at the scene of his crime?

Those last words he had spoken to her had come back into her mind in the long dark hours of the night with a sudden, awful significance. 'You must understand. How can I speak now? I will have to see your grandfather as soon as possible.'

Had he been giving her a warning of what he intended to do? Telling her he needed the money from the theft of the Finderby Star? Or, worse, needed the death of her grandfather for the success of his canal? Susan looked bleakly despairing, as the Earl of Chene came into the room, and Hephzibah quietly shut the door.

He strode rapidly to where she sat, and possessed himself of her hands.

'Susan. My dear. I am more sorry than I can say that this should have happened. I would have come sooner, but I have only just been told. You should have sent for me.'

A small corner of Marcus's heart was bruised that she had not sent one of the farm men hotfoot to find him. He wanted to think it was to him she would turn. But he knew his Susan would always think she could fight on alone.

'You must tell me now what I can do to assist you.'

Susan could not look up at him. Every part of her body ached with the need to trust him, to move into his arms, to lay her head on his chest and let him solve all the problems that beset her, to carry her burdens lightly away. But she could not do it.

She stared at the hands that clasped her own. She could feel her fingers faintly trembling in his grip. Violet's words trickled like poison in her mind. She closed her eyes. She wanted to shout at him. *Was* it him? Had he lied? Was *he* the thief who had stolen their gems and broken all her family tranquillity? Who had stolen her heart and was breaking it, trampling unconcerned over the pieces? But the words remained unsaid. She could neither bear to say them, nor to hear the answers.

She stayed, eyes closed, head hung down, and, torn as she was, she could not move.

Perplexed, the Earl released her hands, and moved away. He stood by the little fireplace, and regarded her, frowning.

She had picked up a quill now, and was turning the pen over and over in her hands, the stiff white plumes rasping softly on her fingers.

'Susan.'

She looked up at him.

He was shocked at the anguished despair in her gaze. He could not understand why this attack, admittedly distressing, should have produced such extremes of misery. His every instinct was to go to her, to hold her, to console her. But something held him back. She was utterly withdrawn into herself; there was nothing to encourage him at all.

'May I arrange for extra nurses to come to relieve you of some of the work?'

'Thank you, but no,' she managed, in a stiff, small voice, speaking to somewhere over his shoulder. 'If we need more help Dr Broadby will send someone from the village.'

'Can I speak to the magistrate on your behalf? What is being done to capture these ruffians?'

'I believe the doctor has done all of that for us, thank you.'

Her face was pinched and pale, and, if anything, had grown paler while they spoke. Dark rings showed starkly beneath her eyes, which had a bruised look, heavy with unhappiness. It seemed it was an effort for her to raise them to look at him.

'Is there *nothing* I can do to help you, Susan?'

His voice was quiet. He felt there was something here he did not understand.

She shook her head.

'Nothing, my lord,' she managed to say.

'Why?'

He spoke urgently, suddenly angered and confused by

this unaccustomed apathy. Of all the responses to disaster that he might have thought to find in his intrepid Miss Finderby, it was not this frozen despair. 'Why?' he repeated.

She looked at him then, her face full of pain.

'We manage very well, thank you, my lord. We have no need of any assistance.'

He strode back to her, and gripped her shoulders.

'That is not what I am asking, and you know it. Why will you not allow me to help you?'

His hands were tight on her small shoulders as he fought the impulse to shake her.

Desperately she wanted to confide her worries to him. She needed to tell him all that was said about him; part of her heart still ached to take his part and defend him against such calumny. But she could not find the words to speak such monstrous accusations to him; she could not have borne to watch the hurt in his face while she said them, as he realised she almost believed them.

Yet all the while she could not push them out of her mind. She could not look at him and not, horribly, wonder.

Tears stood in her eyes.

'Please go, my lord,' she said huskily. 'Please go. There is nothing you can do here. We have no need of you. Please, just go.'

Hurt and confusion made him angry. He roughly released her, and picked up his hat from the desk. Without a word he walked to the door. He paused there, staring at her from shadowed eyes, his dark brows knit, all his thoughts a turbulent mix of emotions. She thought that he would speak then. She did not know if she could just let him go, could watch them part like this. But he said nothing. He turned the knob and flung the door wide, pulled it decisively shut behind him, then strode out through the kitchen without a glance at Hephzibah. She heard him take his horse from the stall.

Hephzibah crept over to the parlour door and listened. Had all been quiet, she would have ventured in. But she distinctly heard the sound of sobs, quiet and muffled, but long, shuddering sobs. Shaking her head anxiously, Hephzibah crept silently away.

It was a long time before Susan emerged again. When she did her face was blotched and wan, but she insisted on taking her turn in sitting with the invalids, allowing Anne to rest. Apart from discussing the needs of the patients, she barely spoke, and although she would meticulously spoon them gruel she herself ate next to nothing.

A few days passed, and Susan, from choice, saw no one but the family. Both Alfred and her grandfather had regained consciousness, but both were very frail. Alfred's knife wound, however, remained clean and without infection, and the doctor's hopes were high for a total recovery. The Baron was noticeably weaker. He had lost what movement he had had in his arm, and now his speech was slurred and slow. But his mind, amazingly, while he lay awake, seemed as clear as ever. Jeremy's wounds were no more than sore, but they left him irritable and demanding.

Visitors who arrived with gifts and condolences were met by Hephzibah, and told Miss Finderby was too exhausted by her nursing labours to be seen.

Most understood, and were sympathetic, although Mr Chapley-Gore was affronted at not being called upon to arrange everything for Miss Finderby. He took care to inform Hephzibah that Miss Finderby could rest assured that he would personally visit the magistrate, and lay before him all that was known by the people of the village against his lordship, the Earl of Chene. He confidently expected that an arrest, all due to his own exertions, would immediately follow, then all their troubles would be over. He was certain such news could not fail to reassure and impress Miss Finderby's faint and female heart. He made Hephzibah repeat the gist of it twice before he trusted her to deliver the news to his satisfaction.

Violet, who had accompanied him, was equally disappointed not to receive preferential treatment and be
whisked through to see Susan for herself. But Hephzibah
considered that young lady had done enough harm
already, and sent her away frustrated. Violet was able to
make much in the village later, however, of whispered
comments upon Susan's inability to show her face to
anybody, even her dearest friend.

When Benjamin arrived, with a basket of fruit from
the Chene hothouses for the benefit of the invalids,
Hephzibah accepted it gratefully. She was quite angry
with Susan when she came, dull-eyed, into the kitchen,
and quietly insisted that the Earl be thanked for his kind
thought, but it was not necessary. The Finderbys needed
nothing from Chene. The basket of fruit was to be sent
back.

Hephzibah argued fiercely against such ill manners,
and against depriving those who were ill of such choice
morsels. But Susan would not be moved. The fruit was
to go back, and Benjamin did not at all relish the prospect
of informing the Earl of that fact. Despite a quick kiss
behind the dairy door from Becky, he departed gloomily.

The Earl, as all of Chene realised to their cost, was no
longer whistling about his daily tasks. His temper was
almost as bad as his mother's, and freely displayed, in
his short, sharp, sarcastic answers, to all who had
dealings with him. Several of the newer staff, recruited
when Chene was reopened, began to regret their once
prized places, and a couple of underfootmen and a maid
all threatened to resign. Bowdler watched the situation
gloomily. Oliver, having had his head bitten off several
times, was now keeping a low profile, and the dowager
and the Earl could hardly bring themselves to speak to
each other at all.

The news about the returned fruit did not improve
matters, but Benjamin survived delivering the message
without losing his place. Indeed, the sudden bleakness
he had seen in the Earl's eyes as he had delivered it had
given him a sharp sympathy and, oddly, an increased

loyalty to his employer. When all in the servants' hall were bitterly complaining, Benjamin kept thoughtful, and quiet.

The Earl was not surprised, as Oliver was, at the contents of a note received by him from Jeremy. Oliver had sent commiserations, had invited Jeremy over to ride when he was recovered, and had asked Jeremy to organise a day when he was well enough for them to look at the coal-seams together. Jeremy had politely declined all the offers, and announced he had no further interest in developing the coal on Finderby land.

'The alarm of the attack must have addled the boy's brains,' Oliver said, shocked and affronted at such a rejection from a mere schoolboy. 'Why, you couldn't have met anyone keener when he was here. He couldn't talk of anything else. Picked my brains endlessly. It is absurd. A burglary doesn't alter ones plans for a coal-mine, does it?'

He ran his fingers through his elegant Brutus crop.

'One would not have thought so.'

Marcus was holding Jeremy's reply, gazing at it with a puzzled frown. He was uncertain whether or not to take comfort from the fact that the boy rejected them also.

He was convinced that he had not mistaken the way Susan had shared his emotions. She had no artificial wiles to entrap him with meaningless flirtations. She would not know how, and that was something that had drawn him irresistibly to her from the start. No, the feelings she had shown him were as true as his own. He had been certain that something more than just a casual change in her feelings had been involved. His understanding of her made no sense without. But what?

For a week the Earl made no further attempt to contact the family at Finderby. Indeed, he tried his very best to put them out of his mind. There was much work to be done on the estate. Although Blake had been an excellent and efficient agent, always keeping the best interest of the family in mind, Marcus had found many instances where he himself would have leavened that efficiency

with humanity. He was endeavouring to make good
where he could, and to train Blake in his humanitarian
ideals. It was uphill work, and kept him absorbed and
busy. The evenings, however, had begun to seem long,
empty, and lonely.

Oliver suggested inviting up a party of friends to spend
a few weeks at Chene. Usually Marcus would have
jumped at the idea. Now he refused it out of hand. He
had neither the time nor the inclination at present, he
said.

When the Earl did eventually arrange to return to
Finderby it was to visit the vicar, and inspect the
foundations of the school, newly laid out. All his hope
was that, whatever shock or anxiety had distressed Susan
when he saw her last, time would be working to heal it,
and their shared interest in the school would bring them
together again. He sent a short note to Miss Finderby,
merely informing her that he would be there, had she
anything she wished to discuss. He hoped against hope
that a note from her would arrive. But it did not. When
he met Mr Stanbridge he learned that Susan had excused
herself from the meeting. She entrusted the vicar to make
decisions on her behalf. She was still too busy with her
nursing; she had no thought for other, lesser concerns.

The Earl, his hopes rebuffed, made polite enquiries
about the health of those at Finderby, and received
neutral replies. He felt the vicar was perhaps not as open
with him as he had been before, and this, with his hurt
disappointment, made him resort to cool, aloof reserve.
He seemed uninterested.

The vicar had certainly heard all the gossip that swirled
about Finderby. He was accustomed to receiving village
gossip, and receiving it with the scepticism and generous
pinch of humour it invariably deserved. The tales now
circulating did seem particularly pointed, but despite the
damning look of them he still found that he did not in
his heart believe the Earl to be at the back of this gang.
He preferred to make his judgements on personal obser-

vations, not third-hand talk, and all he had seen of the man he had liked.

He toyed with the idea of speaking to the Earl himself about the gossip that was rife, for he could make a fair guess at what Susan must be feeling, and the confusions between the two of them to which this would give rise.

But the aristocratic reserve into which the Earl withdrew was too much for a country vicar, however outspoken, to breach, especially upon a matter so potentially delicate. Mr Stanbridge returned to his vicarage unhappily feeling he had failed someone, though he was oddly uncertain whom.

The Earl, riding in moody discontent back through the village street, paid no attention whatever to the nudges and whispers and looks that accompanied his progress. This was a pity, for the phenomenon might have aroused his curiosity, had he considered it. As it was, he returned home disappointed, secret hopes that he might see Susan dashed, and he spent the evening becoming steadily drunk with a singularity of purpose that was unusual.

CHAPTER TWELVE

THE magistrate nearest to Finderby village, Mr Horatio Vance, of Cedar Lodge, Findham Parva, was of a dyspeptic tendency. It was his habit to nurse his digestion tenderly, frequently resting his small, spare frame, and avoiding all undue stress or excitement. On the whole, however, he enjoyed the demands made by his magisterial role, and the regular misdemeanours of the district caused him no qualms. Justice was dispensed to drunks, brawlers, petty thieves and the occasional poacher pompously, but fairly, in Mr Vance's thin, dry voice, and with a strong aroma of peppermint lozenges.

He had no ambition whatsoever towards greatness or fame, and the arrival of the Gradeley Gang in his area had filled him, not with revenging enthusiasm, but with reluctance and disquiet. He was prepared, naturally, to do his duty, but hoped it would not be to the detriment of his digestion.

He was not pleased, therefore, when Eustace Chapley-Gore presented himself importantly in his study one morning, and informed him that he must immediately take horse and make haste to arrest the Earl of Chene.

'There can be no doubt, my good man, no doubt at all,' Chapley-Gore insisted, marching up and down Mr Vance's study carpet till he was like to wear away the design, and giving Mr Vance nervous qualms of the digestion just to watch him. 'Everyone in Finderby knows the truth, and now is the time to act. Before another dastardly attack takes place. I have an elderly mother—poor, frail creature; she swears she is not safe in her bed! It is an appalling state of affairs, and one that must not be allowed to continue. We rely on you to act at once, sir, at once, and apprehend this vicious villain.'

Mr Vance was startled, to say the least. He eyed his

148

visitor narrowly, ushered him to a chair, and sniffed the
air, hopeful for signs of drunkenness, or even insanity.
He had no liking for Mr Chapley-Gore, having long
privately considered him to be an opinionated bore, but
in fairness he had to admit to himself that he had never
previously had cause to doubt his word. He sighed.

'What proof do you have for your accusations?' he
asked, extremely dubious, seating himself, and fumbling
into his tail-coat pocket for his lozenge box. He sucked
gratefully at the peppermint, straightened his wig in an
effort to look authoritative, and prepared to consider his
visitor's extraordinary announcement.

'Proof?' Eustace was astounded at this dragging of
heels. He had envisaged them instantly galloping
together over to Chene to take the fellow, amid much
local glory, and acclaim from the ladies. 'What proof do
you need?' He leaned earnestly forward, and counted
points off on his fingers. 'He has the intelligence, he
needs the money, he has the men to command, he knew
about the Finderby jewels—had just been told—and
nobody else did. . . Why, 'tis as plain as the nose on
your face.' He was blustering.

'Hmm. Well. I do not know. You may be right,
sir. . .but, as a magistrate, I cannot act wilfully. Intelligence is no crime, I trust?' He gave a dry little laugh.
'Nor is the shortage of ready money, or my gaol would
be very much fuller than it is today. And then, do you
have any proof that he needs money?'

Mr Vance sucked hard on his lozenge, frowning, and
readjusted his wig.

'The evidence of my own ears.' Chapley-Gore spoke as
if this was decisive. 'I hear he is to rip up all his estates
and turn them into mines and manufactories. A man
must be desperate with need and greed to contemplate
such measures.'

'Hmm.' The magistrate sucked reflectively. 'I am not
certain I can agree. Not entirely certain. If what you say
is true, I would have thought it more probably proof that
he has money sufficient to invest.'

'This is ridiculous quibbling, sir. I am affronted. As magistrate, your job is to convict the villain, not defend him. I do half your work for you by discovering and reporting the name of this fiend, and then you propose to ignore me? Must I take the matter to a higher authority?'

Mr Chapley-Gore was spluttering, red-necked and outraged. Mr Vance swallowed his lozenge, and sighed heavily. He steepled his fingers, rested his chin lightly upon them, and eyed his visitor severely.

'You may rest assured, Mr Chapley-Gore, that I will take every proper step. I will undertake to interview the Earl of Chene personally, and investigate the matter. You may safely leave it in my hands.'

'So I should think. So I should think. Can't have such a fellow moving into our district and being accepted at all the best houses when he is no more than a common criminal. No, indeed. Apprehend the man and all his wicked followers. At once. Hanging is too good for them.'

When Mr Chapley-Gore had departed at last, much disappointed that no headlong gallop to Chene had resulted, but comfortably aware of having excelled in his civic duty, and eager to report the fact to his friends and neighbours, the magistrate sat slowly down in his chair. Already the unaccustomed stress of such a visit was taking its toll in painful digestive twinges. He rang the bell to order a tisane of camomile, took off his wig and perched it on his knee, and rubbed his bald head. Interviewing the Earl of Chene on possibly unfounded accusations of capital crimes was not a prospect he relished.

He arrived at Chene a few days later, after a suitably plain luncheon of boiled fish and a little cold chicken meat. He was daunted, on being admitted by the impeccable Bowdler, and announcing his business, to find himself being surveyed with distaste through an ornate lorgnette by a vast-bosomed lady who was regally descending the stairs. However, she swept away without a word, and he was admitted to a private interview in his lordship's study.

The dowager, wanting a target for her displeasure, discovered Oliver in the library.

'Your brother has another ridiculous visitor,' she pronounced loudly, swirling into the room and staring aggressively about her. Oliver nodded non-committally from by the fireplace, a book on principles of engineering still held in his hand, and silently hoped she would swirl out again. 'Some underbred little man who announced himself to be the local magistrate,' his mother continued, undeterred, 'and had the extraordinary temerity to hint he wished to discuss the Gradeley Gang with Marcus. Marcus really must learn how to depress the pretensions of these little men with their parochial concerns.'

Oliver shook his head irritably.

'It seems to me perfectly proper that the man should wish to consult Marcus over such a matter. This gang is a scandal to the area. If Marcus, as the largest landowner and employer in the district, can give the support and men needed to hunt them down, why, the sooner, the better.'

His mother glared.

'There is no reason at all for him to concern himself. He should be above such matters. He employs Blake to deal with persons of the class of this magistrate.'

Knowing it would be more sensible to keep quiet, Oliver spoke anyway.

'After the attack on Finderby Manor, I know Marcus will consider it to be very much his concern, and rightly so. We may have our disagreements with the family, but they should be protected from such outrages.'

The dowager's face flushed an ugly purple.

'I might have known! I might have know that Miss Finderby would be somewhere behind this. Marcus has not been himself since the day she had the audacity to traipse into this house. Why the house of such paupers was singled out for attack anyway, I cannot imagine. I shall speak to Marcus and tell him to have nothing to do with any of these people. The sooner we are back in Town and he renews his acquaintance with the Duke of Nare's daughter, the better it will be for us all.'

'I don't think Marcus will welcome your comments, Mother,' Oliver ventured wryly, 'any more than he relished the attentions of the Duke of Nare's daughter!'

'That, my boy,' she said grandly, 'is no business *whatsoever* of yours.' And she swept back out of the room, leaving Oliver slowly shaking his head.

The dowager would have been a great deal more irate at the underbred little visitor if she could have known the content and implications of the message that had brought him to interview the Earl. He was not finding the interview at all easy, particularly because the Earl was so affable and helpful.

'Everything in my power to help,' the man was saying, having sat Mr Vance down to an excellent glass of port. 'I am most keen that these ruffians should be apprehended.'

'Er—yes. Thank you.' Mr Vance hesitated, seeking words. 'It was particularly suggested to me that I should speak to *you* about this matter. . .' He paused.

'Yes, indeed. Quite right. I certainly have men I can release to form a search party if you should so wish.'

The Earl smiled encouragingly. He had the impression that the little magistrate was nervous. He had not thought himself so very daunting, and reflected he must do his best to set the poor man at ease.

The magistrate had brought out a large white handkerchief, and was wiping his forehead in anxious dabbing gestures. He suddenly stared at the handkerchief as if he had only just noticed its existence, frowned, and stuffed it back into his coat pocket.

'Well—er—it was more a case of *where* we should be looking. . .' he ventured.

'I fear I cannot be of much help on that.' The Earl endeavoured to sound a positive note. 'Perhaps I could institute more extensive questioning on your behalf to establish if anything was seen or heard after the last raid at Finderby Manor?'

Mr Vance sighed and, without thinking, felt in his tail pocket for his lozenges. The Earl was so plausible, so helpful. He appeared such a pleasant and honest man. The magistrate narrowed his eyes, the lozenge box still clutched in his hand, and concentrated his attention on Mr Chapley-Gore's accusations. He spoke severely.

'It is felt in the neighbourhood that it would need a leader of some social eminence to organise the gang,' he said, endeavouring to study the Earl's face for any sign of a guilty reaction, 'a man who needed money urgently, could command men, and would know which houses were worth robbing.'

'Well, that seems sensible,' agreed the Earl reflectively, 'but I am afraid that I cannot truthfully tell you that anyone springs instantly to mind.' His dark eyes seemed the soul of honesty. 'I will certainly give it some thought.'

'It would need,' the magistrate persevered desperately, the sweat breaking out on his forehead again, 'to be someone who knew about the Finderby jewels.'

'Yes, that is curious, for I believe I am correct in saying they had not been worn for many years. One would think they had been forgotten. It is quite a problem, Mr Vance, but you may rely on me for any assistance you need; you have only to say the word.'

The Earl stood, indicating that the interview was at an end. Mr Vance was beginning to feel foolish, and angry at Mr Chapley-Gore for precipitating him into this ridiculous situation. He would have left believing Chapley-Gore to be an utterly misguided fool, had not the Earl finished reflectively, 'You see, I have something of a personal interest in the business.'

Mr Vance, whose carriage had been rung for, turned from his progress towards the door.

'And what might that be, my lord?' he heard himself ask in accusatory tones.

If the Earl was surprised at the personal question he made no sign.

'That is a private matter,' he said, with an air of finality, and a small, inscrutable smile. Mr Vance left the room feeling suddenly unsure. He might have dared to raise the matter again, if the large lady had not been standing in the hall to view his departure with all the affability of an iceberg in a blizzard. She seemed eager to speak to the Earl, and the magistrate was surprised by a twinge of masculine sympathy as he made his escape.

Whatever his ambiguous feelings towards the Earl, however, of one thing he felt quite certain. There was no possibility, without an overwhelming amount of firm evidence, that he would contemplate endeavouring to apprehend the Earl of Chene. He had seemed affable and keen to help this afternoon, certainly, but there was a steely strength about the man that Mr Vance would not care to cross. And if that daunting lady had been the dowager, and he crossed her path. . .

Mr Vance's imagination shied away from following that thought any further, and he felt for his lozenge box once again.

The dowager had indeed accosted Marcus as soon as the magistrate had departed from Chene. She had followed him belligerently back into his study, and demanded that he have nothing to do with the magistrate, the hunt for the gang of robbers, or particularly with Miss Finderby.

The dowager was not truly certain even in her own mind why she mistrusted Miss Finderby so much. But she had sensed a danger to her own peace of mind from the moment she had first seen that bedraggled brown figure enter her house, and events were more than proving her right.

She had been outraged to discover from her maid that Marcus was not only paying for repairs on the Finderby estates, but also seemed to have taken the brother under his wing, *and* was financing a school in their village. It seemed proof that the girl must be some unprincipled gold-digger who had mysteriously anchored her claws in him, and was doubtless holding out on the use of the land for the canal in the hopes of extracting other financial advances.

Then, just witness, she thought angrily, Marcus's reaction to her motherly insistences that he break all contact. He had angrily pronounced that his visits to Miss Finderby were nobody's business but their own, he would visit her whenever he wished, and whether his mother liked it or not was of no concern to him. At thirty years of age he would act as he saw fit, and she would have to learn to accept it. He also intended to assist the magistrate in any way he could, in order to aid the speedy arrest of the Gradeley Gang.

The dowager glowered to herself at the memory. She had been glowering and sulking for three days, steadfastly refusing to speak to Marcus at all—a state of affairs which seemed to cause him no distress whatever.

It was while she was sitting glowering that the idea came to her, took root, blossomed and came to fruition. If Marcus was proving so blind to reason, she thought, it left her no alternative as a responsible mother but to go and warn off this upstart little social climber for herself.

The dowager was not one to waste time. The following morning, without a word of her intentions to either of her sons, she ordered round her large and ponderous crested carriage, and, with driver and two armed footmen in attendance in case this irritating gang were in the area, for she considered herself and her pearls to be a desirable target, she set off for Finderby Manor.

The drive that led round to the front of the Manor had long been disused, for everyone who visited the family knew that the great hall had been uninhabited for many dusty years. The dowager, however, took one glance at the drive that ended in the farmyard, with access to what could only be a kitchen door, and ordered the carriage on. The horses swept around the house in knee-high grass bright with meadow flowers, and pulled to a halt in an area that might once have been a forecourt, but was now an open field, grazed by a scattered flock of geese. With a look of disdain from the carriage window, the Earl's mother waved an impatient hand at one of the footmen, summoning him down to knock on the vast studded wooden door.

It was Susan herself who heard the unaccustomed knocking. She was sitting with her grandfather. Leaving him sleeping, she ran lightly across the landing, down a passage to the front of the house, and ducked through the tiny arched doorway where the passage joined the gallery that ran around the great hall. Skirting round the gallery, she peered outside. It was just possible to make out the wheels of a carriage through the cobwebbed windows.

Perplexed, she ran down the spiralling staircase to the ground floor, fought back the huge, unyielding bolts, and dragged the door ajar. It had sagged on its hinges, and it was only with the help of the footman, one whom she had not seen before, and eyed with some astonishment, that the door was opened. Hands and apron dusty from the struggle, Susan stepped breathless on to the doorstep, and saw for the first time the visitor, who was now descending heavily from the vast carriage, an imposing vision in voluminous cerise skirts and a dark purple turban. The girl straightened her back in a small, defiant gesture, and frowned.

'You honour us, Lady Chene,' she remarked drily.

'Yes.' The dowager glared about her. The flock of geese had advanced to survey this improbable invasion of their grazing land, waving their long necks and hissing sulkily. 'I intend to speak to you. You may invite me inside. You——' she gestured at her footmen '—wait here with the carriage.'

She sailed towards the door, certain of her entrance, and, with a small shrug, Susan stood aside and let her pass.

The dowager looked about her, at the high bare stone hall, the threadbare hangings, the single great oak table that was all the furniture, and the festooning cobwebs.

She brought her gaze back to the girl who stood before her.

'You need not,' she stated repressively, 'offer me refreshment. We will merely talk. You will listen to what I have to say.'

Susan smiled. She wondered fleetingly what refreshment the dowager feared she might receive. As for listening, unless she ran away it did not appear she would have much choice.

'Yes, ma'am,' she said demurely. She could see how much the smile infuriated her visitor.

The dowager paced towards the huge table, her purple kid boots clicking on the worn flags, then turned and began to pronounce.

'Ever since your uninvited eruption into our life at Chene my son has been disturbed by you, your family and your affairs. Naturally, in the elevated position he holds in Society, he has been troubled by those who wish to impose upon him, or more probably upon his fortune, all his life. I trained him early to dismiss such importunate nobodies without compunction. Why he has not rid himself of your unwanted attentions as speedily as I taught him to dismiss those others, I do not know. But I do know that these unwanted attentions have continued for long enough. Too long. We have no need of your kind at Chene, Miss Finderby, and my son is not to be bothered by you or your family in the future. You will give me your word that you will have nothing further to do with my family. That is all I have come to say.'

The swaths of purple turban contained one single ostrich feather, which dipped and swayed in dancing accompaniment to the chilly words. Susan found she had been watching it more than she had been concentrating on the speech. She realised that the dowager was obviously waiting for her to make the desired response. The gold lorgnette had been raised, and Susan was being subjected to a forbidding scrutiny. She gave a small smile, which might, perhaps, have passed as apologetic.

'No,' she said.

The dowager's face froze, and began to darken in hue.

'I beg your pardon?'

'I said, no.'

'Do you not understand, you ignorant, impudent girl?
I am forbidding you to see my son. Forbidding you.'

'But you must surely understand, Lady Chene, that
you are in no position to forbid me to do anything?'
Susan pointed out, sweetly reasonable. 'Certainly you
have made plain to me that you do not wish me to see
your son. I have heard you, and understood. What I do
about that—well, that is entirely my affair, don't you
think?'

There was no one, except her son Marcus, and then
only after he came into the title, who had ever spoken to
the dowager with such defiance as this. She could hardly
believe what she was hearing. The Finderby hussy was
watching her, as cool as you please, as if they were doing
no more than discussing a recipe for marmalade. She
forced herself to speak.

'You are refusing to obey me in this?'

'I am telling you that whom I see is my own concern,
not yours, Lady Chene.'

'Then you *are* refusing to obey me. You will give me
no guarantee that you will cease seeing my son.'

'If you insist, ma'am, then yes. I am refusing. If I
should wish to see Lord Chene, I shall do so. Naturally,
I regret if this disobliges you. Was there anything else
you wished to discuss?'

'Impudent, impudent girl. How *dare* you speak to me
so? I have never before been so insulted. I shall. . . I
shall. . .' She paused and drew breath, vast bosom
heaving, ostrich feather dipping, unable to think what
she might do. Turning on her heel, she swept across the
hall to the door, skirts swishing on the dusty flagstones,
raising dancing clouds in the sunbeams. Her heavy face
was quivering and ugly.

Watching this departure, Susan realised that she was
shaking. She gripped her fingers together, and forced her
face into a polite smile. At the door the dowager paused.

'I shall not forget this, Miss Finderby. I am seriously displeased. Seriously. Indeed, I am affronted. I had not thought to meet with such unregenerate wickedness, not even in these uncivilised parts. It is a shock——' she placed one large white hand on to her buttressed bosom '—to one who is gently nurtured. Not,' she said, with a certain satisfaction, 'that that is anything *you* would understand. I do not wish to see you again, Miss Finderby.'

'I can assure you, Lady Chene,' Susan responded sweetly, knowing she was giving way to temptation, 'the feeling is *entirely* mutual.'

With a glare of pure fury the dowager flounced through the door. The vigorous hissing of the geese told Susan that she had an enthusiastic escort hastening her path into the carriage. She heard the coach pull away, and still she stood, unmoving. It was not until two snaking necks and sharp-eyed heads wound curiously round the open door that she pushed away her thoughts and hurried over to shoo the geese out, and force the great door shut.

She had been wondering at her own obstinacy in insisting upon her right to see, if she should wish, a man she knew she hoped never to see again.

The dowager was not over-endowed with good sense. She found it impossible, at dinner that evening, to refrain from giving an account of her afternoon's interview at Finderby. It so filled the narrow confines of her mind.

She launched into her tale, bristling with outrage at her insulting treatment by this impossible upstart girl, quite oblivious to the warning signs of anger on her eldest son's face. She truly expected her sons to express their outrage on her behalf. Oliver, watching her, marvelled that she could be so obtuse, and waited resignedly for the explosion from his brother. He was surprised, therefore, when Marcus asked his mother to repeat the end of the tale a second time.

'Weren't you paying any attention, Marcus?' his mother snapped. 'She *refused* to obey me. Stood there in a filthy apron, like any common chambermaid, and had the audacity to tell me she would see you if she so wished. Refused flatly to give me any assurance that she would stay away. Can you credit such impudence?'

She stopped abruptly to stare at her son. He was gazing beyond her, down the table, apparently into thin air, with a faint smile hovering on his lips. His eyes had lost the heavy look of anger that had darkened them earlier.

'Are you listening to what I say, Marcus?'

'Yes, indeed, Mama. And thank you. You have told me much that I wanted to hear. I had not thought you could be so obliging.'

To her fury he nodded to her with a sudden bright, speculative smile, and raised his glass in a silent toast.

CHAPTER THIRTEEN

THE announcement by Mr Vance, in response to a peremptory visit from Eustace Chapley-Gore demanding news, that he could see no reason whatever to apprehend the Earl of Chene, was predictably unpopular. Violet, who had invested much thought and emotion into the theory, was insulted by the magistrate's conclusion.

'I suppose it is only to be expected,' she snapped, pouring bowls of tea for Eustace, her mother and herself in the chilly neatness of the Netheredges's best parlour. 'Mr Vance is well enough for local concerns, perhaps, but in an outrage of these proportions he is plainly afraid to act. Either that, or he is a fool who cannot see what is clear before his nose.'

Eustace was shaking his head sympathetically. Mrs Netheredge, reclining on a fat sofa covered in striped satin, looked sharply from one to the other, her smelling-salts clutched in her hand. Violet eyed Eustace's solemn expression, and made an effort to moderate her harsh tones to a more dulcet sweetness.

'What a pity, Mr Chapley-Gore, that Mr Vance has not your bravery and determination.' Her face broke into a soft, endearing smile as she offered him the plate of sugared biscuits. 'Poor misguided Susan has been wickedly led astray by this evil man. *I* seem to have lost my closest friend, and *you* have lost. . .' She paused and sighed heavily. 'But I will not distress you by speaking further on a subject that can only raise bitter memories for you of what might have been.'

She sighed again, prettily, then leaned over and laid a gentle, comforting hand on his arm.

'I must be hard for you to see her acting thus.' Violet shook her head in sorrowful wonderment, and took two biscuits for herself.

'I fear,' Eustace remarked heavily, 'that Miss Finderby is not at all that I believed——'

'Don't go on!' Violet leaned towards him, wide-eyed. 'Don't speak words you may yet regret. Perhaps it may not all be over for you. Do not despair. Even Susan's disastrous ride with him through the village *may* eventually be forgotten. No, no! Say no more.'

Violet's face was flushed with more than usual colour, her lips parted about her protruding teeth as she gazed at him in earnest sympathy. She pressed her arms forward into her lap, squeezing her small breasts upwards in her demure lilac gown. She smiled at him. Eustace goggled slightly as an unexpected thought struck him. He leaned towards her and laid a damp, heavy hand over hers.

'You are so good, Violet,' he said solemnly. 'A good and loyal friend. It much distresses me to see your friendship abused and scorned. But do not feel that your selfless concern for others passes utterly unnoticed and unappreciated. There are those not so very far from here who can see true worth——' he lowered his voice '—and know its value.'

Violet was blushing, and simpering in coy surprise, when Mrs Netheredge interrupted pettishly.

'Are you never going to pass *me* the biscuits, Violet? And I *would* like another bowl of tea, *if* you can spare your ailing mother the time?'

She waved her sal volatile vaguely towards her nose, setting the bows and ribbons of her cap nodding.

They both hastened to make much of her. But although she had spoken with her customary pettishness she did not appear to be displeased. She had long privately considered that such an upright and worthy gentleman as Mr Chapley-Gore would be wasted on eccentric Miss Finderby. She nursed hopes of him.

Many people in the village agreed with Violet's assessment of Mr Vance, and his statement after his visit to Chene did nothing to quell the rumours. There was muttered talk of bringing in the Bow Street Runners, but no one was quite certain how to set about securing the services of these famous sleuths. However, they were all very certain that not one of them wanted to volunteer to pay for those services.

It was inevitable that the talk would reach the ears of the Earl eventually, although no one dared to speak of it to his face.

The Earl had been giving quiet consideration to how best to approach Miss Finderby, now that the extraordinary report from his mother had given him some trickling of hope. He had given long and painful hours of thought to why she had rejected his offers of assistance so absolutely, why her feelings had so abruptly changed, and no explanation had offered itself. Now, at least, he hoped, they might talk again.

In the meantime, several invitations had been sent by the Earl to local people. He had many initial courtesy visits to repay. It could not escape his notice that a growing number of these were apologetically but firmly refused, which he found puzzling. Then, on market day in Findham, Marcus could not help but notice that he seemed to be an object of especial interest to the populace, though he could deduce no reason why this should be.

It was Oliver who learned of the reason.

Both the brothers had been invited to eat dinner with George Pembleton, in the company of Sir William Gantrey and Colonel Parkins. The Earl had cried off, for a friend of his was stopping at Chene for the night, on a journey north into Scotland. Oliver thus travelled over alone.

He was unimpressed by the Pembleton house, as he surveyed it, riding up at a leisurely trot. A pleasant place once, of no great size but suitable for a gentleman's residence, it had been allowed to decline, and now showed tell-tale signs of lacking any regular maintenance. Paint was peeling, wood cracking, and occasional red pantiles missing from the roof. Outside the hedges were in need of clipping, and an untended ditch had clogged up with debris and flooded over the drive, leaving thick, churned mud. Oliver frowned in silent disapproval.

The welcome was warm enough, however, and, whatever else George Pembleton was slacking on, it was not his cook, or his cellar supplies. The food and drink were both exceptionally good. Despite these temptations, Colonel Parkins had cried off, pleading a sudden bilious attack, and Sir William Gantrey, after a subdued evening to which he contributed little, made his excuses early.

'I begin to feel I carry some plague about with me,' Oliver remarked, only half in jest, as he and George sat over the port. 'People are crying off from invitations, or avoiding me in the town, just as if they believed we had the smallpox at Chene. Is there any talk of infection? If there is I have certainly heard nothing of it. Yet only a few weeks ago people were clamouring to make our acquaintance, what with the canal plans, and introductory social gatherings.'

George looked up at his young guest with an expression that was oddly hard to read, delicately balancing a pinch of snuff upon his wrist.

'You have not heard the talk, then?'

He raised his wrist, bent his head, and sniffed, keeping his cold eyes fixed on Oliver's face. He snapped shut the enamelled snuff-box lid.

'What talk? I have heard nothing.'

'About the so called "Gradeley Gang"?'

'Naturally I have heard of their exploits. Everybody has. It is a scandalous matter. But how does that concern us at Chene?'

'Only,' began George, walking over to the fire and placing a log upon it, despite the warmth of the evening, then turning to look curiously at Oliver, 'only the gossip concerning who is organising the gang. It would appear, dear boy——' and Pembleton gave a small, bitter smile '——that local opinion has assigned this role to your brother, deeming him the only man hereabouts with the necessary intelligence.'

'Marcus? Organising the Gradeley Gang? But how absurd!'

'Yes. Yes, it is, isn't it? But I think you will discover that that is the cause of your abrupt loss of popularity. People hear, they talk, they wonder, they suspect, and then they back away. It happens, dear boy. Absurd, as you say, but it happens.'

'But. . .but. . .' Oliver did not know whether to laugh or rage. It was so ludicrous. 'But why?'

So George Pembleton explained at detailed length all the reasoning that had led Violet to conclude that the Earl must be the villainous leader of the Gradeley Gang. Flatly told, accompanied by regular inhalations of snuff, the reasoning sounded unpleasantly convincing. Oliver suddenly found himself wondering whether Pembleton believed it to be true. He was watching Oliver's reactions shrewdly from piggy eyes above round pink cheeks. Did he hope to expose the truth and apprehend them? More probably his thoughts were turning on blackmail, or sharing in the profits, Oliver thought in an upsurge of anger.

They played a few desultory hands of cards, but Oliver's mind was not on the game. He found he was losing with an unaccustomed regularity. He called a halt, paid his debts, made his apologies and took his leave.

Oliver rode home thoughtful. His first reaction to Pembleton's words had been outraged dignity that any gossip could so besmirch the family name. Now his thoughts took him further. A massive collapse in confidence in Chene would inevitably result in the withdrawing of investment from the canal-building scheme. And without outside investment and goodwill the entire plan could never be more than an outline on a drawing-board. The more Oliver thought, the more angry he became. That so many plans and hopes could be set at risk by such ridiculous talk. . . He spurred on the chestnut horse to a long-legged canter, despite the overcast darkness of the night, anxious to talk with Marcus.

He was to be frustrated, however. Marcus and his

friend, Viscount Rame, had spent an amiable evening in alcoholic reminiscences, and were in no mood for serious talk. Oliver excused himself, unable to join their mood, and went to bed.

It was the following afternoon before Oliver found he could speak to his brother privately. Marcus had suggested they ride together, after Rame's departure on his way north, in an attempt, as the Earl said wryly, to clear his fuddled brain. They set out across the park, at a suitably gentle amble, and almost at once Oliver began to pour forth everything Pembleton had told him. The resulting silence from his brother was so long that Oliver wondered if he had been listening at all.

'Have you nothing to say, Marcus?' he enquired in frustrated exasperation.

'I was merely reflecting,' the Earl remarked, 'that what you have told me explains a great many things.'

He was staring ahead, his heavy brow furrowed, his dark eyes giving away nothing of his feelings.

'Of course it does,' said Oliver irritably. 'It explains why we are being treated with all the enthusiasm that might be lavished upon a couple of rabid dogs. It explains why my canal may never see the light of day. It certainly explains a great many things. More to the point is what are we going to do about it?'

Marcus turned to face his brother, and his black brows were lifted in surprise.

'I should have thought that must be obvious. Naturally, we are going to discover who really is leading the Gradeley Gang. Discover them, bring them to justice, and clear our own good names.'

'Is that all?' enquired Oliver sarcastically. 'When the combined attempts of all the victims and magistrates in the district are utterly bemused, we will merely snap our fingers and solve the crimes, I suppose?'

Marcus gave a wide smile. His teeth were very white, his eyes bright and hard.

'Yes, little brother. Do you lack faith? You heard of the efforts of the magistrate. Do you truly not think we can do better? And remember, I am the man with the wit and the nerve, and the men to command, and the ruthless desire to gain my own ends, am I not? All those people cannot be entirely wrong! Let us put these talents to good use, and outwit this Gradeley Gang. I think they have done harm enough. It is time, little brother, that they were stopped.'

Looking at him, Oliver suddenly found himself believing that it was possible. It was only a matter of time. When Marcus was in this mood, anything could happen. There was a blazing, angry keenness about him, and Oliver grinned, swept forward by that same determination.

'So!' he said, with satisfaction. 'We prove all the gossips wrong, and watch all the faint-hearted social sheep come trotting back to us, eh?' He laughed. 'Well, then, big brother, where do we begin?'

'It will need some thought,' remarked Marcus. 'We will apply our minds to the problem as we ride, and compare notes in my study when we return.' And he kicked the great black horse, Bo'sun, into a rushing gallop away across the park, leaving Oliver laughing, floundering to catch up.

The Reverend Mr Stanbridge had been calling regularly at Finderby Manor, and on the whole he was pleased at the progress of all the victims of the cruel burglary. The prayers he had said anxiously over Alfred and the old Baron were now, he thought with relief, less urgent. Alfred was sitting up in his bed, and even worrying about the care of his master, and the Baron was complaining at the fussing of females around him, and asking petulantly for his valet.

The Baron was weak, and angry at his helplessness over all that had occurred, angry that he could no longer defend his family and care for them as they deserved. It was plainly obvious, he had muttered to the vicar, that young Jeremy was too headstrong and rash to be left alone to care for his sister and to run the estate. He fretted over his family's future, but otherwise he was much recovered.

Jeremy was mending apace, having crept downstairs and stolen back his clothes from the kitchen when Becky had run out to meet Benjamin. *That* young man seemed able to create errands to run in Finderby village, or beyond in Findham, almost every day of the week, as Hephzibah tartly observed. Jeremy was even going out to the fields now, supervising the men and undertaking what light work he could manage. It was only Susan, Mr Stanbridge reflected, studying her thin, pale face, who did not seem to be recovering from the effects of the burglary.

The vicar had felt that he failed before, when he found no way to convey to the Earl the things that were being said about him. But he had no qualms about speaking to Susan. He invited himself firmly into her little parlour after descending the creaking stairs from the Baron's room, flung his wig irritably on to the floor, flicked wide his dusty coat-tails, and sank heavily on to a protesting cane-seated chair. He pleaded for tea and Hephzibah's scones, and decided he would speak his mind. Anything was better than watching that bleak look in her eyes. Their grey, once so bright and clear, was now like the flat grey of the English sea beneath a leaden English sky, devoid of all promise of sunshine.

She sipped her tea, perched on the edge of a chair before him. She was staring blankly out of the window. Mr Stanbridge had the feeling that she could have been drinking anything, she was so unaware. He frowned and spoke abruptly, plunging to the heart of his worry.

'I know what they say about Chene, Susan. I have heard it all. Gossip always reaches the vicar, and is always brought with the purest possible motives.' He allowed the anger to show in his voice. She had turned to look at him, at least. 'And I don't believe any of it.' He continued roughly, 'It is malicious nonsense, invented tittle-tattle. Spread mostly out of mischief-making and jealousy, I should guess.'

He saw the flicker of hope then, as she stared at him, still in that unaccustomed silence, and he hoped to God that he was right. His instinct about a man had never let him down before. He saw no reason to mistrust it now. He put his trust in his God and spoke on. 'The Earl of Chene is a good man, Susan, and he is being maligned. He needs his friends to believe in him.'

The hovering hope was piteous in her eyes. He knew now that he had not been wrong in what he thought had occurred between these two. He would have given his blessing at once to such a match. He had never viewed Chapley-Gore's pursuit of Susan with any enthusiasm. He would have married those two only with the profoundest sadness. But Chene! That was another matter altogether. And, he reflected, with a spurt of irritation, he could think of no better man than the Earl for the Baron to entrust his family to, if only the obstinate old man could be brought to acknowledge as much.

'I have been trying so hard to accept his guilt,' she said, in a monotone so quiet he could barely hear her. 'It seemed so conclusive—what else could I think? But I have not been able to truly believe, and the uncertainty has been eating away at my heart. The attack was so cruel. My family suffered so much. How could I think with any fondness of a man who might have perpetrated such a despicable act? I felt a traitor to my own people. Yet those feelings, that conviction of his innocence—it would not die. But how could I see him——' and she raised an agonised face '—knowing what everyone believes, what everyone would say?'

She stared at him, desolate, and the tears welled up in her eyes and ran unheeded down her cheeks. 'Now you speak to me as if I have deserted him, and you fill me with shame.'

'My dear Susan!' The vicar fumbled in his tail pocket and managed to disentangle a cleanish handkerchief, which he pressed into Susan's hand. 'No, indeed! I never meant to shame you. Oh, dear me, no, no. Merely to give you strength. To let you know you are not alone when in your heart you believe he is innocent. Despite all that is said, I believe that too.'

She wiped her cheeks and blew her nose on the vicar's handkerchief, and clutched the damp grey bundle in her hand. 'No need to see him till it has all died down,' the vicar continued anxiously. 'Maybe better not, with all the tattle-mongers about; but don't lose faith. I believe the truth of it will emerge. Mr Vance found nothing to proceed on, so he told me. Indeed, he was impressed by Chene, considered him an amiable and helpful man, if a touch mysterious. Whatever that may mean! Come, now. Put a brave face on it. Perhaps if we put our heads together we can come up with some ideas for Mr Vance to consider. After all, if the Earl is innocent, then we must look for the villain somewhere else.'

Susan was looking across at him. Eyes red and tears smudged on her cheeks, yet she looked more alert and thoughtful than she had since before the burglary.

'Of course, yes,' she began. Then her face fell again. 'But this idea of a gang leader. It may not be true after all. Perhaps they are merely robbers and highwaymen who are luckier than most. *Then* how do we trace them?'

'Give it some thought, Susan. You have a lively mind. Use it now to seek out the truth, tell me any ideas you have, and we shall send to the magistrate to carry them out.'

He sounded so keen, so determined that for the first time in many long, weary days Susan felt a glimmering sparkle of hope, which grew stronger and brighter after the vicar had gone, and she seriously began to apply her mind to the problem. With a new determination, Susan went through to the kitchen, and startled Hephzibah by solemnly putting a square of damp grey linen in a pan to boil.

'That man deserves white handkerchiefs,' she pronounced, defiantly mysterious, and vanished back to her parlour.

Despite his optimism to his brother, the Earl of Chene was nursing a well of angry hurt. Initial relief at realising

the almost certain cause of Miss Finderby's chilly rejection was rapidly followed by the worming hurt of
betrayal, an indignant pain that she could ever have
believed him guilty. It hurt his pride, as well as his heart.
Accustomed to privilege and approval, even flattery and
pandering, he found it harder than most to accept the
villainous role cast for him. Brought up almost entirely
as a town dweller, he was unfamiliar with the power of
country gossip. Susan, he thought, suddenly furiously
angry with her for the pain she caused him, should have
been above such petty considerations, above listening to
such spiteful idle talk. She should have believed in him.
He thought, with an aching certainty, that he would have
held faith in her beyond the ends of the world. Still
smarting, unsure whether that faith in her also encom-
passed forgiveness, he sat down to write a letter.

He arrived with the letter the following morning at the
kitchen door of Finderby Manor. It was early, too early
for social calls. Impatience had driven him forth. The
men were only just setting off for the fields. Barnaby had
met him in the yard and taken Bo'sun, but after a look
at the Earl's face had made no remark. As he led the
great horse to a stall he heard the thudding of the Earl's
fist, harsh and loud on the old timbers.

Susan was still in the kitchen, clearing dishes, while
Hephzibah was speaking to Anne in the larder about
some missing gooseberry pie. Surprised at the racket, the
two servants' faces peered out in breathless silence
around the larder door-frame as the Earl, without waiting
for a reply to his knocking, strode defiantly in. Susan
stood rigid, the colour draining from her face, a stack of
greasy plates piled before her on the table.

The Earl had thought endlessly as he rode, considering
what he would say to her. Sometimes he decided that he
would merely leave the letter with Hephzibah and go. Or
he would angrily demand to speak to Miss Finderby. Or
come upon her quietly, take her hand, and seek understanding. No scenario satisfied him. He did not know
what he would do.

He stood now somewhat at a loss. He had never envisaged the two staring faces in the larder, the table and the pile of plates between Susan and himself, the wariness in her eyes, and Ranger, suspicious at the loud knocking and the sudden tension in the room, stretching and pulling himself out from beneath the table, a long growl rumbling in his throat.

He had not envisaged how thin she would look, and pale and tired. It was two weeks since he had seen her. She looked as if she had barely slept or eaten for all of that time, and this realisation made him angrier, irrationally guilty. He should have discovered and scotched this absurd talk immediately, he thought, not let her suffer. But, and he shook his head slightly, *she* should not have believed it. How *could* she have believed him capable of such things? Had he not bared his heart to her? He was glowering at her with an intense, daunting fury. He could not read the emotions in her face. She merely gripped the edge of the table with white-knuckled hands, and gave him back stare for stare.

All the speeches he had prepared, of recrimination, of pacification—of any sort—deserted him. His reaction to the sight of her was entirely physical. He wanted to hold her, grip her, shake her, even strike her, to smash through the web of false words that held them apart. He wanted to kiss her, to drown her in furious kisses, to drive that deadened stare from her face and feel her body come alive under his hands. She did not even look desirable, only small, wan and weary. But he wanted her as he had never wanted anyone before. He almost hated her for that.

The dog prowled round his legs, sniffing accusingly at his top boots and rumbling ominously. The girl Anne gave a brief hysterical giggle, instantly stifled, her face blushing plum-red. Susan never moved. A corner of the Earl's mind told him that very soon this scene was going to deteriorate into either bathos or farce. He did not think he could cope with either.

He reached into his waistcoat pocket, and brought out

the letter he had written the previous night. Still looking
at Susan, he stepped forward and laid it on the table.

'Read it,' he said.

She had flinched as he moved forward, as if afraid of
him. He glared at her, bitterly insulted, unaware that she
read the violence in his face.

'I will call back tomorrow morning to speak with you,'
he said grimly. 'I *will* speak to you then. Privately. Do
you understand? This *cannot* go on.'

He turned on his heel, Ranger snapping toothlessly at
his boot at the sudden movement. He strode out of the
kitchen and away across the yard. For a long moment
the kitchen remained frozen. Then, as if sleep-walking,
Susan picked up the letter, and walked out of the room.

Anne and Hephzibah crept out of the larder, eyes
wide. Anne was agog. But to her intense disappointment
Hephzibah would not discuss the extraordinary incident
at all.

'You keep your nose out of other people's concerns,
and your fingers out of my gooseberry pies,' was all she
could be drawn into remarking.

Anne flounced out to the dairy.

CHAPTER FOURTEEN

THE letter was terse.

> Miss Finderby,
> It has come to my attention that it is necessary for me to actively clear my name. This is regarding certain malicious gossip concerning a purported connection between myself and the activities of the so-called Gradeley Gang.
> I would also deem it an honour were I able to apprehend the perpetrators of your family's loss and distress.
> Towards this end it would assist me if you would agree to discuss the events of the burglary at the Manor with a view to discovering the culprits.
> Yours,
> Chene.

The letter was spread open on Susan's desk the following morning. She, standing beside it, had her elbows rested on the window-sill. She leaned at the open casement, and stared blindly across the garden. The pink hollyhocks beside her were filled with the busy drone of fat, pollen-dusted bees. Ranger lay snoring on the brick path that led down towards the vegetable patch.

Susan heard the sounds of someone's arrival, but she did not stir. She waited upon events with the same strange, fated inactivity that sometimes invaded a dream-world. It was only after Hephzibah had announced his name, and she had heard the door shut, leaving them alone together, that she slowly turned around. She stood very still, her ears still full of the droning bees, and looked at him.

He had taken off his hat, and held it in his hand. His short black hair was full of shadows, and his frowning brows shadowed his eyes, as his hook of nose shadowed the thin line of lips below. His cravat seemed a bright and startling white beneath such sombreness. His eyes were bright too, staring at her with an intensity that daunted and accused. She was hardly aware of the dark green jacket, fitted so closely across the muscles of his shoulders, the cream breeches, and the bright shine of his polished top boots, gleaming where they caught the golden square of sunshine that spread across the floor. Her eyes were held remorselessly by his stare, as if his gaze mesmerised her.

Her hands still rested behind her on the window-sill. Susan found she was gripping the worn wood as if it were a lifeline to dry land. She was pressing her body back against the thick stone of the house wall that had defended her family through so many centuries. She did not know what to say to this man. Every phrase that had sprung into her tormenting mind through the long night had seemed to say too much, or too little. She did not know how to explain the complexities of her heart, not even to herself. She could not speak.

The Earl was suffering from the same indecision. Nothing had prepared him for a situation so ambiguous, and all his customary assurance had deserted him. Anger, hurt, doubt, and a fiercely possessive protectiveness warred within him as he watched her. He felt unable to look away from the grey eyes, huge in her pale face, which gazed at him, like those of a threatened animal, from beneath a tumble of brown curls. Words could not tell her fast enough all the contradictory things he needed to say. He felt helpless before her gaze, and this angered him.

He moved towards her, never taking his eyes from her. As he put his hat down on her desk, he thought she braced herself, as if uncertain whether he might not harm her. Bitterly hurt, renewed anger surged up in him. He was standing close against her now, and he gripped his hands on to her shoulders. She flinched, and he knew his hold had hurt her, but in his anger he only gripped her more firmly. He could see his knuckles show pale against the brown of his skin. Her bones seemed fragile, and very vulnerable, beneath his hands.

She was staring up at him, tears beginning to well into her eyes. Her lips were trembling. Still she stood passive, pressed tight back against the wall, the sunlight from the open window behind her streaming through her hair to give her a halo of gold.

'For God's sake, Susan.' His voice was raw and husky. '*I* have no part in this gang of robbers. It is all lies. You *know* that. You *do* know that, don't you?' He found he was shaking her, pulling her to and fro against him. 'Don't you?'

He fought to quell his rising anger. He knew that he could hurt her, and knew that a corner of his mind he had thought long subdued through his years of maturity wanted to hurt her, wanted to punish her for the hurt she had caused him. She was staring up at him, the tears welling out and running down her cheeks.

Slowly she nodded.

'I could never truly believe it, whatever they said,' she whispered. 'But what could I do?' She closed her eyes, squeezing the tears over the thick brown lashes, and hung her head.

With a sudden sigh some coiled tension within the Earl relaxed. He slowly ungripped his fingers from their bruising hold on her shoulders, and slid them in a gentle caress down her back, pulling her against him. Her small brown head rested on his chest, and he gently held it there, laying his cheek softly against her hair and lightly fondling her curls between his fingers. His eyes rested idly on the bees still bumbling heavily from flower to flower.

After some little time he felt the tautness begin to leave her body. She fumbled for a handkerchief, and, head still bent away from him, she blew her nose. He smiled with a gentle fondness at the top of her head. He felt her push the handkerchief back to wherever she had found it, and her hands creep up his chest as she pushed herself back to look up at him.

Susan knew she had irrevocably committed herself. With that one small nod she had allowed her heart to dictate her future. She had committed herself to following where it led, in defiance of all the arguments of reason. Only the vicar would support her. No one else in the village would understand at all. Even her family might despise her. She had pinned all her faith in this one man. Yet she knew she would not regret it.

She had been aware of his anger, then of his arms about her, his hand in her hair, soothing her as he might gentle an injured animal. Now she felt that anger had gone. That glaring fury that had chilled and shamed her yesterday had died away. Now, she thought, with profound relief, they could talk.

She meant to speak, to begin to explain. She needed to tell him of all that had been said, the inevitability of the hideous conclusions that had tormented her. But when she looked up at him, and her eyes met his, still so dark and filled with unfathomable emotions, her heart seemed mysteriously to fill her breast with its thudding, and breathing was difficult so that she must open her mouth to draw breath. Where his hands still touched her, her skin seemed to tingle and quiver, and a sudden turbulence of her emotions filled her mind with confusion. Her body ached for more of his touch.

He was pulling her closer, and with one hand he tilted back her chin. She thought the racing pulse in her throat beneath his hand would stifle her. Her breath came quickly. She realised part of the throbbing pulse she felt was his heart beneath her hands. He was bending over her now, and she knew she ached for this kiss more than anything she had ever wanted before. Her eyes closed, as he lowered his lips to hers.

It was a long time before either became aware again of the bees buzzing in the sun-drowned spears of hollyhocks. When eventually the Earl released her, yet still he kept her in the circle of his arms, as if afraid she might vanish if he quite let her go. Perhaps both had managed to tell more of their confused emotions than could have been told in hours of talk. He gazed down at her, and she managed a shy, shaky smile. With a sudden grimace he pulled her hard against him, kissed the tip of her nose, and laughed.

'Oh, Susan, sweet Susan,' he whispered. 'Thank heavens, thank heavens!'

She blushed, and laughed, and the look she gave him as she gazed up at him made it inevitable she would be kissed again.

It was later again before they sat down to discuss the burglary, Susan at her desk, and the Earl on the cane-bottomed chair that had protested beneath the weight of the vicar. At the Earl's request Susan repeated to him everything she knew of the robbery of the Finderby Star. He had borrowed paper and pen, and noted down details of the men involved, everything she could recall of what Alfred and her grandfather remembered.

'Oliver is visiting as many of the victims as we know of, and as will agree to speak to him. Every detail we can add will help to build up a picture of these men. Have you talked with people in the village? Surely someone heard the men ride through? Some cottager up with a child? It is improbable they would have tried to make their escape over the fields with such a maze of dykes and hedges to penetrate.'

'I have not been out to ask.' Susan flushed slightly, then looked at him firmly. 'I have been so tired with all the nursing, and. . .and I could not bear the talk. Everyone had condemned you. They had all watched me drive through the village with you after we met to plan the school. Even the kindliest would take some relish from seeing me discomposed after they believed me proved so catastrophically mistaken in my trust of you. I had no way to argue against them. Reason proved them right.'

'But *why*, Susan? Why did this gossip have the power to affect even you? Oh, I have been told what they are saying, and it makes a pretty enough case for a village gossip to believe, but what so distressed you?'

He could ask her calmly now. Already the raw hurt was in the past.

'Because the Gradeley Gang knew about the Finderby Star.'

'But what does that prove? Surely, there are many people who remember your mother. Older people who might talk of it?'

'No, you don't understand. It is more than that. They knew *exactly* where to look for it. Well. Not exactly. But they knew *just* as much as Jeremy had told you and Oliver when he spoke of the jewel on that picnic at Chene. Those are details that no one outside the family would know. No one. That is why all my reasoning led me back to accusing you, even though my heart cried out your innocence. For who else could have known those details? I can list for you the people who know. Grandfather, myself, Jeremy. . .' He watched her with a quiet delight as she earnestly checked off the names on her fingers. 'Alfred, who is grandfather's valet, Hephzibah, then Oliver and yourself. Not even Anne and Becky knew. That knowledge seems to me, and to Jeremy, for we have discussed the matter endlessly, the single most important clue to finding these men. The only road it led me down was one I could not follow. But without his heart to convince him otherwise, Jeremy of necessity believed the results of his reasoning.'

Marcus was frowning. Pembleton's gossip had not contained this apparently damning fact. It made Susan's dilemma starkly plain for him.

'My poor girl,' he said. 'I had not realised it was so conclusive. I am astounded now that you allowed me into the house at all.' He paused, thinking, then resumed slowly, 'Could Jeremy not be mistaken? Reflect how readily he spoke to my brother and myself about the Star. Acquaintances not long known. Perhaps he spoke as casually to others?'

Susan shook her head.

'He swears he has not, and I believe he remembers aright. You must know that you and Oliver were more than passing acquaintances for Jeremy. You had become the most trusted friends of his life, and he spoke to you both with a freedom which is unusual. He would know if he had mentioned the Star elsewhere.'

'Hephzibah or the valet had spoken to no one? Or your grandfather?'

'No, I have asked them. And why should they? No one has even thought of the Star for years. It has been quite forgotten since my mother's death.'

'Then what explanation can there be? How did these men know of the Star?'

Susan looked at the man she loved with a small shrug and a smile.

'You see?' she said. 'It *must* be you!'

His returning smile was more of a grimace.

'This is absurd. Soon you will convince me of my own guilt! But I know *I* mentioned the Star to no one; I forgot about it as soon as told. And I do not believe Oliver mentioned it either, though I will ascertain for sure.'

He leaned forward in his chair and possessed himself of her hands.

'We are left with a ridiculous conclusion, are we not? The only possible answer to this riddle is one which I know for an absolute fact, and you honour me by believing, to be wrong.' He slowly shook his head, then continued, 'But if the obvious conclusion is untrue, then there must, necessarily, be another. The only problem then is to discover it. I mean to do that. Will you help me, Susan?'

She smiled at him.

'Yes,' she said.

They talked for a little while about what had been stolen, how victims had been chosen, where the jewellery might be sold, and by whom—all topics that Oliver and the Earl had discussed the night before.

After some while the Earl rose reluctantly to take his

leave. Susan stood and smiled up at him shyly, wanting
him to kiss her as he took his leave, uncertain if he
would. He laughed, held her to him, and kissed her lips
lightly.

'There is something of grave import that I quite forgot
to say to you, Miss Finderby,' he said. His face was
suddenly solemn, and she stared up at him, anxious. 'I
know this is not the ideal time,' he continued, 'and I had
fully intended to do the honourable thing and speak first
to your grandfather, but what can I do? You have utterly
overwhelmed me. When all this foul business is over,
Susan, and you can do so without feeling shamed in the
eyes of the world, will you do me a great honour? Will
you marry me?'

Oddly, despite all that had occurred, she had not
expected this. She gazed at him, her thoughts whirling.
She thought of Violet and her vicious talk, and of
Eustace, with his ponderous unwanted courtship, and
his prudish pomposity. She thought of Grandfather with
his bitter prejudices and hatred, and of Jeremy, so
young, left alone to manage Finderby Manor. She
thought of the Dowager Countess of Chene, her disdain,
and the ambitions she must hold for her son. She thought
of her own daily life and realistic expectations. Reason
was stirring its miserable head, telling her this was not
an offer she should accept. It would not be right for her
to accept.

She saw the hint of doubt darken his eyes and just
crease his forehead as he watched her and waited mutely
for her reply. That uncertain flicker of misery put paid
to all chance reason had of ordering her life. Spurning
the unwanted reasons why she could not say yes, she
smiled up at him.

'Yes, my lord,' she said.

'Marcus,' he insisted, frowning in his surge of relief.

'Yes, Marcus,' she said, mock-obediently.

Then, of course, he kissed her again.

After the Earl of Chene had left the Manor Susan
ventured shyly out into the kitchen. She knew there was

no possibility of fooling Hephzibah. The little old woman was kneading dough in a huge earthenware bowl at the kitchen table. To gain the necessary height she stood on a battered beechwood stool which had served this purpose for as long as Susan could remember. Her sleeves were pushed hard up her stringy arms, and flour covered her to the elbows. She fixed Susan with a sharp, shrewd eye.

'He left looking very pleased with himself,' she remarked. Hephzibah was not one to come over subservient at the sight of a title. 'Come here where I can see you, my girl. Come on, no hiding there in the shadows.'

Susan walked over to the table, catching blurred glimpses of her passing shape in each of the polished pewter plates on the dresser. Hephzibah rested her hands on the sides of the bowl and studied the girl.

'Huh!' she said. 'So it's like that, is it?'

Susan flushed a deep pink, but she was smiling. She sneaked her hand into the jar of raisins that stood open on the table and took a few, eating them one by one.

'At least he has put some colour back in your cheeks.' Hephzibah sounded dour. 'We should be glad of that at all events.' She returned to her dough with a renewed ferocity. 'Well? Are you going to tell me all about it?'

Susan popped another raisin into her mouth and grinned. She felt absurdly light-hearted.

'Tell you what, Heppy?' she asked, airily.

'Don't come your tricks with me, Miss Susan.'

Susan waited. She knew Hephzibah would suffer torments until she knew just what had occurred.

'Now if you had a caring mother alive and well, or even your aunt Catherine, God rest her poor soul, I wouldn't take it upon myself to ask, as you well know.' Susan raised an eyebrow and grinned, and Hephzibah thudded the dough determinedly. 'But you haven't, and I would be failing in my duty to this family if I didn't take a care for you, Miss Susan. Now, you tell me. What did he say, this Earl, to send you dancing out here like the first day of spring?'

'Heppy,' Susan began, eating another raisin, and wondering even as she said it if it could possibly be true, 'when we have discovered the *true* Gradeley Gang, *and* cleared the Earl's good name, why, then I shall marry him.'

Jerking back, startled, Hephzibah's feet shot from the stool, and she tumbled off backwards in a flurry of flour. She sat heavily on the stone floor, agog with surprise, bony legs in warm knitted stockings and heavy boots sticking out from a jumble of skirts and flannel petticoats. She still stared at Susan, open-mouthed.

She shut her mouth like a trap and glared as Susan smothered a giggle.

'Well,' she remarked crossly, 'it's no surprise! I can't say that I didn't have my suspicions!'

'Of course you did, Heppy. I know I can't hide anything from you.' Susan was chuckling. She helped the old woman up, and sat her in one of the rocking-chairs. She moved the kettle into the heat of the fire, and reached down the teapot. 'You sit there a minute,' she said. 'I'll make us both a cup of tea, and I'll tell you all about it.'

She knew she could talk Hephzibah round to her way of thinking. Hephzibah could ferret out any forgotten information in the village, and would make the staunchest of allies against the Finderby gossip-mongers.

Later, still glowing and serene, the secret of her engagement secure in her heart, Susan went upstairs to sit with her grandfather. The old man was awake, and in a querulous mood.

'I hate these young girls to care for me, Susan,' he muttered, his voice slower than before the attack. 'I need a man to care for me. It would be more fitting. That old fool Hephzibah tells me Alfred is still not well enough, and I've told her to take on another man. Or send up one of the footmen. I will not be proud. He needn't be a trained valet. Fetch me up a footman to care for me, Susan; don't leave me with these girls.'

Susan sighed. They had held this discussion before.

'There are no footmen any more, Grandfather. We cannot afford footmen. And there is no money to take on another valet. The outside men are all needed on the farm, what with bringing in the hay, and tending the livestock. They have no time to sick-nurse. Be patient with the girls, Grandfather.'

'No footmen? No money? What is wrong, Susan? The Barons of Finderby should not be so impoverished.'

Susan took a deep breath.

'There *is* coal beneath the estate. We could work the coal to restore our fortunes.'

She saw the vacant, querulous look vanish from the old man's eyes, and he regarded her sharply from beneath bushy white brows.

'This is that Chene whelp's talk. Canals and coalmines. Enticing Jeremy with his ideas. I know. You can't hide much from me. I have the vicar singing Chene's praises each time he calls, prattling on about schools and thatching. Telling me this man is a good man, nothing like his father. And Colonel Parkins talking about wealth from this canal. Then, of all things, young Eustace Chapley-Gore telling me Chene is the leader of the gang that broke into my bedroom! Pompous young fool! By God! The Chenes don't break into bedrooms to steal the odd jewel. They crawl to the throne and sweet-talk away a man's land acre by acre. The Earls of Chene may be every damn kind of villain I care to name, but they don't have the petty, sneak-thief mind of a house-breaking gang, or of Eustace Chapley-Gore!'

The old man was glaring at her, and Susan reached for his medicine, but she could not help but smile. Of all the people who might have believed in the Earl's innocence, her grandfather was the last she would have imagined.

'You think I don't hear things, lying here,' the old man went on. 'But there's nothing wrong with my ears, or my mind. And I have a lot of empty hours in which to think. Stanbridge can be an obstinate old devil, but he is nobody's fool. He thinks Jeremy may have a talent for all this new-fangled mechanical nonsense. He says there is money to be made, and we need to make it.'

He was eyeing Susan, while he docilely swallowed his draught, as if trying to sum up her response.

'I think Mr Stanbridge is right, Grandfather,' she said.

'Humph. The man has too many damned opinions for a vicar. Should keep his nose in his Bible. Go away now. I am tired. But. . .damn it, send Jeremy to me later. I want to talk about his God-forsaken canals and coal-mines.'

Blinking in astonishment, she went.

That night Susan dreamed she was at Chene. It was a confused dream in which the dowager kept appearing on staircases, her eyes protruding and her huge index finger pointing at the door as she ordered Susan out of her life. Yet the door always vanished as Susan turned towards it, and as she wandered the corridors, searching for the way out, at every corner a footman bowed and offered to refill her glass of wine.

She woke, it seemed, from very deep sleep, with the idea crystal-clear in her mind. Pictured sharp in her mind's eye was a memory of the picnic, and the three men reclining on their cushions, talking. Jeremy, talking about the Finderby Star. And behind them, moving competently about on silent feet, was a footman. In her memory there was no face. But she could see feet in polished shoes, with white clocked stockings above, and a liveried arm, reaching down over the spread tablecloth, quietly pouring wine. And that forgotten face, of a servant trained to be forgotten and faceless, was, of necessity, hearing everything that was said.

Unable to sleep as her mind raced in excitement over the possibilities thus conjured up, Susan fumbled for her tinder-box and struck a light. Shielding the fluttering candle with her hand, she flitted down through the slumbering house in nightgown and shawl, and sat at her desk. She was smiling, enfolded in memories of that morning, as she sharpened her quill and, setting the candle to best light the paper, penned a brief note to the Earl of Chene.

When she had folded and addressed it she sat for a long time, smiling in the flickering light, her mind five miles from the restless rustling and creaking of the ancient Manor as it grumbled and settled in its sleep.

CHAPTER FIFTEEN

VIOLET was astounded. She stood at the white painted gate of her house, scissors in one hand, trug of cut flowers in the other, and stared down the village street at the retreating curricle. It swayed gracefully along behind a pair of highly strung matched greys, and was quite unmistakable. Sitting in it, shameless beside the villain of all Violet's conjectures, sat Miss Susan Finderby.

Violet gasped, whirled round with a speed that set the broad rim of her straw hat flapping and her ribbons flying and hurried indoors to tell her mama. Her busy mind was conjuring all sorts of errands to take her scurrying down the village street in the wake of that extravagant equipage.

'Are you still feeling brave, little Miss Finderby?' the Earl asked, as they left Violet's riveted figure behind them. She held her head high, he noted with pride and an affectionate smile. An indomitable little figure in her light brown dress, her shawl, and sensible bonnet, she was looking severely at any gaping passer-by.

'Yes indeed, my lord. I have been a fool hiding at the Manor, when there are schools to build, gangs to capture, new villages to plan. The shock of the attack must have addled my mind. Never before have I allowed mere ignorant gossip, or even mistaken public opinion, to influence my actions, and I can assure you I don't intend it to happen again.'

She had spoken severely, pushing those days of torment firmly behind her, but she shrugged and smiled when she caught the Earl regarding her with quizzically raised eyebrows. He grinned.

'There speaks the Miss Finderby who stormed my fortressed heart with one lashing of her tongue! And together we shall defy the ignorant and achieve all our purposes.'

'Indeed we shall, my lord.' She spoke very demurely, but she sneaked a mischievous smile up at him from under her bonnet. 'Tell me what you have done about the footman.'

They were approaching the vicarage, and the foundations of the school, which had been their objective, the Earl having persuaded Susan out of the house with a plea to her sense of duty.

'Ah. In that case we will leave the school,' he said, acting immediately upon his words by urging the greys onwards down the road that led out of the village, 'and call at the vicarage on our return. It will do you good to see something of the countryside after so long. Have you any preference as to where we should drive?'

'None at all, sir, if you will only answer my question. I woke in the night and quite thought I had discovered a vital clue. Are you not as excited as I am? *Did* the footman disclose all our family secrets, and will he lead us to the gang?'

'Hold hard, hold hard, my girl.' The Earl was frowning to remember the lane he wanted. 'I thought we might drive up along the ridge road over the Gridby Hills. The views are superb.'

'It is the next turning you want, then,' said Susan, with the familiarity of one born and bred in the area. 'Left by the oak at Annie Packard's cottage, cut through Blagg's farmyard and out through the ford, not the gate, then follow the track till Gallow's Cross. Now, will you tell me about the footman?'

He laughed. 'Yes, ma'am,' he said. 'I spoke with Oliver, and neither he nor I could remember which man was there, though indeed you are right—there was a footman, for I can clearly recollect holding out my glass to the man while Jeremy was speaking of the Star. The sunlight caught it, and I remember likening it idly in my mind to the sparkle of diamonds. But so many of the staff are new to us, I am not yet familiar with all their faces.'

'At least I was right. He was there.'

'Oh, yes. He was there. You were right, my clever girl. It was at this point that Oliver and I decided to include Bowdler in our investigations. He has been with the family so long he is quite above suspicion. We put the whole case to him. He claimed it would have been one of two men who served us—Noah Spode, or Jared Williams. Personally, he suspects Spode, but he has no more proof than an opinion that the man looks insolent!'

'He may well be right. I would respect Bowdler's judgement.' Susan looked thoughtful, frowning at the swishing tail of the horse ahead of her. 'What you need to discover is the person to whom the footman could have passed the information. It is too much to suppose that all your staff hurry off to perpetrate vile crimes, without you so much as noticing. The gang is surely not operating from your house. If the footman is to blame, then it logically follows that he must have accomplices outside Chene.'

She was engrossed in the problem, with the same total concentration that she would put into planning schools, or villages, or anything that held her imagination. He smiled.

'Our thoughts exactly,' he said. 'We decided that Bowdler should watch both men about their duties indoors. Then, whenever they go out, we recruit his nephew.'

'Has Bowdler a nephew? I didn't know.'

'Nor did I. Obviously he does not believe in using family influence for advancement! But he swears by this lad's honesty, so we sent for him, and he will follow either man whenever they go out.'

'Who is this nephew?'

'A young groom in my stables. A well set-up lad. His name is Benjamin Foot.'

Susan laughed.

'Oh, yes,' she said. 'I know Benjamin very well.' The

Earl glanced down at her in surprise. 'He is such a regular visitor at the Manor that he almost has his own place laid at mealtimes! I hope for Benjamin's sake that your suspected footmen regularly travel in the direction of Finderby!'

'Whatever do you mean?'

'How little you know of your staff, sir. Benjamin has been utterly smitten by our dairymaid, Becky Marsh, since the first time he set eyes on her, when he delivered your letter to my grandfather. They have been walking out together ever since.' The Earl was frowning. 'It is not a cause of concern,' she said. 'They make an admirable couple, and you have made a good choice, entrusting the investigating to Benjamin. He is a quick-witted lad, and certainly honest. He will serve you well.'

'I was not doubting him. I was reflecting with shame upon how much better is your knowledge of my staff at Chene than is my own! The sooner you come to be the mistress of the house, the better, my love.'

Susan blushed and looked up at him uncertainly. This was the first direct mention he had made to his proposal of yesterday, and she was still finding the thought of a future with herself as mistress of Chene difficult to believe. He glanced down at her, and smiled.

'It was not all a dream, my dear. You did accept me. Are you regretting it already? I shall not take kindly to being jilted, you know.'

They had passed Gallow's Cross now, and the Earl allowed the horses to slow to a walk as they began the long pull up on to the ridge. On the lower slopes the lane was sunken between steep banks, and overhung by huge elms, the track made rutted and stony by winter rains.

'I am not a girl who "jilts", Lord Chene,' she said with careful dignity.

'No,' he replied, and the smile he gave her set her heart tumbling erratically in her breast. He muttered something impatiently, halted the greys abruptly in the middle of the lane, put an arm about her and pulled her to him. 'I have been wanting to do this all morning,' he

said, kissing her. He held her back and stared intently at
her. 'This fresh air must be doing you good,' he told her
with a half-smile. 'The colour it has brought to your
cheeks makes you utterly irresistible.'

She blushed yet more as he kissed her again.

'No,' she said, after a moment, reluctantly pushing
him away. 'Someone will see us.'

He laughed. 'Let them!'

But when a vast wagon laden with hay rounded the
bend at the bottom of the lane behind them the Earl
released her, and urged the greys on.

'Have you considered your mother?' Susan voiced a
doubt that had been much troubling her. 'She will not
take kindly to me. I am certain she must have other plans
for you.'

'Indeed she has! The Duke of Nare's daughter! A
dreadful girl, with buck teeth and a voice like a neighing
horse, to whom I have given no encouragement whatsoever, to my mother's oft-repeated chagrin. I look forward
eagerly to clearing my name of this slanderous talk, so
we may announce our engagement officially and ensure
my mother's disappointment. And Lucretia Nare's!' He
gave a flashing, white-toothed grin. 'I console myself by
indulging plans for my mother. I own a very convenient
dower house.'

Susan's feelings of relief that the dowager would not
live with them were only to be crushed at the thought of
her residing just across the park.

'I believe I have seen it,' she remarked in a small voice.
'On the road that skirts Chene Park.'

'That is certainly *a* dower house,' her beloved said,
amused. 'But the one I had in mind is on my Irish
estates. A small but charming residence, delightfully
remote, and well out of the common crowd that so
disgusts my mama. In fact it is so individually retired it
is almost impossible to travel from for at least nine
months of the year!'

Susan giggled.

'Your sentiments are unfilial, my lord,' she said.

'So would yours be,' he replied grimly, and he sped the horses up the last of the rise and out on to the hilltop, where the road stretched like a white ribbon before them over the open heath. With a sideways grin at her that lit up his dark face, he sent the curricle flying forward in the bright sunshine.

They called at the vicarage on their return, and walked over with Mr Stanbridge to view the foundations of the school. Work had been proceeding steadily while Susan had been sunk in her own problems. The builder from Findham was there, ready to discuss the work, but they had no complaints. Everything had been done as Susan wished, and the walls of the building would soon be rising from the trampled mud. She regarded it all with deep satisfaction.

Mr Stanbridge regarded the couple who stood before him with satisfaction, too. It did not need the glowing smile Susan gave him to reassure him. He had some bad news for them, however.

'I have heard there was another attack by the Gradeley Gang last night,' he said gloomily. His informant, he did not need to add, had been quick to place the blame on Chene's massive doorstep.

'I thought things had been very quiet since the attack at Finderby,' the Earl remarked, with interest. 'I thought perhaps my purported greed for ancient jewellery and dented silverware had finally been sated, but obviously not. Where am I deemed to have attacked now? Either my brother or I will wish to speak with the victims to gather what information we may to aid us in tracing this gang.'

'By all accounts it was a house some fifteen miles off, by Redcliff. There is talk of strings of pearls, much prized, and, yes, silver tableware. A family called Penwright. I am afraid I have no more details.' The vicar flapped his black cloak irritably. 'I wish you *would* track these people down. They are causing so much misery. And——' he glanced at Susan '—I would dearly like an end to this malicious talk.'

'So would I, sir,' the Earl replied. 'And soon. I think you may rest assured that they will be apprehended.'

The vicar looked at him sharply, then smiled. 'Indeed, I think they will. Good luck to you, my lord.'

The Earl drove slowly back through the village. Susan made a defiant point of waving greetings to all her friends and acquaintances.

It was a couple of days later that the Earl received another note summoning him to Finderby Manor. He had been intending to call, for he had news for Susan, but the note took him quite by surprise. Lord Finderby desired to meet him, and requested an interview as soon as was convenient. The note, in Susan's hand, had clearly been dictated. He stared at it in astonishment for some moments before slipping it into his pocket, and calling for his curricle.

Susan had walked down across the meadows, ostensibly looking for flowers for Hephzibah's medicinal potions, in reality watching for the dip and sway of the curricle behind the prancing greys, or listening for the gallop of Bo'sun's great hoofs over the turf. She saw him as soon as he turned on to the bridge over the stream, and stood waiting, a small figure in sprigged muslin, dwarfed by the wind-ruffled meadows stretching to the hazy horizons. The greys swept up, frisking and dancing, sensing the Earl's excitement on seeing her, but they slowed to pace demurely when he leaped down beside her, and he led them as he walked with her back towards the Manor mound.

She was eager to hear of the footmen.

'Nothing.' The Earl shrugged. 'Both Bowdler and Benjamin report nothing more than the performance of their normal duties, and an occasional walk down to the Chene Arms in the village. Jared Williams spends some time with the blacksmith's daughter in the sheds behind the forge, but Benjamin did not conclude this was for villainous purposes. At least, not as far as we are concerned. The blacksmith might take another view of it!'

Susan laughed.

'Poor Benjamin. How miserable for him to be spying so.'

'I think he is enjoying himself. Fancies himself as a Bow Street Runner! I shouldn't worry about Benjamin. But it seemed to Oliver and me that if it was merely a question of passing on likely information—and perhaps this gang has contacted greedy servants in any number of houses—then he would only make contact if he had information to pass on. We aim to hurry things on a little. We will create some information, and watch to see what happens.'

'What will you invent?'

'I am not certain yet. Some tale of easy pickings that should seem difficult to resist. We will make sure both footmen hear of it, and then—well—we will follow, and hope!' He smiled to himself, and, glancing at his face, Susan reflected that she would not envy the burglars when eventually Marcus discovered them. 'If we are lucky the bait will catch a minnow which will lead us to the pike.' He turned to look at her, and his expression softened. 'But now you tell me. Why does your grandfather wish to see me?'

'On that, I am no wiser than you,' Susan said. She added nothing more, and kept her hopes to herself for fear they should be unfounded.

'His speech is slow,' Susan said quietly, as, some while later, she led the Earl up the dark stairway to her grandfather's room, 'but I think you will understand him well enough. He would not tell me anything of what he means to say to you. I think he wants to look at you before he decides!'

The Earl merely smiled, and stood back to let her enter the room before him.

Anne was there, busy smoothing the old man's sheets to a chorus of bitter, muttered abuse about fussing females. Anne bobbed an apologetic curtsy at the Earl, and hurried out.

Lord Finderby stared at his visitor with a steely eye.

The Earl, standing relaxed at the bedside, returned his regard calmly. He was very aware that Susan had unconsciously positioned herself protectively close to him, glancing anxiously from his face to her grandfather's, and that the Baron's acute gaze had not missed this fact.

'How do you do, my lord?' the Earl began. 'I have long been hoping for this meeting.'

'Humph. Have you indeed?' the old man growled. 'After more of my land, that's what it is. To think it should come to this. A damned Chene at my bedside! Hah!' He glared at the younger man from beneath jutting white eyebrows.

'Grandfather——' Susan began, but the Earl laid a quietening hand on her arm.

'It's all right,' he said. 'Let your grandfather speak.'

'Let your grandfather speak,' the old Baron mimicked angrily. 'Don't you patronise me, my boy.'

'My lord,' the Earl replied with a faint smile, 'I wouldn't dare.'

The old man glared at him again.

'Damned Chene,' he muttered, half to himself, his gaze wandering about the room. 'Impudent young whelp. Doesn't have much of a look of his mewling, whingeing father—there's that to be thankful for. To think I would end my days talking to a Chene.' He focused sharply back on to his visitor. 'The Finderbys had owned this land, and half the county, for fifteen generations before the Chenes stole the most of it.' His tones were accusing. 'Fifteen generations! And the blood of Celtic kings and Saxon thanes was running in their veins. While your family were nothing. Nothing! Drabs and peasants, kitchen menials, serfs and slaves.'

The Earl blinked, surprised, and raised an enquiring eyebrow.

'You don't like to hear the truth, heh?' The old man gave a wicked, yellow-toothed grin. 'Fancy name—Carlleon. Eh? Fancy. Like to pretend it's Norman, I dare say?'

The Earl did not like to deflate the old man by

admitting that, unlike his mother, he had never given
the origin of his family name any thought at all. He
shrugged non-committally.

'Hah! I knew as much. Well, let me tell you something, Lord Chene. Before that smooth-talking upstart
forebear of yours had endeared himself to Queen Bess
and made his fortune, his name was not Carlleon. Oh, no.
I have traced back the family records, and it's there for
all to see. Your name had a similar sound, but nothing
like as grand. No. It was much more homely. Scullion!
Scullion, that was your family name! And scullions they
were. Scrapers of greasy dishes, carriers of pails of offal,
spit-turners and turnip-peelers, those are your forebears.
And likely they worked here, in this very Manor kitchen.
What do you say to that, then, Earl of Chene?'

His tone was filled with triumphant dislike as he
grinned up at the Earl from his mound of pillows in the
threadbare lace-edged pillowcases. It was gloomy where
he lay, beneath the heavy, dusty tester and the sombre
carved bedposts. The sun was golden outside, but no
brightness penetrated here.

'You don't surprise me,' the Earl remarked mildly.
'My mother, in misguided hope, spends long hours
searching for mythical Norman ancestors. I have frequently distressed her by my declared belief that we
came from far more disreputable origins. I have to
confess that I had considered tricksters and con-men
more probable than offal-carriers, but I dare say one
could trace them all somewhere in the family tree.'

The Baron stared. He had expected bluster and outrage, pomposity and self-consequence. Almost despite
himself, he gave a reluctant smile, and irritably sup-
pressed it.

'So you see yourself as a descendant of con-men and
tricksters, eh? And you hope to be a credit to them, no
doubt, with your schemes to take other men's acres for
your canals and your mines. Oh, don't you worry. I have
heard all about it. All just a con, is it?'

'I certainly endeavour to live by the use of my wits as

much as by the exercise of my consequence and position.
But to honest ends, I trust. In the case of the plans for
the canal and the mine, I can assure you there is no trick.
It will be a working and profitable venture.'

'He has inherited the family smooth-talking tongue.'
The old man still glowered, muttering to himself. 'Old
Stanbridge approves of him, of course. And Chapley-
Gore thinks him a villain. That can only be a point in his
favour. Pompous young bore.'

He turned his glare back at the Earl. 'You just stand
there, meekly taking all my insults. What are you? A
man? A man, or a sugar-tongued milksop? Heh?'

Having experience of the Earl's explosive temper,
Susan had been listening in increasing anxiety. Now she
was chewing her lip, her forehead wrinkled, offering
silent prayers. To her astonishment, the Earl laughed.

'As you well know, my lord, there is often more of the
man in the one who can rein in his temper than in the
one who lets it fly. Can we not agree to consign my
ancestors to the dregs and sweepings of history? It is no
doubt where they belong. I must confess that my concerns are all with the future.'

'Huh.'

The old man lay for some minutes, staring at the two
who stood at his bedside, thoughts rambling in his head.
Somehow the pleasure he had taken in his bitter hatred
had faded. Perhaps he was growing too old, too tired.
Perhaps it had never really mattered. That interfering
vicar had told him a great many things recently that he
had not wanted to hear, but he had thought long and
hard about them afterwards. Now it seemed that perhaps
some of the scorned ideas that the vicar had planted in
his unwilling mind had had some basis in truth.

Anxious at his long silence, Susan spoke.

'Do you feel poorly, Grandfather? Shall I give you
your medicine?'

'Stop blathering, girl.' He moved his head impatiently.
'Tell me, sir. What are these concerns for the future?'

'Three things primarily concern me at present, sir.

Firstly, the apprehending of the so-called Gradeley Gang.
I mean to catch them. I would hope I could offer to
return your Finderby Star when I track them down, but
I fear it may be too late for that.'

'It's not important.' The old man shook his head
dismissively.

'Whatever do you mean, Grandfather?' Susan burst
in. 'It was all we had left.'

The Baron cleared his throat, and gave his granddaughter a glance that could only be described as
shamefaced.

'Paste,' he growled.

'Paste? How do you mean, paste?'

He sighed irritably at being forced to explain.

'It was a copy. I needed the ready cash. Done when
your grandmother was alive.' The old head shifted
uncomfortably. 'And don't take that poker-faced look
with me, my girl. It's just the look your grandmother
gave, when she found out, and I wouldn't tolerate it
from her either. It was back in the old days. Too long
ago for me to worry about it now. There was a little place
in Paris, very discreet. Man by the name of Georges
Strass. Jeweller to the King. He obliged many a young
gentleman in need of funds, with a timely copy in paste,
and many a wife was none the wiser.' He closed his eyes.
Marcus gave a meaningful glance at his beloved, and she
gave an angry little shrug, and carefully rearranged her
expression. 'The only thing that gave me any pleasure
about that burglary,' the Baron remarked, his eyes still
closed, 'was the thought of their faces when they realised.
It was a very good copy, you know. Fooled that flibber-
tigibbet mother of yours. She never knew the truth.
Flaunted the damned thing everywhere.'

Susan bit her lip and made no answer.

'Well? Well, Lord Chene? What is your second concern, then, sir?'

The Baron was keen to abandon talk of the Finderby
Star.

'The construction of the canal,' the Earl replied. 'We

are still keen to route it over your land, if you would consider the plans. It would, in addition, be an opportunity for you to develop the coal-seams that lie beneath your estate.'

Susan thought of how much this meant, both to Marcus, and to Jeremy. She found she was holding her breath, waiting for her grandfather's response.

'I'll make you no promises,' he growled eventually, 'but bring your plans and drawings and what have you next time you come, and I will look at them.'

'Thank you, sir.'

'I make no promises!' the old man repeated.

'I understand that, sir.'

'And the third thing?'

'Sir?'

'The third thing you are concerned with? What is that?'

The Earl hesitated only for a moment.

'The third thing is your granddaughter, sir.'

Susan gasped. She had never anticipated that the Earl would mention this. She waited in terror for the outburst of fury, the condemnations, the banishing.

'When I have discovered the perpetrators of these crimes, and cleared my name of the slanders which you have no doubt heard, I mean to marry your granddaughter, Lord Finderby.'

The Baron's eyes had flown open, and he was glaring at them both with all the rage Susan had anticipated. She instinctively looked to the medicine bottle, and almost called out for Alfred, forgetting he would not be there.

'You *mean* to, do you, my lord? No "by your leave"? No requesting her hand?'

'It will make us both very happy, sir——' here the Earl put a hand on Susan's shoulder and drew her nearer to him '——if you will give us your blessing. We would like, when we announce the engagement, to have your support. But I should tell you that, whatever you decide, I do intend to marry her anyway.'

The old man's forehead was puckered.

'Can this *truly* be what you want, Susan? I can't believe it. Marriage to a Chene?'

She found she was shaking, but she managed to nod her head. She realised that her grandfather's protests sounded oddly half-hearted.

'Yes, sir,' she managed to say.

Once again Lord Finderby closed his eyes and lay still. Susan looked up at the Earl, who was watching the old man's sunken face sombrely. He caught her glance, and gave her a reassuring smile.

'Hah!' said the old man eventually. 'It is not what I would have chosen. And I won't say it is, not to please any of you. But I suppose it is one way to get those stolen Chene acres back into the family!'

CHAPTER SIXTEEN

VIOLET had found it almost, but not quite, impossible to believe that Susan was willingly consorting with a man who, she was convinced, had so brutally wronged her family. She had always regarded critically what she termed Susan's wilfulness and eccentricity, but this behaviour reached beyond the bounds of eccentricity. It was wicked folly. She declared as much to anyone who would listen.

Although many in the village held Susan in great affection, it was widely feared that she had been duped. No one wished to suffer the contempt of Violet's sharp tongue by contradicting her, and most, therefore, at least for appearance's sake, agreed with her. Only Mrs Peters and young Jimmy declared that they did not believe a word of what was said against the Earl, and no one listened seriously to the opinions of a miserable drab and her son from Mill Cottages. As for the vicar's doubts, it was well known he was a saintly man, but sorely lacking in common sense.

It was not long before Violet persuaded herself that it was her duty as a friend to point out to Susan the evil of her ways.

'I take no concern for my own reputation,' she emphasised to Eustace, on the afternoon of the day that the Earl of Chene met Lord Finderby. 'I am not so selfish as to draw back from my duty to one who was once my dearest friend. If her behaviour now leaves all who know her filled with shock and horror, still I will risk the social unacceptability of visiting her house. It is my Christian duty to show her the evil of her ways.'

Eustace was deeply affected by this selfless good-heartedness.

'I will accompany you,' he said. 'With myself as escort,

no one can cast a slur upon your good name, no matter
what depravity is accepted at the Manor.'

Eustace had heard so much of Violet's fevered imaginings that it was no longer beyond his foolishness to
picture Finderby Manor quite taken over by the
depraved followers of the Gradeley Gang, with the old
Baron bed-ridden and ignorant, if they had not already
done away with him, and Susan living the life of a gang-
leader's moll!

Once this errand of mercy was decided upon they were
zealous to be away, and set out immediately in Eustace's
gig.

It was some disappointment to them both to find the
yard of the Manor drowsy with the buzzing of flies and
the drone of bees from the gardens, empty of highwaymen's horses, or indeed of any horses at all. Tying up
the stout roan gelding which pulled Eustace's gig, the
pair ventured to the kitchen door.

Hephzibah was busy at the table beating a cake mix
with a wooden spoon. She looked up. Her old face was
pink from exertion and the heat of the open fire.

'Good afternoon to you both,' she said, straightening
up to regard them, and pushing a stray wisp of grey hair
from her eyes with a wipe of her arm. She was friendly,
but her tones lacked any real enthusiasm. 'Come in,
come in. I'll put the kettle on the fire, and make us all
some tea. It is many a day since we saw you.'

Both the visitors were disconcerted by the peaceful
kitchen, redolent with the warm aromas of new-baked
scones.

'The men are all in the fields of course,' Hephzibah
continued, answering the questions she assumed they
would want to ask, 'and Jeremy with them, for he is
quite recovered now. Even Alfred can sit in his chair out
in the garden now, and shell peas or suchlike. And the
old lord is as well as he will ever be.' She smiled. 'We
are all going on very well. But you will be wanting Susan.
She is out sowing lettuce seed. I'll call her.'

'No, there is no need,' said Violet hastily. 'I will go out and find her.'

'And I will pay my respects to Lord Finderby, if I may,' pronounced Eustace heavily, determined to ascertain for himself the Baron's safe progress, 'and I will join you ladies later.'

He was glad to leave the kitchen. It distressed Eustace more than Violet to be entertained in a kitchen, like in any common farmhouse, for it offended every sense of what was due in the home of a Baron. His sense of order was affronted. He lacked the feelings of smug complacency in the superiority of her own establishment that Violet gained from being welcomed in such a way.

Just now, in addition, Eustace did not wish to think that he was any less proper in the execution of unpleasant but necessary duties than Violet herself. He knew he was obliged to explain to the Baron the full horror of his granddaughter's behaviour. He steeled himself to fortitude as he mounted the stairs.

The ominous silence from the bed, as Eustace solemnly retailed the shocking fact of Susan's openly travelling in the curricle of a man known to all the county to be a hardened villain, should perhaps have warned Eustace of his impending reception. But he was not a sensitive or imaginative man, and could only suppose Lord Finderby to be struck dumb with horror, and with gratitude at being thus informed.

'I am only sorry,' Eustace concluded with earnest self-satisfaction, 'that I must bring you such deplorable— nay, devastating news. News of your granddaughter's reputation blackened. . .and to think that once I cherished hopes of becoming a part of your family. . . I offer my heartfelt sympathies, sir. You suffer a heavy blow.'

He shook his head solemnly, privately congratulating himself on having escaped any binding connection with the family before this scandal broke. Complacent in his thoughts, the slow voice of the old man came as a shock.

'I had rather,' Lord Finderby began, his voice thick with dislike, 'that my granddaughter was scandalising half the nation with a man such as Chene than settling for the pusillanimity of marriage to you. I would not care should Chene be making his fortune by stealing rose-painted piss-pots via a gang of harlots! At least he is not a posing, prosing pomposity. At least he has the courage and convictions of a man. You, sir, you carry all the conviction of a cockroach. I scorn your mendacious tittle-tattle! I despise you for the contempt you pour on my granddaughter's good name. I will not have you ever again in my house. Go!'

Lord Finderby closed his eyes with the finality of dismissal, and, after a few moments of ineffectual blustering which was completely ignored, Eustace made his way back downstairs.

Violet had fared very little better in the garden.

Susan had looked up warily from where she crouched over the string that marked the row of seeds. She stood up to face her erstwhile friend.

'I feel it is my duty to speak with you.' Violet sounded defiant, her voice pitched high. 'Someone needs to give you the word, and it seems there is no one but me.'

'You are all kind consideration,' Susan rejoined.

Violet flushed. 'I am not one to shirk a duty.'

'No one could ever accuse you of it, Violet.'

Susan was leaning on her rake, hands grubby from the rich loam. Violet frowned in distaste.

'You fill all proper-minded people with disgust. Parading about the neighbourhood in the company of a robber, highwayman, probably a murderer! A man who cruelly harmed your own family! Are you so utterly sunk in depravity that you are impervious to the demands of public opinion? Are you happy to trail the dregs of your reputation yet further through the mire? Save yourself, Susan! Put a stop to this wickedness. Banish this man from your life, whatever his fascination for you, and aid the law in apprehending him for his crimes! Your folly could eventually be forgotten. Do not condemn yourself to a life utterly beyond the pale!'

Violet was rather pleased with this speech. Impassioned but fair, it expressed everything a devoted friend could possibly be expected to plead. However far sunk in vice, surely Susan could not resist its plea. How great was Violet's surprise, then, when Susan gave a burst of laughter.

'Oh, dear, Violet, forgive me, but really you deserve no more. What foolishness you talk. Can you not see that this is nothing but your misguided imaginings? I should be angry with you, but——' she laughed again '——I can only see the absurdity!'

Stung, Violet flushed an ugly red, her pale eyes narrowed angrily.

'I do not deserve your mockery! I came as a friend to save you from your own wickedness. It seems I am already too late!'

She turned with a flounce, purposely treading over the line of seeds. She saw Eustace coming down the garden, and hurried towards him.

'Don't try to speak to her,' she cried, flinging herself at the man so that he was obliged to catch her against his chest. He soothed her with awkward embarrassment. 'We are too late! She scorns me with mockery and contempt. There is no longer a path to her heart. That my friendship should be treated thus!'

Eustace made as if to put her aside, and go to speak his mind to Susan, who was watching this affecting scene with mixed contempt, exasperation and amusement. Violet, however, wanted none of that. She leaned closer, clinging to him.

'Do not leave me! I do not think I can support myself without you. Take me home, Mr Chapley-Gore. There is nothing for us here!'

'Indeed, I believe you are right,' Susan heard Eustace remark in troubled tones. 'For I do believe that poor old Lord Finderby has finally addled his wits. There is no doubt about it. You should have heard what he said to me. The old man is not right in the head!'

Supporting each other in their afflictions, the two vanished around the corner of the house. Susan stared after them for some minutes, then shook her head. She raked over the line of lettuce seeds, and debated the necessity of a further sowing of radishes.

The Earl, Oliver and Bowdler planned to lay their trap at dinner that evening. The two suspected footmen were to serve the meal.

It was a more elaborate spread than usual, for the dowager had an old friend, Lady Watson, staying with her. The vicar of Chene, with his good lady, had been invited up, as well as the curate who hoped to succeed to the living, with his wife, to swell the party. Neither couple was likely to offend their benefactor by refusing his invitations, no matter what rumours circulated. He could be pronounced a Bluebeard, and they would pray for his soul, but eat his dinners. Lord Chene considered that the extra time necessary to serve the guests would give him ample opportunity to lay his bait.

'I received a letter recently,' he began, 'from a cousin of ours.'

'And whom would that be?' enquired the dowager, instantly keen to criticise.

'Mrs Kelsteven. If you remember, her husband died some months ago, and her son succeeded to the property. A handsome estate,' he explained for the benefit of his guests, 'with an elegant house. Unfortunately her daughter-in-law had never regarded Mrs Kelsteven and her daughters kindly, and the son is a selfish young man, much under her influence. Now it appears that the rift between them is so great that it is essential they leave the family home and find other accommodation immediately.'

'Well,' put in the dowager, 'I fail to see what concern it is of yours. They are only distant cousins, after all, and cannot presume to have any claim upon you.'

The Earl merely looked at her.

'I have always found Mrs Kelsteven a pleasant woman,' he said. 'I would have no wish to hear of her hardship when it is in my power to offer a remedy. I have decided to lease her the Chene dower house, and have written today to tell her as much.'

'The use of the dower house?' The dowager was outraged. 'What folly is this, Marcus? It is bad enough to hear that one *possesses* encroaching, impoverished relations, without encouraging them to sit upon the doorstep.'

'It is a charitable solution,' the vicar ventured, pacifically, and the curate nodded solemnly, but no one paid any attention to them.

'I have decided to improve the furnishings at the dower house, of course,' Marcus continued, 'and I thought I would send down two of the sets of silver tableware. There is so much we never use, I dare say Bowdler will rejoice to see less of it on his shelves. There is one set of silver with a particularly hideous epergne decorated with obese cherubs studded with pearls. Do you remember it? I am certain our cousins could find a use for it. I will have it all sent over in the morning. Perhaps one of these two could carry it down?' He nodded towards the footmen, ensuring he had their attention.

'Certainly, my lord,' murmured Bowdler discreetly.

'This is ridiculous!' exclaimed the dowager. 'Bad enough to *let* the dower house, but to hand over our silver? Why, it is worth I don't know how much. Hundreds of pounds! Thousands! What could a woman like Mrs Kelsteven want with such things? And she not even a close cousin!'

'She has been accustomed to everything of the best, Mother. It will please her to have the use of them. And she is not so distant a cousin. If you remember, it was her great-great-grandmother who inherited the Galesby diamond pendant that you always swear should have come to your grandmother and thus become yours. I know Mrs Kelsteven owns it now, and it will certainly come with her. I trust they will be here inside a fortnight.'

The Earl thus had the satisfaction of helping a needy

relative, baiting a trap for any traitorous footman, and annoying his mother exceedingly, all by one easy deed. Oliver was grinning at him in approval, and the brothers continued the meal in great good humour. The footmen could not help but overhear, and Bowdler had every reason to continue discussion of the valuable property to be left scantily protected in the dower house once the meal was over. They could hope for speedy results.

The dowager, who had always exclaimed at tedious length that nothing would induce her to retire to the dower house—she would rather be banished completely to the ends of the earth than suffer such a rejection at the hands of her son—could hardly now complain when she was effectively denied any possibility of doing so. She consoled herself with the reflection that Lucretia Nare was a sweet girl who had always shown her every consideration, and who, when the time came, would certainly beg her to live with them at Chene.

Oliver excused himself from the party as soon as dinner was over. It had been arranged that, after the meal was cleared, and after careful examination of the silver to be moved by Bowdler and the two footmen, Bowdler was to excuse the men from duties for the rest of the evening. As Benjamin could not follow both men, Oliver had volunteered to join him.

The two sleuths met up in a storeroom near the butler's pantry. They could hear Bowdler busily wondering why the Earl should be giving away such valuable silver to a lady who already owned a diamond pendant that would, by all accounts, buy half the Indies. Oliver smiled.

'Whom do you wish to follow?' he asked Benjamin.

The young groom shrugged bashfully.

'It's for you to say, sir.'

'We will toss for it. You call. Winner takes Noah Spode!'

Oliver lost the call, and grinned disappointedly. 'I dare swear I know where I will spend the rest of the evening, if what you have told us is true! Eavesdropping outside the store at the back of Bailey's forge. What a bore. I guess you will have all the excitement, Benjamin!'

Benjamin grinned back, eager to go. He privately agreed. He suspected Noah Spode, with his shifty eyes and meticulous politeness. He disliked the way Spode hovered, just a little too close, to anyone holding a conversation, as if permanently eavesdropping. He very much hoped Spode would be their man, and he the hero who tracked him down.

They heard Bowdler dismiss the men, and Williams telling Spode he would take the chance to go down to the village. Oliver, who had, like the young groom, pulled on dark clothes, top boots, breeches and jacket, purposefully buttoned the jacket up to the neck.

'Are you coming out?' they heard Williams ask.

'Perhaps later,' Spode said. 'Don't you wait for me. You don't want to keep her waiting!'

Williams chuckled. 'She's always ready and waiting.' But they heard him move away, and Spode turn back towards the kitchens. With a brief wave and grin to Benjamin, Oliver moved off after his quarry.

Benjamin slipped out moments later. As he entered the kitchen, thinking Spode would have hurried through and out of the house, he paused, startled, at seeing Spode seated at the great deal table, his feet among the racks of pans that ran beneath it, hunched over a sheet of cheap paper, laboriously scribing a letter with a pencil. Benjamin was surprised, impressed, and deeply suspicious at this evidence of learning. He lingered in the shadowy edges of the huge room.

'I'll have back my taper and pencil, Mr Spode, *if* you've quite done. I've my requirements for tomorrow to finish.'

Benjamin had not noticed the cook sitting by the long range, squinting at a list she had been preparing, unable to see without her light.

'I shan't be troubling you any longer, Mrs Batt. I'm going out now.'

As soon as he heard this Benjamin went ahead, out of

the warm kitchen, down a flight of stone steps, and along a length of stone-flagged passage smelling of mildew and damp, which led out into a side courtyard. It was deserted and silent in the darkness. He crossed the yard, and stood inside the open doorway of a store, hidden in the dense blackness, where he could watch the doorway opposite for Spode's exit.

He did not have to wait long. He watched Spode pause as he reached the yard, and, by the light of the half-moon, watched him tuck the paper he had been labouring over into a shirt pocket, then carefully button his coat up over it. With a glance around to see he was unobserved, Spode then made off at a brisk walk, through the outbuildings and gardens, and into the park.

It was not difficult for Benjamin to follow at first. The moonlight was fitful, for clouds were passing regularly overhead, and the buildings, and the shrubs of the garden, offered generous cover. The breeze generated just enough noise in the undergrowth to mask any sound of stealthy footsteps.

Once in the park it was more difficult. Where Spode chose to enter the park, it was divided from the gardens by a ha-ha, beyond which stretched open grass interspersed with a few fine old trees. Spode, having again looked warily behind him, but missed observing Benjamin lurking behind a dense holly bush, jumped nimbly down the ha-ha, and set off across the open grass at a loping run.

Benjamin instantly ran to the wall edge, and jumped down. He remained there for some moments, hidden in the dip from Spode's sight should he chance to look back, and wondered what to do. While the moon shone, Spode was plain to see against the open silvery grass, and Benjamin knew that he would be equally obvious. Making a hasty decision, he ran, bent double, along the base of the ha-ha until he had a huge old oak between himself and his quarry. Then he broke from cover, and ran as fast as he could to the tree.

From then it was largely a question of luck. Benjamin

tried to keep a tree between himself and Spode, but sometimes he relied on the passing clouds, and ran with all speed in what he hoped was the right direction. Once he thought he had been spotted. The moon emerged, bright and clear, as Benjamin sank perforce to a crouch in the open grassland, and Spode paused to catch his breath, and survey the park behind him. He stood for what seemed an age, while Benjamin strove desperately to exactly resemble a bush, or a tree stump, without in fact moving so much as a finger.

But Spode moved on, more slowly now without giving any indication of having seen his follower. A thick band of woodland extended around the edge of the park, dividing it from the public road that skirted the boundary wall. To Benjamin's dismay, Spode plunged confidently into the darkness of the wood, and vanished from sight.

It took considerable resolution on Benjamin's part to jump up and approach the deep shadows of the trees, uncertain whether or not he had been observed, and what reception might be awaiting him among those shadows. He felt horribly exposed crossing the moonlit meadow. However, he walked on boldly now, deeming secrecy foolish if he had been spotted, and pointless if he had not, and Spode had merely hurried on through the wood. As he went he busily invented reasons, just in case he should be stopped and challenged, to account for why he should be leaving his bed in the Chene stables to sneak out of the park at midnight. He began imagining the entire bloodthirsty Gradeley Gang waiting for him in the trees.

In fact the trees were empty, at least of humankind. As he reached the spot where Spode had vanished from sight, he realised there was a narrow but distinct path leading onward. Hurrying now, afraid he had lost Spode altogether, he ran through the rustling darkness.

It was pure good fortune that he avoided colliding directly with the footman. The narrow path led directly to the base of the red brick wall that skirted the park. Here a fallen tree had long ago rested against the side of the wall, and, with some minor adaptation to its branches, had obviously been serving as a convenient ladder for a considerable while. Spode appeared to have just returned down this ladder. He stood at the base of the old tree, buttoning up his jacket, and there was just time for Benjamin to step back behind the bushy bole of a lime tree before Spode hurried past him, clearly returning from whence he had come.

Benjamin waited only as long as he was safe before hurrying over to the tree, running up to it, and looking over the wall.

On the far side a neat pile of brushwood had been stacked, screened from the road by a clump of hawthorn bushes, and providing a simple means of scaling the wall. Pausing only to see that he was alone, Benjamin climbed down. There was nothing to see. The road was completely empty as far as could be seen in either direction, and, no matter how much he strained his ears, Benjamin could hear no sound beyond the whispering and creaking of the trees. If Spode had met somebody, that person had vanished as rapidly as had the footman.

Frustrated, Benjamin sat down on the pile of brushwood to think.

If Spode was indeed their man, as Benjamin suspected, then it was sensible to assume he wished to convey news of the silver to be left in the dower house to the other gang members. Indeed, Benjamin had assumed that the note being so painstakingly lettered on the kitchen table at Chene was to give that information. He had brought the letter with him. How, then, had it been delivered? To whom? When?

Benjamin pondered. He had watched Spode place the letter inside his jacket. But, he thought with a start of excitement, when Spode came back over the wall, he paused to button his jacket again. Surely, then, he had opened it to remove the letter. So he *had* delivered it. But to whom?

The more Benjamin puzzled, the more perplexed he became. Spode had not known he would have the information to pass on that night. He had no way of arranging for anyone to meet him. He had visited no house or tavern where he might meet someone. Yet now he was returning to Chene, and it was reasonable to suppose that he had delivered his note. So where?

Standing up abruptly, and startling a dog fox which had been sauntering confidently down the centre of the road, Benjamin began to look for a letter-box. He did not know what he was seeking, only that it would have to be close to the crossing of the wall, for Spode was gone so short a time, and presumably sheltered from wind and rain.

He began by searching for hollow trees. None of the hawthorns was old enough to provide the necessary hole, but there were several other trees that took some while to explore. He found nothing. Next he examined the wall, pulling and poking at the bricks for any that might be loose. It was difficult in the darkness, and he frequently tripped and stumbled in the brambles that grew near the foot of the wall, but his only reward was a conclusion that some previous Earl had employed a bricklayer who was an expert in his trade. Not one brick was loose. The pile of brushwood yielded nothing either.

Benjamin was beginning to wonder whether he was not mistaken. He sat down on a flat stone at the roadside, to give the problem more thought, and the slab tilted gently beneath his weight. Jumping up, he raised the heavy stone. There beneath it, burrowed into the soil, was a rusty tin box. And inside the box was Spode's note. Benjamin gave a broad grin, and carefully replaced everything as he had found it.

He had not opened the note, for he could not read it if he did. And he saw no reason to take it. It would say, he presumed, just what the Earl wanted it to say. The important thing to discover, the young groom decided, was who came to collect the note. With that in mind he took a small bundle of brushwood from the stack, waded into a bramble patch which would hide him, yet give

him a good view of the stone, spread the brushwood into
an apology for a bed, and lay down. He knew it might be
a long wait.

It was daylight when Benjamin suddenly awoke, and
memory came to him instantly, along with the stiffness
and chill of his night on the roadside. He was about to
ease his limbs and stir, when he realised he was not
alone, and he froze to immobility.

'Spode is proving his worth again, after that fiasco of
the Finderby Star,' a voice remarked, and there was a
thud and jingle as a horse shifted its position. 'I had not
thought we would have the good fortune to relieve Chene
of any of his worldly goods. The house is far too well
locked and staffed. But the dower house. That will be a
much easier nut to crack. Here, read it for yourself, if
you can decipher it.'

Again, the shift of horses, and the rustle of someone
smoothing out a sheet of paper. Hoping they were both
engrossed in the letter, Benjamin opened his eyes, and
slowly turned his head. There were two men only. Both
were mounted, but both had their backs to him, and he
could see nothing of their faces. As Benjamin set himself
to remember every detail of their horses, their clothes,
their voices, one handed the letter back to the other, and
they began to move on down the road.

'It must be worth our consideration,' the first man
remarked. 'We can discuss it at the Dale House. There
have been no other communications of such interest.'

Then, just as Benjamin, straining his ears, was considering how best he could follow them, the horses were
urged into a canter, and they speedily vanished round a
bend in the road. Any chance of keeping up with them
had gone. Repeating every word he had heard to keep it
fresh in his memory, Benjamin rapidly scaled the wall,
and set off at a run through the wood towards Chene,
spurred on by an eager enthusiasm to break his news to
the Earl, and a hearty desire for his breakfast.

CHAPTER SEVENTEEN

THE Earl arrived once again at Finderby Manor later that day.

His explanation to Oliver, who as yet knew nothing of his commitment to Susan, but only that the old Baron was prepared to look more favourably on their plans, had been to plead Susan's extensive local knowledge. Not one of them at Chene knew of anywhere called Dale House, and study of all the maps of the district that the Chene library could produce drew a similar blank. Blake, the agent, had heard of no such place. Benjamin's buoyant enthusiasm was undiminished as he cudgelled his brain for any memory of such a house, but his results were disappointing.

Marcus had persuaded himself that appealing to Susan was a necessity. In reality, the hours without her were empty. He was finding it increasingly difficult to stay away.

When he arrived he found no difficulty in persuading her to drive out with him. Susan's release from the long days of doubts and misery had left her light as air, singing and laughing through the Manor house, sweeping aside Grandfather's dampening comments, Hephzibah's head-shaking and Jeremy's doubts and worries with the same happy unconcern with which she had regarded Violet's interference. Nothing now could sway her conviction of the Earl of Chene's innocence, his honour, his integrity and his good-heartedness. She was certain they would clear his name, and her dreams often moved on, if not quite to their life together, then at least to their joint plans for his ideal village.

Her face glowed with pleasure when she saw his figure silhouetted in the kitchen doorway. There was none of the endless waiting while she changed her clothes that the Earl had found so irritating among the previous young ladies of his acquaintance. Susan greeted him with a wide smile, took her apron off, reached her bonnet and shawl from behind the kitchen door, and pronounced herself ready.

'Have you never spent hours preening yourself to go out?' he asked, amused, as he handed her up into the curricle. 'In your speed of departure you are, to my knowledge, unique among females.'

'And I dare say your knowledge is extensive?'

'Very wide,' he agreed solemnly.

She chuckled. 'I should have known.' She paused, then continued lightly, 'Of course I used to primp and preen. Every girl does. But it brought me no other joy than the heavy-handed admiration of grandfather's friends, and the need to dodge any encounter with them on the back stairs once they were befuddled in their cups. No, wait! I lie. It also brought me one offer of marriage from a wicked old goat of sixty-seven, with a bald, pointed head, a straggle of beard stained yellow by dribbled tobacco, a sagging belly and legs that would make a sparrow seem a prize fighter! He suffered a convulsion and died within six months of my refusal. I could not mourn him!

'Beyond that, my lack of fortune and my woeful outspokenness deterred would-be suitors. There were only the earnest attentions of Mr Chapley-Gore. Solemn, worthy, virtuous, tedious Eustace. Poor man. I truly think he believed that with a little more effort he could so order my mind as to make me worthy of the offer of his hand. No longer, however! I am deemed beyond recall since the day I chose to associate with highwaymen and robbers!' She laughed at him. 'But you can see why I have ceased to preen, and my mirror has almost forgotten who I am!'

'My poor girl! So undeservedly unappreciated! But I fear I should be offended. Does not even the arrival of your affianced merit a quick glance in the mirror?'

'Preen for you, my lord? Indeed, no. How could I

hazard such a thing? It is plain to me that I captured your heart by the novelty of my bedraggled clothing and shrewish tongue! What else could it have been? I dare not risk losing you now, at so delicate a stage in our relationship, by attempting any alteration! Perhaps once we are safely married, then I shall dare to use my mirror again! I might even, on occasion, risk a new bonnet, or dress!'

'Miss Finderby, how you underestimate my devotion! No be-ribboned bonnet could deter me! Nor even a pretty new dress! Even a London modiste could make no difference in the world,' he said, in exaggerated tones, his gallantry belied by his grin. 'To me you will always seem perfect!'

'Now that is very charming!' she remarked judiciously, her head on one side 'A most sweet compliment. But one, I fear, sorely designed to encourage me in my idle ways. But enough of this. I do not wish you to become conceited now you realise what opposition you had to overcome to win my hand, and how I slave to keep you by me! Tell me, my lord; did you set a trap for your footmen, and did it work?'

They had headed away from the Manor on the road towards Chene, the Earl keeping the greys to a steady trot. After they had paused to admire the gleaming gold of the new thatch on Mill Cottages, completed now, and greeted young Jimmy who cavorted before them gleefully on his crutches among the squawking chickens, he spent some time telling Susan all that had occurred the previous night.

'So you see,' he concluded, 'Benjamin was quite the hero of the hour, and poor Oliver had the dreariest time among the blacksmith's roosting chickens, waiting for the indefatigable daughter of the establishment to exhaust the passions of Jared! To add insult to injury, when at last Jared headed for home, and Oliver moved to follow, the hens set up such a cackling commotion that the blacksmith set the dog out to catch the intruder, and Oliver only escaped with his breeches whole by vaulting over a wall into a pig-pen!'

She laughed. 'But it was done in a noble cause, all to clear the good name of Chene. Now we know our villain! But where does he lead us? Where was the place these men mentioned?'

'There we have the problem. They said they would discuss Spode's note at the Dale House. That is all we know. And I can find no trace anywhere of anything called the Dale House. You know every inch of this countryside, Susan. Do you know where it might be?'

To her great annoyance, she did not. She worried at the name continuously as they drove, muttering under her breath, engrossed in her thoughts, determined to solve the puzzle. She looked up, after some little while, to find the Earl regarding her with amusement.

'It sounds like the chanting of an African witch-doctor! What are you mumbling to yourself?'

She laughed. 'I am following lanes in my mind, naming everything along them. The Dale House must be somewhere. It must be on a track. If I trace enough in my mind, perhaps I will remember it.'

'Relax! If you know the name, it will come to you without such endeavours. I refuse to spend my day with a young lady, however charming, who does no more than hide beneath her bonnet and mumble.'

He had turned the horses off the road to Chene, and was almost allowing them to pick their own course, down lanes that were no more than grass and mud tracks joining farmyard to farmyard through the fields. Susan gave him her attention again, and told him of the visit of Violet and Eustace the previous day. She spoke humorously of the encounter, but he was angered on her behalf, and his dark brows pulled together into a quick frown.

'My poor girl! She is a dreadful creature. No matter. When my cousin Kelsteven is established at the dower house, I shall introduce you to her daughters. They are charming girls, far better suited to be your friends. We will entirely cut Miss Netheredge's acquaintance. And Mr Chapley-Gore's, of course, lest I become jealous!'

'I was sorry that I could only laugh at her, and not fight to clear your good name. But I could not take the risk of her believing me, and spreading any news that you were no longer the guilty one, or we might have warned the true gang that we were searching elsewhere.'

'And the continued ill fate of my good name in Finderby village is a mere nothing in the circumstances.' He was solemn, teasing her. She loved to watch the way his face moved, the quick frowns, or the crinkling of his eyes and twitching at the corner of his mouth when he was privately amused.

'Very true,' she answered severely. 'You must submit to the present evil in order to gain the future good.'

'Yes, ma'am.'

'And when we have discovered the true villains, I shall take great pleasure in informing Miss Netheredge of the fact myself!'

They continued in this vein for some time, talking and teasing, until Susan looked about her in surprise.

'Where are we? Oh, yes, I believe I know. If I am right, if we turn left here it will lead us down to. . .'

She paused, her mouth still open to speak, staring at nothing. Marcus looked at her queryingly, reining in the horses. She laid a hand on his arm, and stared up at him.

'The Dale House! Could he have misheard? How close was Benjamin to these men? Might he have been mistaken in the name?'

'Perhaps. Why?'

'Because—well—let me explain. There is an estate down there. A small estate. I can remember Grandfather telling me of it when we once drove over this way. It has been the subject of an inter-family dispute for many, many years, and because ownership is disputed nothing can be touched. The land is utterly neglected. At some time the house was burnt down—deliberately, many believed, to prevent anyone inheriting it—and it is now little more than a shell. I had forgotten it. No one speaks of it now. It has been deserted so long, the whole place seems forgotten.'

'But why should this be the place we seek?'

'Its name. It was known as the Vale House.'

They stared at each other. Her eyes were sparkling in anticipation, her lips half smiling, a trail of brown curls straying on to her cheek. The Earl remained thoughtful for some moments, then began to smile.

'I suppose it could just be possible as a gang's hide-away. Hidden, forgotten, on nobody's land. Any number of tracks wind around the fields and doubtless lead in and out of the old estate. And Vale and Dale could be mistaken by a man straining his ears in a bramble patch. Yes. Susan, my clever girl, I believe you may have something.'

'Such a cautious man. I *must* be right. Let's go and look.'

'Is that wise? If you are correct, the last thing we want is to alarm this gang. We should be taking our suspicions to the magistrate, and organising a party of men to apprehend them.'

'How can we alarm them? We will only be driving along the lane, as we have all these other lanes. People must, on occasion, pass by. And more, how will you ever discover if I am right, if we don't have a look? At the moment we have nothing more than a wild guess to put before the magistrate. We may be totally mistaken, and very foolish we would look then, with half the county out on a wild-goose chase.'

The Earl had been considering this fact. He had been privately deciding to return Susan safely home, then to come back under cover of darkness, with Oliver and Benjamin, to investigate further. But, looking at the excitement on her face, he was loath to disappoint her entirely. As she said, there could be little harm in passing by the estate on the public highway, such as that highway was.

The Earl shook his head, but he turned the horses, and they set off down the lane to the left. It was soon

obvious that they were passing through the disputed
estate. Evidence of neglect was on every side. The fields
were a rank tangle of lank grass, nettles, dock and sapling
trees, rapidly encroaching on the pasture and on the once
ploughed land. The trees along the lane grew so dense
and close that they totally overhung the way, and the
curricle bumped and jolted through a green gloom. Even
the lane showed no sign of use. Grass, and even brambles
grew across it, long and untrampled.

'From the look of the lane, I am afraid we are
mistaken. This road is not in regular use by anyone, let
alone a busy gang of men,' the Earl remarked, frowning
as the curricle hit hit a particularly large stone hidden in
the undergrowth, and lurched precariously. 'It would be
sensible to turn back, if we can find somewhere to turn
the horses, before we both land in a ditch.'

Susan sighed. The curricle jolted and swayed violently,
the ash-wood springs creaking and complaining. 'You
are probably right. I wonder exactly where the old house
is? We have not seen any sign of it yet.'

A couple more twists in the track, and Susan's query
was partially answered. Two great brick gateposts
loomed up in the tangle of brambles alongside the lane.
They were topped by stone leopards, much worn by the
weather, and almost strangled by ivy. Wrought-iron
gates hung crazily from the posts, themselves locked
forever open by the strands of ivy and swarming bryony
that held them fast. Chene stopped the curricle, and they
stared about them. Susan shuddered.

'It is a desolate place. And you must be right. No one
is using it. That drive has been impassable for many a
long year. No one could have brought booty along here
at dead of night without breaking his neck. But how
disappointing.'

'No matter. We will trace Dale House eventually. I
think I can turn the carriage here, but it will be tight. I'll
lead the horses round.'

Marcus jumped down, and paused to look more closely
at the decaying gateway. Intrigued, Susan clambered

down the steps of the curricle, and jumped to the ground. While Marcus endeavoured to decipher the markings on the stone coat of arms on the gateposts, she climbed up the slope of bank beside them, hoping for some view of the burned ruin.

'*Someone* comes here,' she remarked suddenly. 'Though on foot, not horseback. There is a path here, just inside the boundary. Look.'

Loosely tying the greys to the old gate, the Earl jumped up to join her. He studied the winding path below them.

'Poachers, probably. This must be a poacher's paradise, neglected as it is.'

'Let's follow it a little way. I would like to catch a glimpse of the house now that we are here. And look, the path seems to turn to follow the drive. Come on!'

He shrugged. 'The horses will be all right for a short while. But I think you will be disappointed. There will probably be little to see.'

'Nonsense! How can you be so unimaginative, my lord? This whole place is a Gothic extravaganza! Feel the oppressive silence of the ancient forests, devoid of all trace of birdsong! Does it not cry out of evil deeds in times gone by? Look at the drive—a tangled epitaph to aristocratic decay! Imagine what ruins we will discover. Gaunt and towering blackened stone, circled by ravens croaking of doom, and owls hooting of destruction! The trailing ivy will cover all traces of the hidden doorway to the passage that leads to the leaden casket covered in the black velvet cloth, and the casket will contain. . .' She laughed. 'What would you prefer? The body of a beautiful young heiress, wickedly done away with by her vile stepmother? Treasure and jewels, left by the evil count in incalculable amounts? Or the vulture-picked bones of the villain a-scurry with rats? Any would do, you know!'

The Earl was laughing as he held back the branch of a sycamore to let her pass.

'I did not know you were an enthusiast of such novels.'

'Surely, my lord, everyone reads such novels, if they

would but say. There is no pleasanter way of passing a
long winter evening. Admit it. You were instantly familiar with all the eventualities of which I spoke!'

'I see I have no option but to plead guilty. But I still
do not believe we will discover anything more exciting
here than some old bricks standing amid a great many
brambles!'

'You begin to worry me, sir. I had believed we shared
our every thought in common. Now you confess that you
lack any of the sensibilities of a hero! How are you to
make all a girl's dreams come true?'

'That must surely depend upon what those dreams
may be!'

She looked up at him then, which was a mistake, for
he was laughing at her in that certain way which softened
and brightened his face, and left her heart beating too
erratically to continue teasing him with any confidence.
She took his arm, and smiled at him.

'You should not angle so shamelessly for compliments,
sir. You know very well what my dreams might be.'

He kissed her then, of course, in the heavy silence and
the watery green light of the sleeping woods.

'Shall we go back to the horses now?' he asked, a little
later.

'Oh, no. I insist upon seeing the house. It can't be far
now.'

She led him on down the path, and very soon it was
plain that they had entered what had once been elaborate
gardens. Paths, with traces of their gravel still to be seen,
wound between woody and straggling shrubs, through
shaped rocky outcrops, and beneath artificial rock archways, all thick with moss and trailing ivy. Susan was
enchanted.

'It could not be a better setting for a Gothic ruin! I do
believe that whoever designed the gardens was the one to
ignite the house! He had always planned to encompass
the charred remains into the original design!'

'He must have difficulty in selling his designs!' the
Earl commented drily.

'There!' Susan said. 'Look through the bushes. That must be the house. If we take this path we will reach it.'

Ahead it was just possible to distinguish chimney-pots standing above the trees. The path she indicated dipped downwards towards them, and soon the two were descending slippery steps of moss-covered brick. Somewhere near by a spring must have left its intended channel, doubtless blocked with many winters' leaves, and now ran down beside, and on to the steps. Steep, rocky banks soon enclosed them on either side. A huge rock archway, almost a tunnel, spanned the end of the flight of steps. It was dank and running with water inside, green with lichen and slippery underfoot. At the far end ivy hung down from it in a curtain.

'One could not devise a more dramatic opening on to the ruin,' Susan said with satisfaction, as they entered the cool shadow beneath the arch. 'Open the curtain, my lord, and reveal all!'

Marcus was laughing as he swept the ivy aside with one hand, and stepped through.

The barking explosion of the gun ripped through the summer silence. Susan leapt back beneath the arch, and for a fraction of a moment she thought it was only poachers, and was almost ready to laugh at her folly. Then Marcus staggered after her, stumbling on the wet brick, clutching at his arm, and came to rest leaning back against the wall, head bent, raggedly gasping for breath. In the same instant she felt the stinging on her neck and shoulder, and looked down in astonishment at the welling blood. Instinctively, she turned to Marcus.

'Run!' he whispered painfully. His eyes were closed and his face white. 'Back up the path. They have not seen you yet.' He was gasping to catch his breath. 'Run back to the curricle and escape. Quickly.'

She could see now the torn fibres of his jacket above his elbow, and on his chest, and the blood oozing through from beneath. It welled up between his fingers, gathered, and trickled over, and she watched in a frozen horror as it ran down his wrist and into the ruffles of his shirt sleeve. The dark stain on his coat was spreading rapidly. She hesitated, unable to leave him.

'I will help you. Give me your arm. We can go together. I cannot leave you here. You are badly hurt.'

'For God's sake, Susan, please don't argue now. You must go. They have seen me! They know I am here. But you can escape if you hurry.'

'Oh, no, sir, if you'll forgive my correcting you,' drawled a voice, 'but we have been watching both of you for some little time now. . .' the voice paused and chuckled '. . .and the good lady would get no further than yourself.'

There was a scramble on the bank behind them, and a tall man jumped down into the path behind them. His face was concealed behind a dark scarf and black hat, and he was holding a serviceable pistol. Another, similarly clad, pulled open the curtain of ivy ahead, and waved a blunderbuss at them threateningly.

'This way, if you please, ladies and gentlemen,' he said with a leer.

Susan looked from one to the other with what she hoped would pass for haughty disapproval.

'Don't be absurd,' she said, fixing her eyes on the man with the pistol. He seemed to be the leader of the two. 'This man is seriously hurt. We need to fetch a doctor immediately.'

The masked man gave an idle shrug, and she thought he laughed.

'No doctors around this part of the woods, ma'am. But we'll take you to a nice quiet room where you can lay him down to rest.'

'What do you mean, no doctors? Fetch an apothecary, then. The need is urgent. You *must* help. Do you know who this is?' She was furious and afraid.

'Oh, yes, ma'am.' He advanced on them now, waving them forward with his pistol. 'I know very well. This little plum falling into our hands is the Earl of Chene. Now——' and his voice was sharp with threat '—will you assist his lordship? Or shall I?'

'But he may die!'

The man merely shrugged, and deliberately cocked his pistol. Reluctantly defeated, angry at her helplessness, Susan put an arm about the Earl.

'You must walk now,' she said quietly.

He made no response, and it seemed he was barely conscious, but when she spoke more urgently he frowned, opened his eyes, and pushed himself off the wall. His face tightened in a grimace of pain, but he followed where she guided, and, dividing her anxious glances between Chene and the armed man behind her, the two ventured slowly out of the rocky shelter, and down towards the Vale House.

The ruin was as gaunt and towering as Susan could have wished. Floors, doors, windows and roof—all had been destroyed in the flames. Only the solid brick remained, walls blackened and charred, punctuated by lonely fireplaces high above which led up to chimney-pots that scraped the sky. But there was no delight to be found in its desolation now. Reality was too horrible already.

Marcus had put an arm across her shoulders, and his weight was heavy against her. Once she stumbled and thought she would fall, taking them both to the ground, but the man behind grabbed her arm and hauled her upright, then waved her forward without a word.

They were taken into the ruin, up cracked steps pierced by nettles, through what must once have been a french window on to the gardens, and across a wide expanse of marble floor. Its black and white tiles were splattered with droppings from the jackdaws which circled above, chacking irritably.

Once they were through to what must have been the kitchen quarters, Susan found that here the damage had been less severe. The rooms were damp and the windows broken, but the fire had not reached this far: the roofs sagged but held, and pantries, sculleries and storerooms could be distinguished. Leading them through several, the man with the blunderbuss eventually threw open a

stout door. He cursed while he struggled to light a
candle, then, once successful, led the way down a musty
stone staircase into the cellars of the old house. Susan
looked in despair at the man with the pistol, for she
knew she could not assist the Earl down the stairs alone,
and the man, with a shrug, half lifted him to the bottom.

It was impossible to judge the extent underground, for
they passed several storerooms, and still the space
stretched away into the darkness. The air was cold and
damp. Another door was flung wide. Susan and Chene
were waved through, the Earl stumbled and sank to his
knees, and before she could turn to plead for help the
door had been slammed shut, and she heard the grating
of a heavy bolt being drawn across.

They were imprisoned.

CHAPTER EIGHTEEN

SUSAN flung herself at the door, and beat upon it with her fists, crying out for help. No one came. The door was so tightly bolted, so solid, and fitted so securely in its frame that her frantic efforts produced barely any sound, and certainly no response from beyond. She paused, forehead rested in despair against the wood, tears on her cheeks, and, apart from her own sobbing breaths, the silence was absolute. So absolute that a further dread overwhelmed her, more awful than any other. *He* was not breathing! Wheeling around, and running to where Chene lay collapsed on the floor, her heart stood stilll, and she was certain he was dead.

It seemed to Susan that for some minutes she was frozen in a nightmare, unable to think or move. Yet she was kneeling beside him immediately, fumbling to unbutton his coat, feeling with shaking hands for the beating of his heart. But it was not necessary. At her touch the Earl groaned, rolled over, and made an attempt to sit up. She snatched off her shawl and bundled it into a pillow. Weak with relief, rubbing the tears angrily from her cheeks, she urged him to lie down again and allow her to examine his wounds.

It was only at this point in time that Susan appreciated that they had not been left in absolute darkness. The cellar they were in was not quite below ground. A small window, of tiny panes with a solid iron frame, was set in the wall at head height, and looked out at ground level on to a tangle of nettles. It did, however, let in sufficient dim green light for Susan to be able to attempt an examination both of her surroundings, and of the man stretched at her feet.

The room was not large. It had not been a wine cellar, but some more general store place. Now it contained little of use. A stack of wooden crates in one corner were plainly empty, and the only other things she could discern were a broken wine bottle, a snapped fishing-rod, and a solitary top boot, green with mildew. This glance around was the work only of moments. Seeing nothing of assistance in her plight, Susan turned her fearful attention to the Earl.

His eyes were open now, and she saw with a welling of relief that he was conscious.

'I need to look at your injuries. We must bandage them, and stop the bleeding. I must remove your jacket.'

She forced her voice to calmness, but still she heard it quaver. She had opened the front of his coat, flinching in horror from the mess of blood and torn cloth, and done no more than place a tentative handkerchief over the chest injuries. But the sleeve was too tightly fitted for her to examine his arm. He nodded slightly, and she knew he had understood, but his gaze shifted to her shoulder.

'What of your injuries?' he whispered, frowning.

Until that moment Susan had forgotten the stinging and bleeding she had noticed while they were under the archway. In her fear and fury, and her anxiety over Marcus, she had no thought for herself. She glanced at it now, and gave a shrug that became a wince.

'It is nothing. Only a graze. Look, it is not deep; the ball merely glanced across the skin.' She was impatient at his concern, frightened he might be dying at her feet. 'How we are to remove your jacket? That is the real problem.'

The Earl whispered that he had a penknife in his pocket. Susan fumbled to retrieve it, and with much trepidation cut away the sleeve of the coat, then of the linen shirt beneath, both heavy with blood. It seemed to her inexpert and fearful eye that the ball had not lodged, but had passed clean through the flesh, and, owing to the fineness of the Earl's shirt linen, the wound did not appear, in that dim light, to be embedded with fragments of fibre. Anxiously trying to remember everything Dr

Broadby had said about treating the blunderbuss wounds
Jeremy had suffered, Susan took Marcus's own handkerchief, and, making as thick a pad as she was able, bound
it tightly around the injured arm with her sash, and tied
it fast.

'Thank you.' Marcus's voice was still very weak, but
he managed to smile for her. It was almost enough to
reduce her to a sudden flood of tears. Sniffing hard,
scowling angrily at herself, she forced herself to jag and
saw away at the side of his coat, and, with dread at the
severity of what she might find, to expose his injured
chest.

It seemed that a cluster of shot from the blunderbuss
had hit together in a small area of his right side, one ball
through his arm, and three or four into his ribs. As she
cut away the shirt and exposed the ripped and bloody
flesh, Susan found the tears she had fought back had
made their way regardless. When she angrily blinked her
eyes clear, the tears ran unheeded down her cheeks, and
dripped hot on to her nervous hands.

It was at this moment that the door juddered, and
opened, someone placed a loaf of bread and a bottle of
wine on the floor, and the door slammed shut again—all
before she could begin to move. Once again she flung
herself towards it, and shouted wildly for help, for a
doctor, even just for water and bandages. But there was
no answer whatever, only mocking silence.

'There is no chance of fetching a doctor,' she heard
Marcus say. He sounded angry and bitter. 'It is plain
they do not intend anyone to know we are here. There is
nothing to gain by distressing yourself over it. I brought
this injury on myself—I must make the best of it. And,
by God, I deserve it. How could I have brought you
here? I cannot forgive myself for that. Ever. How could
I have acted like such a blind fool, when we knew and
suspected so much? It was an irredeemable folly.'

He was frowning, fretting angrily at himself, clenching
his fist. Furious at having exposed her to such danger,

discomfort and fear, he was furious too at his own helplessness.

Made yet more anxious by his outburst, Susan hurried back to his side, bringing the wine, which at least had been uncorked for them. After insisting she drink first, Marcus managed a few sips before she set about the frightening business of cleansing his chest wounds. Her handkerchief was sodden and useless now, and she tore portions from his ruined shirt to use as swabs. He watched what she did critically, and, when she discovered two of the balls still lodged against the bone, insisted she take the penknife and ease them out.

It was almost a relief when he lost consciousness, and she could quickly remove the shot, and another fragment she discovered, while he was still insensible. She used some of the wine in an effort to wash the wounds clean, then, quickly removing her petticoat, she folded it into a large pad and placed it over the wounds. Tying it into place with his cravat was more of a problem, for his was a dead weight and she could barely push the cloth beneath him, but eventually she had contrived something more or less to her satisfaction, and the bleeding seemed to have slowed. Very gently then, she raised his head, and offered him wine to drink, but he remained insensible, and made no attempt to swallow.

Shaking with misery and fear, Susan took her shawl from beneath his head and wrapped it about him. Then she sat by him on the damp brick floor, and pillowed his head in her skirts, anxiously stroking his hair and his forehead. Spasmodically she shivered, apprehensive and cold.

It seemed to Susan an eternity that they remained there. Her legs were stiff and numb, but she dared not move and disturb Marcus. She took comfort in listening to his regular breathing, and occasionally reaching her hand down to feel the pulse at his neck. It beat with a reassuring steadiness that made the discomfort of her position, and the soreness that she now felt on her neck, of little importance. Yet still she studied him, and lightly touched the heavy brows, the proud nose, and the dark lashes lying soft on the cheek. She was storing memories against the bitter, gnawing fear that the whisper of breathing would falter and cease, and in that passing breath she would lose all the delight she thought that she had found.

It was while they remained thus that the door opened once again. The man with the pistol slouched in. He casually gestured towards them for the benefit of some-one behind him, then stood back. Another man, similarly masked, moved calmly past him into the room, carrying a bracket of candles, which he then held high. The flames swooped, and steadied. Susan stared angrily. He was tall, stout, and stood with an arrogant assurance. He glanced rapidly about the darkening room, then stared at the prisoners for some moments.

'He is not dead?' he enquired coolly.

'He is not,' Susan replied, furious. 'Though, for all the help we have had, he should be. What do you want with us? Can you not let us go, if you will not bring a doctor here? Even an apothecary could help. It is mon-strous to treat us so.'

'But I have no great fondness for the Earl of Chene, Miss Finderby,' the man replied indifferently, ignoring Susan's gasp of astonishment at the use of her name, 'and only a financial interest in whether he lives or dies.' He turned now to the man with the pistol, and gestured him out of the room. 'You are right. I am sure this can be turned to good account.' He spoke quietly, but Susan could still just distinguish his words. 'It will be a new venture for us. I shall return home now, and devise the ransom note. Expect me back with it within the hour. It can be delivered in the early morning, before the house-hold are awake. I am sure even the unloving dowager can be persuaded to pay a pretty penny for a dear son's safe return. Otherwise. . .' The man shrugged, with an abrupt gesture of one hand. He looked back into the room then, and saw Susan's face, but he merely turned away, gesturing for the door to be shut.

'This is inhuman,' Susan cried. 'Will you do nothing to help or comfort us?' But she might as well have saved her breath, for both men ignored her, and the heavy door slammed shut once more.

It was not long after this that, when she reached to feel the pulse on his neck once again, Marcus reached up his hand and gently clasped hers. For a few moments he lay holding her hand pressed against his neck, then he turned his head and she thought he kissed it.

'I am afraid I have slept,' he said, frowning, and twisted his head a little to look up at her. He winced, and with a struggle he pushed himself up until he sat facing her.

'You have done a professional job. Thank you.' He briefly indicated the bandages. 'I feel considerably stronger now.'

It was clear that he would have no energy to spare for her emotions, only for conserving his own strength, and for considering their dilemma. Keen to get off the cold damp of the floor, and oddly shy after that long spell of unconscious intimacy, Susan arranged the wooden crates into rough seats, and Marcus was able to move stiffly across and sit down. Susan made her shawl into a sling for his arm, and, when it was tied, he assured her he was completely comfortable. She was not at all sure she believed him, but they shared some of the bread and wine, and he seemed to gain more colour in his face.

While they ate Susan relayed to him what had been said when the stranger had come to view them.

'What I can't understand is, how did they know my name? You are a notable figure, but I am not. . . It has been teasing my brain. I believe I have heard his voice before—this tall, stout man. But it is just an odd notion. Try as I will, I cannot place it.'

'It is odd they knew either of us, for I have been such a short time in this part of the country. It all adds weight to the surmise that this gang is organised by people we know. Tell me again what was said.'

Susan again repeated all she remembered.

'This man even knows the character of my mother! So—someone who has visited at Chene, perhaps?'

'But certainly not one of your staff. This man had the voice and the assurance of a gentleman, even if he lacked the manners.' She paused. 'I suppose the financial interest he has in you is just in collecting a ransom? It couldn't be anything else, could it?'

'Not unless he hopes to make his fortune by joining in our canal-building.'

'*Could* the leader of the Gradeley Gang be someone you have approached over the canal?'

'Why not? Circumstances are so bizarre, it seems it could be anyone!'

'No! Not *anyone*.' Her voice rose a little in excitement. 'He did not intend me to hear, but he said he would return *home* to write the ransom note, and that he would be back within an hour. Surely, that must mean that he lives within twenty minutes' ride of here, for one must allow some time for the stowing of his horse, and the writing of the letter.'

Marcus was nodding, sturdily making efforts to eat the dry bread, and studying the room in the rapidly fading long rays of evening sunlight while she talked.

'So, do you know who owns the surrounding estates?'

'I should. Indeed I should.' Susan sighed. 'But I am sorry—I cannot even seem to think properly now.'

'My poor girl. You are quite exhausted. Eat some of this bread. Hunger won't help us, and we must make the best of what we have.'

He handed her the loaf, and stood up carefully, adjusted the sling with a grimace, then walked over to study the window.

'It is a solid iron frame,' Susan said gloomily, but he continued to study it, then to poke about at the edge of it. Taking his penknife, he inserted it into a crack in the mortar at the side of the window, and, after a few moments of effort, levered a section out. It fell with a smack, and a scatter of sand, on to the floor.

'But not, I think, indestructible,' he said, with quiet

satisfaction. 'The iron frame may be strong, but the
mortar it is sitting in shows its age. I do not know how
long we have before they return, or what guards they
might have posted outside, but I am willing to make a
bid for freedom. It seems unlikely to be any more
dangerous than our present situation. What do you
think?'

Susan had jumped up from the box where she sat. A
sudden vision of action and escape revived all her
energies.

'Only let me help. We must work immediately, while
there is still a little light. Oh, if only we can escape!
What shall I use to work with?'

It was not too difficult to find a piece of broken crate
with a nail protruding, and break it free. Armed with
this, she set to work, scratching, digging and levering,
constantly frustrated by the need for silence.

It took much longer than either had thought. The light
was soon altogether gone, and they worked by touch.
Frequently Marcus had to rest, and working with his left
hand was at best difficult. Susan took over the penknife
while he rested, and worked as quickly as she could. She
almost wept when the blade broke, but she carried
doggedly on with the broken end, worrying at the
cracked cement, fumbling at the loosened fragments with
fingers now raw and sore.

It had been dark a long time when Marcus decided to
risk breaking the glass in the tiny panes, and attempting
to tug the frame free. No one had come near them, they
had heard no sign of anyone inside, or seen guards
outside. Still, as a precaution against being heard,
Marcus held the sleeve cut from his coat across the
panes, while Susan hit them with the heel of the abandoned top boot.

The crack of each pane breaking seemed terrifyingly
loud in the silence, but although they waited, heart in
mouth, straining for the slightest sound, nothing
resulted. Cautiously they took hold of the frame. With
the cloth wrapped over the jagged edges of broken glass,

Susan and Marcus together pulled at the rusted old iron. It would not move. It resisted so long, and the pain of pulling at it was so great, that Marcus had stepped back, trying to disguise his grunts of pain, not telling Susan of the renewed flow of blood he could feel now seeping from beneath the bandage on his chest.

In a despairing fury Susan gripped the frame and shook it violently. There was a cracking noise, and she staggered, stumbled awkwardly backwards in a shower of mortar and sand, and dropped the frame heavily on to the floor.

For some minutes they both froze, certain someone must have been disturbed by the noise, but all remained uncannily silent. Marcus shifted quietly over to the window, and looked out. There was no flicker of torch-light or candle-glow between the nettle stalks. No tell-tale smell of tobacco smoke from a thin clay pipe. Not a scuffing footstep or a stumbled oath. Not a sound. A thin moon had just risen, and gave the palest of silver lights. He turned to the darkness of the cellar, where Susan's face showed only as a smudge of grey.

'Well, my love.' He attempted a murmured lightness he was far from feeling. 'Shall we take a stroll by moonlight?'

She had been bringing over a stack of wooden crates to ease the climb from the window for him, but now she crept close beside him and looked out. He put his strong arm about her, and held her close, dropping a light kiss on her curls. Her bonnet had been abandoned long ago. She was shivering. 'Shall we try to reach the curricle?'

She longed for some familiarity, and the safety of speed.

'I am inclined to think not,' he replied, his voice just above a whisper. 'If the men had followed us as they said, they will certainly have discovered the curricle, and almost as certainly have taken it and hidden it from view. Despite the loneliness of the lane, I doubt they would take the chance of leaving it there. Also, if they discover our escape, that is the first direction in which they will search. No. I think we must endeavour to reach a high road by another route, and avoid asking for help at any nearby houses. It would be galling to have escaped our prison only to seek help in the villain's residence! Come on, my love, be brave. There is no time to waste.'

Apart from the nettle stings it was easy for Susan to leave the cellar, and she helped Marcus ease his way out. They set off quietly though the tangle of the old garden, anxious to get away from sight of the house, afraid to hurry. A flicker of candle-light behind one window at some distance from them showed that the place was not deserted, and they were glad when they could put the shelter of a high wall between themselves and the stark shell of the Vale House, black against the starshine of the sky.

They made their way through a succession of walled kitchen gardens, where the broken glass of the hothouses glistened silver in the moonlight, and the bushes, walls and archways cast ink-black shadows, wells of unfathomable silence, deep with menace. Then they were out of the furthest garden, through a rotted wooden gate, into a windbreak of whispering trees. A path led ahead of them through the black, clustering trunks and, with a muttered command to listen closely for anyone approaching, Marcus led the way along it.

The moonlight barely penetrated here, and they could make no great speed, but fear of pursuit kept them struggling on long after the Earl's forehead was bathed in cold sweat and the top of his breeches soaked with blood. It was Susan who first heard movement ahead. She clutched Marcus's arm and pulled him off the path into a dense clump of holly bushes just before someone on horseback, no more than a hunched, dark shape, passed them by, with barely a thud from the walking hoofs, and only a clink from the bridle.

Spurred on by fear after this encounter, Susan hastened onward, and the two walked some way further. But the woods around them showed no signs of ceasing, the dark trunks massed about as closely as ever, and she was aware that Marcus was stumbling more and more frequently.

'It is pointless to go further now,' she whispered. 'We must leave the path and find somewhere to rest. We can travel on as soon as it is light.'

The Earl could do no more than nod, and she could barely sense his gesture in the darkness. She led the way off the path between the trees until the wood thinned, and they were stumbling over great soft tussocks of grass. No longer with the energy to care, Susan sank to the ground in the welcoming softness, and Marcus stretched beside her.

She thought she would stay awake, afraid, listening for danger, unable to sleep under the high, glistening stars and the black immensity of the skies. But Marcus slept, and his breathing was regular, soothing, and soporific.

CHAPTER NINETEEN

THEY woke with the dawn, sore, chilled and cramped, but the daylight brought new hope. They were quickly up and away. The blind, stumbling panic through the blackness of the previous night need now be no more than a cautious walk, alert for dangers. It led to a rapid sighting of a road. A passing carter, shocked from his early morning torpor by their appearance, carried them to a village some miles on, where they were able to procure the loan of a jacket and a shawl, a hot breakfast, and the hire of a gig, all at the local tavern. They were in Finderby village by seven o'clock, to the gaping astonishment of the residents, and reached the Manor a little later.

Hephzibah met them at the door. All her night-long anxieties, all her efforts to convince herself that Susan was only staying at Chene rapidly crystallised into horror and dismay as she chivvied them inside.

Two hours later, Dr Broadby was leaving the Manor, complimenting Susan on her handiwork, and the Earl of Chene on possessing the constitution of an ox. Oliver was rapidly approaching the Manor, in response to an urgent summons from his brother, and Mr Vance was climbing on to his horse, bound for the same destination. The Earl was lying, reluctantly, in bed, wearing one of the Baron's nightshirts, and Susan was supervising Hephzibah preparing gruel. The Dowager Countess of Chene was demanding to know precisely where both her sons had gone, and why Oliver was in such a turmoil, and Violet was busy regretting to anyone who would listen that poor Susan Finderby had not only lost her senses, but also her reputation, for she had run off overnight with the wicked Earl of Chene.

Eustace Chapley-Gore had heard nothing of the excitement, and was eating ham, eggs and kidney while perusing the previous day's *Morning Post*, and wondering whether to spend the morning in visiting Miss Netheredge, or in inspecting the turnip crop on his home farm.

Oliver arrived at Finderby agog with curiosity, and ran up the stairs to the Earl's bedroom at the Manor, clutching maps, a letter and a flat case of duelling-pistols.

'I was never more glad to see anything in my life than your man with that note,' he said, as he flung into the room, and straddled a wooden chair that stood near the bed. He grimaced at the bandages, but he laughed as he saw his brother dutifully drinking a bowl of gruel under Susan's watchful eye, and Marcus caught his eye with a rueful grin.

'I am afraid I lie constrained here under doctor's orders,' he apologised.

'Since when did you ever bother with doctor's orders?' Oliver replied. 'You lie there under petticoat government, if you ask me!' But he was grinning at Susan. Seeing them together had explained a lot of things, and Oliver was not one to cause a rift with his brother, or to hold a grudge.

'If you did but know that is precisely what it isn't!' Susan retorted, laughing in her turn, but she would not elaborate.

'You realise we had a ransom note? It arrived at the kitchen door about six o'clock this morning. Some young boy from the village brought it. He had been given the letter by a man he had never seen before, and the idiot could no more describe him to me than begin to write an ode to a Grecian goddess, or attempt to fly to the moon! I believe, had the man had two heads this dolt would not have noticed. I was never more frustrated. No hope of tracing him. They wanted ten thousand pound for your safe return! Ten thousand! I spoke to Blake, and he was just off to consult the magistrate when your note arrived. Vance should be here shortly. But I have not dared tell Mama yet. Probably just as well. You can explain it all yourself, and good luck to you, I say!'

'If they actually sent the note, then they can't have discovered our escape until this morning.' Susan was incredulous. 'All the time we feared pursuit, they must still have been ignorant that we had gone.'

'Yes. They must have discounted any possibility of escape by such a heavy-framed window, and concentrated on guarding the door.'

'But *who*? Where were you? What happened?'

Oliver was so impatient with curiosity, he must be told everything immediately. Between them Susan and Marcus gave an account, much interrupted by questions and exclamations, of the events of the last twenty-four hours. Once done, the three pored eagerly over the maps, discovering the Vale House, and identifying the surrounding properties.

'I have visited two of these recently,' Oliver said. 'This is Hawkby Hall, Sir William Gantrey's place, and over here is George Pembleton's ramshackle establishment.'

Susan was able to name the owners of the other properties, but only the two Oliver mentioned seemed probable, for none of the others had had any dealings with the Earl or his family, and would be unlikely to know them.

'I am happy to suspect George Pembleton,' remarked Oliver cheerfully. 'Gantrey is a good enough sort, but I did not take to Pembleton. He was plainly in urgent need of funds. I believe he hoped to raise enough to make a sizeable investment in our canal, and looked to reap a fortune. That might have made him greedy enough for robbery, if he was of a criminal turn of mind.'

'Is he tall and stout, with an arrogant tone?' Susan asked.

'Why, yes, you could describe him so. You saw him, you know, when he helped Marcus carry that lad with the broken leg down the hill for you.'

'Of course! That was where I heard him! It was the same cold tones, I am sure. Yes, I am certain!'

Susan's sudden cry of realisation and recognition coincided with an exclamation of the Earl's.

'And he couldn't resist putting his name to it, by God! Too vain not to let the world know the authorship of the gang, even if they would never realise that they knew.'

'What do you mean?'

'I was at school with Pembleton. We started new together. He was an officious, arrogant child, forever chanting his name. I have never forgotten it. George Winston Le Grade Sharp Pembleton. Le Grade. Gradeley. Do you see? I think it was a private vanity, to use a version of his own name. He would not expect anyone to remember it. I remember something else. He was often suspected of stealing while we were at school, but nothing was ever proved. And I know there was some scandal when he was a young man, before he went abroad. But since the death of his father, when he came into the property, I have heard nothing against him.'

A knock on the door heralded the arrival of Mr Vance, in a waft of peppermint, and all of the story was once again repeated, the ransom note given into his keeping, and their conclusions voiced. With such a genuine basis for suspicion, Mr Vance rose to the occasion. He lost no time. Barnaby was sent to round up every able-bodied man and boy within reach to help in the capture of the Gradeley Gang.

'As for Pembleton, however——' Mr Vance frowned, looking at the Earl of Chene, and popped another mint lozenge into his mouth '—it does no good for a man who was once a gentleman to be brought to common justice, if it can be avoided. The spectacle presented to the mass of the people, of the degradation of a man who should be infinitely their superior in morals, can only be deplored as undermining the moral and social structure of our nation.'

'I suspect,' the Earl remarked wryly, 'that *he* might also wish to avoid trial, though for somewhat different reasons! I believe the conclusions of the jury to be inevitable, but even should he escape with his life he will always be a ruined man. However——' he nodded towards his pistol case '—perhaps Mr Pembleton might prefer to be offered a gentleman's way out, in return for a complete confession? He always coveted my guns when we were boys. Perhaps now I should offer him the use of one.'

Mr Vance nodded slowly. 'Perhaps you will write a note to him, my lord, explaining the situation. Then, if the house is surrounded, and circumstances permit, I will have no objection to leaving him for a few moments to—er—put his personal affairs in order, as it were. It would be all for the best.'

He noticed, as if surprised, the lozenge box clasped in his hand, and belatedly offered them around to the assembled company.

Mr Chapley-Gore, who had abandoned his turnips for Violet's sake, could hardly credit the tale she now spread before him.

Miss Finderby, it seemed it had to be believed, had finally abandoned all decency. She had run away the previous afternoon! She had been seen at Mill Cottages as she departed, in company with the Earl of Chene. And—they had been together all night! This morning they had been seen returning in a strange gig, pale, dirty and bloodstained. In Violet's lurid mind there was no shadow of doubt. What other explanation could there be? Somewhere there had been a raid by the Gradeley Gang, and these two had taken part. Some brave householder had fought back, and they were deservedly injured. Miss Finderby was openly living under the Earl's protection. It was a scandal the like of which Finderby village, and Violet in particular, had never enjoyed before.

Eustace was shocked to the very core of his conventional being. When a call went around the village that Mr Vance the magistrate was recruiting every able-bodied man and boy to help arrest the Gradeley Gang, Eustace knew he had to go. Even Violet's tender concern for his well-being could not hold him back from performing his duty. With a high regard for his own heroism, he checked the pistol he carried always in his saddle-bag, and went out to urge the villagers on to the Manor.

He was astounded to see young Oliver Carlleon with Mr Vance. He could only conclude that the younger brother had turned King's Evidence in an attempt to save his own skin. This impression was strengthened when Mr Vance gave orders to his gathered troops. Those mounted on horseback were to follow him. Those on ponies, or donkeys, or crammed into carts, were to proceed to the Vale House—he gave close directions as to its whereabouts—and instantly arrest anyone they found there. It was clear, Eustace decided, that the Earl must have suffered such injuries that he had been easily apprehended at the Manor with Miss Finderby, and the rest of the ruthless gang were holed up elsewhere, and, following Oliver's traitorous direction, would soon be within the grasp of the law.

'A splendid thing, this,' he remarked importantly, as soon as they were under way, and he could edge his horse near enough to the magistrate's stout chestnut gelding, 'to take such wicked villains at last.'

'We have not taken them yet,' Mr Vance replied drily.

'No. Well. . .' Eustace looked sideways at the magistrate, and decided he would not mention the arrest of the Earl, if Mr Vance did not '. . .but we will. We will. No doubt about that. Cut off the head, and the body withers, eh!'

'Indeed.'

'And I dare say my information gave you the leads you needed to bring about this arrest, eh, Mr Vance?'

Mr Vance politely inclined his head. 'We have received valuable information from several sources,' he said neutrally.

Eustace Chapley-Gore could have wished for a more generous acknowledgement of his contribution, but he drew back, well satisfied that the Earl of Chene's rapacious antics would soon be at an end.

As the group arrived at Pembleton's house, and crossed the muddy stretch of drive, Mr Vance waved them out to surround the building, and to prevent anyone attempting to leave. He, followed by Oliver and an eager Mr Chapley-Gore, each with his pistol ready, rode around the house to the front door to announce their arrival.

The door stood open and unattended. As they peered within, sudden shouts alerted them from the back of the house. Careering around the corner of the building came the Earl of Chene's curricle, the greys, startled and wild-eyed, leaping at the harness, the driver hunched forward, urging them madly on. Even as Eustace's jaw dropped, and his heart sank in dismay as he realised the Earl was not captured, and would now escape to freedom, Oliver raised his pistol. He rested it calmly on his arm to aim, and fired. The figure in the curricle jerked, flung up his arms, then twisted down out of sight. The greys gave a ringing scream of fear, and fled in a wild stampede down the lane, bouncing their awful burden behind them.

Eustace stared at Oliver in horror. Mr Vance was even congratulating him! This might be British justice, but it made the blood run cold. Had the younger brother only been plotting to expose and dispose of the elder, so that he could succeed to the title? Shuddering in shocked distaste, Eustace drew back from Oliver and Mr Vance.

After the house had been sealed, and a guard had been set at the door, they all moved on to the Vale House. The Finderby villagers had joyfully captured three men, and had already extracted the names of several others. Mr Vance did not press them for the methods used to gain the information. They cheerfully assured him that the men had sung like skylarks, and if they ceased to sing just to hand them back to any public house in Finderby! The captured men stood bruised, bloodied and silent. One spat out a tooth. Eustace, squeamish, edged his horse away. It was one thing to capture gang leaders—he did not feel obliged to concern himself with the riff-raff.

Guards were left at the Vale House also, Mr Vance promising to send men to collect all necessary evidence as soon as possible. The three prisoners were bundled into a cart to be taken to Findham gaol-house. On the road back, some of the men who had chased after the curricle rejoined the group. It had been found, and was being driven back to the Manor. The driver was dead.

There were rousing cheers for Oliver, with much cheerful remark on the sureness of his aim, the ending of the Gradeley Gang and the downfall of its leader. When the comments became unsuitably ribald Mr Vance interrupted. He congratulated everyone on their assistance in upholding the law of the land, and paid them each a shilling in appreciation of their services. This motley collection, many the past recipients of his justice, then even cheered Mr Vance. He placed a lozenge solemnly into his mouth, and sent them all home.

Eustace returned to Miss Netheredge. There was so much he wanted to tell her! It was all most extraordinary!

The Earl remained three days at Finderby Manor, but whether he was more exhausted by his injuries than he cared to admit, or he had merely acquired a taste for the nursing he received, was uncertain. Susan found him the following morning, when she took up his beef tea, sitting by her grandfather's bed, deep in discussion of the opening up of the Finderby coal-mine. Grandfather's voice was vibrant with an enthusiasm that passed all his disabilities.

'This will set up young Jeremy after I'm gone,' he said, taking notice of Susan's entrance for the first time. 'A fine plan. It's a wise thing to invest in such a venture.'

'Yes, Grandfather,' Susan answered, amused.

'I know, my girl. But you can take that smile off your face. I am not ashamed to change my mind and admit I was mistaken. It *is* a good scheme, full of potential for the area, and this young man has a sound mind for the developing of it. Why, he's not like a Chene at all. I dare say the dowager played the old Earl false? No? Well, she wouldn't admit it if she had. We can but hope! But this young man will see that young Jeremy manages our estates to best advantage. After all, it will all be in the family now. A splendid thing. I may express my opinions strongly, Susan, but no one could call me prejudiced.'

'No, Grandfather,' she said fondly.

The old man paused a moment, then continued with a sly grin.

'Besides, he has promised to find me a valet. A man to take care of me. Get rid of these wretched fussing girls. And poor old Alfred can end his days in peace by the kitchen fire, as he deserves. Where he can't be forever tormenting me with medicine!'

Later they spoke about the downfall of the Gradeley Gang.

'At least my greys came back safely,' the Earl remarked. 'No more damage than scratches on their knees where they went through the hedge. Pembleton had a certain impudence, using my horses for his escape.'

'Dreadful man!' Susan frowned. 'So cruel.'

'George Pembleton was always a bad lot,' Lord Finderby put in.

'Did you know him?'

'Knew his father. The boy broke his heart. It wasn't generally known, for they hushed it up, and the parents had the sympathy of the county, but when he was quite a young man he was sent down from Oxford with stories of stealing horses and selling them, violent attacks on other students and cheating at cards.' The old man sighed. 'His father was in despair. Asked me one night what I would do with him. I said I'd take a horse-whip to the boy, then send him overseas to make his own way. But they never whipped him, of course. The mother pleaded on his behalf. And do you know how he rewarded her? He took all her jewellery with him when he left home. Every gem. Stole it all. Terrible business. She forgave him, of course. Fool of a woman. But it broke his father's heart.'

'Did you never suspect it might be he who had organised the Gradeley Gang, Grandfather?'

The old Baron slowly shook his head.

'Why would I think of George Pembleton? That house

of his was empty for years, with only an old couple to
care for it. I didn't even know he was back in the area.
But what you have told me comes as no surprise. None
at all.'

Hephzibah took pleasure in surprising a few people,
however. Calling in at the butcher's in Finderby village,
she listened with no little private amusement to the
variety of tales concerning the demise of the Gradeley
Gang. The only fact everyone seemed agreed upon was
that the young brother, Oliver Carlleon, had brutally
murdered his older brother, the Earl, before any number
of witnesses, in order to gain the title and estates. He
was to be saved from justice only because he had turned
King's Evidence. This was not right, was the general
consensus, for doubtless he still had all the profits from
the gang stored furtively away. Nobody wanted *him* as
the seventh Earl of Chene, however much the menfolk
commended his shooting!

Hephzibah made her purchases quietly, amid suspicious looks. It was not forgotten that the gang had
probably been in hiding at the Manor. Then she paused
by the door, hunched and grinning over her basket of
meat, and slowly shook her head.

'I should stop listening to that Miss Netheredge's
fairy-tales if I were you. You'll find the sixth Earl of
Chene and his new fiancée have considerably more to
offer.'

There was a stunned silence.

'But the sixth Earl is dead,' one foolish woman ventured, perplexed.

'Well, if he is,' Hephzibah retorted, 'it's a mighty
hungry spectre that I'll be cooking this steak for tonight,
I can assure you of that! He's the only ghost I ever met
that ate more than Master Jeremy!'

And she made a dignified exit down the village street,
nose in the air, ignoring with satisfaction all their cries
for her to come back and explain.

It was Becky who told them more, when she walked
into the village to display the handsome young man on

whose arm she leaned. But as he only stood bashfully, grinning and blushing, and her story focused almost entirely on the heroic and dangerous role played by one Benjamin Foot in the downfall of the gang, and rapidly digressed into their wedding plans for the autumn, and the promise that had been made to Benjamin of a cottage, rent free, on the Chene estate, and the beechwood rocking-chair that Becky's grandmother had promised to them, to stand by their very own hearth, not to mention the little wooden cot. . .well, the fate of the sixth Earl of Chene was left uncertain in the minds of most of her listeners.

The following day the Earl himself, with Miss Finderby, drove gently into the village in the now famous curricle. Miss Finderby was handling the reins under the Earl's supervision, for he had his arm in a sling. They were making their way to see Mr Stanbridge.

The astonished faces, staring from every gate, door and window, had Susan beginning to laugh.

'It is true what Hephzibah said,' she began, chuckling. 'They have believed so much nonsense over the past few weeks that now they have believed what Hephzibah told them as gospel truth. They think you are a spectre! There can be no other explanation for so much amazement!'

She could not resist the pleasure of reining in outside Mrs Blaythorpe's, the baker's. Violet was standing there, gazing at the curricle in horrified disbelief, her pale eyes wide.

'How do you do, Violet? I trust your mother is keeping well?'

Violet gulped, and nodded, setting the flowers that trimmed her bonnet bobbing and dancing.

'I am pleased. Do give her my best regards. But how remiss of me. You *do* remember the Earl of Chene, do you not? *What* a blessing he came back to Chene in time to rid us of this plague of criminals, and set Mr Vance on to capturing the Gradeley Gang and that dreadful George Pembleton. Don't you agree? Isn't it astonishing—no

one but he seemed to discover an inkling of the truth?
You must acknowledge him to be the hero of the hour! I
can assure you, Mr Vance does. But we must not keep
you. We have a particular appointment. . .' she paused
and dropped her eyelashes demurely '. . .with Mr
Stanbridge. Goodbye.'

With an airy wave, Susan set the greys moving sedately
on down the village street, leaving Violet rooted to the
spot.

'Hero of the hour, indeed. What a dreadful phrase!
And as for the shameless way you mentioned our visit! I
thought you were a girl who never resorted to such
devious female wiles. Have you been deceiving me all
these weeks?' said Marcus.

She smiled. 'It was wicked of me, I know. But after
the sheer impertinence of her last visit to the Manor—
oh, I could not resist it! Besides, you must know, my
lord, that there is not a woman born who lacks *all* female
wiles. Some of us just use them a little less frequently
than others.'

'I shall have to be on my guard.'

'You, my lord? It is too late. You succumbed to my
natural charm without the necessity of my employing
any wiles at all! I am afraid in such a sorry case you have
no hope of escape now.'

'And what of you? Did my natural masculine charm
lead you irresistibly into my arms?'

'No, no, my lord. You took shameful advantage of my
country innocence. You know that you loosed all *your*
wicked wiles upon me. Think of that first visit I made to
Chene. Your wooing words! Your dulcet tones! It was
unfair. No maiden anywhere could have resisted you!'

They had swung into the vicarage yard, and she
jumped lightly down before he could respond. Mr
Stanbridge burst out of the house, black coat flying, wig
askew, face split by a beaming grin, and ushered them
inside.

'And so,' he said happily, 'you want to fix a date. Very
good! Very good! Let me offer my heartfelt congratula-

tions! And a dish of tea? Or a scone, perhaps? Mrs Bunce
has some incredible scones!'

Not everyone was as happy at the news of the Earl of
Chene's impending marriage to Miss Susan Finderby.
When Marcus returned to Chene, and his mother realised
that he had not been staying with friends, as Oliver had
informed her, but instead had been making himself
notorious by associating with nasty little magistrates, and
gangs of highwaymen, and then, far worse, wickedly,
ridiculously, and unbelievably, offering his hand in
marriage to that Finderby gypsy, she was more than a
little displeased.

'That girl will enter this house over my dead body,'
she raged, her face puce and twitching.

Her son looked up slowly from the letter he was
reading, and raised an eyebrow.

'How inconvenient for you, Mother,' he murmured.
'You will be such a loss to the family.'

She glared impotently.

'I *will* not live under the same roof as that creature!'

'No one would ask it of you, Mama. No one compels
your presence at Chene. But—you will take care,
Mother, just how you speak of my fiancée.'

His voice was mild, but his tone unmistakable. If
possible, the dowager's face turned a deeper purple. She
gobbled like a turkey before she could find words to
speak.

'Only *think*, Marcus! You could be marrying Lucretia
Nare!'

'Rest assured, Mama, that is a reflection that has
frequently crossed my mind.'

'I shall move to the Town house!'

'Susan and I shall be requiring that, I am afraid,
Mother. We will, of course, be travelling up for the
Season each year. We will need to introduce young
Jeremy Finderby about a little. So it will not be convenient to have you there. But—let me think. You may,
if you wish, use the house in Bath. I have no fondness
for it. We will rent somewhere more fashionable if we

wish to visit the town. Tell me, will you be staying for
the wedding? It will take place as soon as the banns have
been called.'

'I will not! Outrageous thought! I would not demean
myself by remaining to watch such an insult to the family
name. I shall leave! Do you hear me? I shall leave at
once. I shall order Jane to begin my packing
immediately.'

'Is it *possible* to insult the name Scullion?' Marcus
mused, but his mother had already stormed out of the
room and was stamping her way up the great oak
staircase.

Violet was consumed with anger, embarrassment, and
envy. Everyone laughed at her theories now. All those
who had made her a centre of importance for so long,
hanging eagerly on her whispers, now looked elsewhere
for news, and Violet felt all the fickleness and prejudice
of village talk.

The Earl and Miss Finderby were warmly spoken of
everywhere, and their contribution to the new school,
and Mill Cottages, not to mention Miss Finderby's many
kindnesses in the past, were all remembered, and mulled
over with new, speculative hopes for the future. The true
story of their bravery in tracking down the Gradeley
Gang was retailed at length by the magistrate when he
came to dine with Mr Stanbridge. He told it all in
glowing terms. He needed to talk, to distract his mind
from the vicarage food. And thus, through Mrs Bunce,
the story spread, and grew gloriously. Violet, sensing the
sniggers behind her back when she walked through the
village, turned to Eustace for sympathy.

But Eustace Chapley-Gore was shocked and embarrassed at the entire business. He was secretly deeply
ashamed at how much he had believed of Violet's tales.
He believed he had been made a laughing-stock. His
dignity was at stake. He took a house in Bath, and
departed with his ancient mother to take the waters. Not
long after, it was heard that he had met a respectable

widow of some fortune, and that he proposed to make her his wife.

Violet reverted to watching Jeremy hopefully, but Jeremy, with farms to run, coal to mine, canals to build, visits to London in store, and Oliver's charming young Kelsteven cousins newly settled in the dower house, was too busy even to notice.

And the Earl of Chene, and his new wife? They spent eight weeks after their wedding touring in the mountain fastnesses of Scotland, without any view of a mill or a mine to disturb their happiness. They arrived back at Chene, in golden autumn sunshine, just in time to attend the official opening of Finderby School to its new pupils.

'What you see here,' the Earl said, on a bright October day, to the assembled villagers, children, and anxious new teachers, just after Jimmy Peters' little sister Martha had stumbled up to Susan with a large bouquet, 'is the excellent result of my first collaboration with the present Countess of Chene.' He put his arm about Susan's shoulders, and everyone grinned. The bolder ones cheered. 'I think I can safely promise you, there will be many, many more such ventures. To drink to which occasions, we hope you will join us in a small celebration.' He gestured behind him.

When the villagers saw the bulging hampers of food and the barrels of beer being humped on to the grass from laden wagons, under the cheerful supervision of Benjamin Foot, there was neither need nor time for any more words.

Look out for the two intriguing

MASQUERADE *Historical*

Romances coming next month

HESTER
Marion Carr

Trapped by the British blockade of Charleston, life was
becoming difficult for the inhabitants, none more so than for
Hester Mackay and her Aunt Kizzy. With brother George
presumed dead, their only recourse would be to take in
boarders, but the only prospects were the British themselves.
When privateer Benjamin Blake requested rooms for himself
and some of his men, Hester's instinctive response was to say
no, for this tall handsome man upset her equilibrium. But Aunt
Kizzy said yes, and that set on course a surprising chain of
events . . .

AN IMPROPER DUENNA
Paula Marshall

Miss Chloe Transome, impoverished dependent of her cousin
Serena, Lady Marchingham, knew that at nearly thirty, her drab
life was not likely to change. But she was wrong. Her old
governess wrote offering a home in Northumberland, and Sir
Patrick Ramsey visited Marchingham. Sir Patrick was intended
for Chloe's charge, Miss Marianne Temple, but Patrick found he
had a marked predilection for Chloe's company, though they
had to be circumspect, for both Serena and Marianne were
jealous of him.

Knowing Patrick had no thought of marriage, nevertheless
Chloe decided to throw her cap over the windmill, and stand
the consequences . . .

Available in May

TWO
HISTORICAL ROMANCES

&

TWO
FREE GIFTS!

MASQUERADE *Historic*

Masquerade historical romanc
bring the past alive with splendo
excitement and romance. We w
also send you a cuddly teddy bear a
a special mystery gift. Then, if y
choose, you can go on to enjoy
more exciting Masquerades every
months, for just £2.25 each! Se
the coupon below at once to – Read
Service, FREEPOST, PO Box 23
Croydon, Surrey CR9 9EL.

--- **NO STAMP REQUIRED** ---

Yes! Please rush me 2 FREE Masquerade historical romances and 2 FREE gifts!
Please also reserve me a Reader Service subscription. If I decide to subscribe, I
can look forward to receiving 4 Masquerade romances every 2 months for just
£9.00, delivered direct to my door, postage and packing free. If I choose not to
subscribe I shall write to you within 10 days - I can keep the books and gifts
whatever I decide. I may cancel or suspend my subscription at any time. I am ov
18 years of age.

Mrs/Miss/Ms/Mr _____ EP2

Address _____

Postcode _____ Signature _____

The right is reserved to refuse an application and change the terms of this offer. Offer
expires 31st December 1992. Readers in Southern Africa write to Book Services
International Ltd., PO Box 41654, Craighall, Transvaal 2024. Other Overseas and Eire,
please send for details. You may be mailed with other offers from Mills & Boon and other
reputable companies as a result of this application. If you would prefer not to share in
this opportunity, please tick box. ☐